Why Rock The Boat When You Don't Know How To Swim?

To Fiona

Annet.

Daniel Sebata

Published by Daniel Sebata
Publishing partner: Paragon Publishing, Rothersthorpe

ISBN 978-1-78222-293-4

Book design, layout and production management by Into Print
www.intoprint.net
+44 (0) 1604 832149

Printed and bound in UK and USA by Lightning Source

Dedication

For my brother, Eiffel, who has difficulties with his mental health.

Chapter 1

THE MEERKAT COURT

Sitting and rocking on a sofa at a secure psychiatric hospital lounge in Bournemouth, UK, I'm wondering what has happened to my life. What has turned my life, in a country that promises heaven on earth, into a nightmare? Turning my dreams into visual hallucinations. I'm a hopeless bystander, watching my life being torn apart by wild animals, each bite they take, stuns my brain into further disorientation.

A Meerkat Court has set and decided my fate. It concluded that I'm insane. Giving the right to the nurses and doctors to keep me in hospital against my will and to forcibly inject me with the most potent antipsychotics available. If I dare to refuse the injection, I am savagely pinned onto the ground by four nurses, who qualify to be bouncers in their body stature and demeanour, the fifth nurse jabs my backside with an injection the size of a poison tipped bushman's spear. I must be injected with two doses; one for being insane and the other for lacking insight into my illness. Punished for being sick.

The Meerkat Court had neither a heart nor a soul. Three white men, in their seventies, sat behind a huge desk, separating them from the rest of us. They were the judge, everyone referred to as 'My Lord,' who sat in the middle, flanked by his subordinates, 'His Excellence' on his right and 'The Duke' on his left. I, my solicitor, the nurse and the doctor, sat in a row, directly opposite the learned gentlemen. Soon the introductions were over, while I was still in a lucid dream like state. The judge then said to the doctor, "Doctor, in your report you said that Mrs...eh...Spider...eh... never mind, suffers from Post Traumatic Stress Disorder (PTSD) and Postpartum Psychosis Disorder (PPD)?" The doctor shifted a bit from his chair and responded,

"Yes, My Lord."

The judge continued, "Could you please describe the nature and the degree of her illness." The doctor leaned forward, cleared his throat and said, "Thank you My Lord. She's a long history of insanity consistent with PTSD currently exacerbated by underlying PPD. Because she has never been properly diagnosed, her insanity has never been treated. There's no doubt that she's barking mad My Lord. The depth of her illness is so severe that if she's left untreated, she's a danger to all of us here. As you know My Lord, she attempted to ..."

"We know, we know." The judge interrupted the doctor, nodding his small grey haired head and using hand gestures too, to stop him from saying more. He thanked the doctor and turned to his right, "His Excellence, do you have any questions for the doctor?"

The bald headed, His Excellence, responded, "Thank you My Lord." Turning to the doctor, he asked, 'Doctor, are you absolutely sure that Mrs... eh...is absolutely insane?" Smiling, the doctor said, "Yes His Excellence, I've no doubt. I've twenty years of experience as a consultant psychiatrist. I know insanity like the back of my hand. Madness is my bread and butter, it pays my mortgage, My Lord. There's only one way to describe her; she's barking mad." Everyone smiled including my solicitor. I didn't know what to do or say, I was just too drugged.

The judge continued, "Thank you doctor," and turning to his left he asked, "The Duke, do you have any more questions for the doctor?" The Duke looked well for his age, he responded, "Yes My Lord. Thank you." Turning to the doctor, he asked, "Doctor, you said that she's psychiatrically ill, isn't she possessed by some ethnic spirits? Are you sure that her presentation doesn't conform to some form of backward African practices? Some form of voodoo worshiping, which has nothing to do with mental illness, but a common and backward practice in her country of origin?" The doctor quickly hit back,

"I've never been to Africa or worshiped some satanic fetishes, My Lord. Whether she presents with true symptoms of insanity or some backward African practice, it's neither here nor there. The issue is: she's living in cuckoo land. The land resided only by her kind, My Lord." I just looked on in a comatose state. Then the judge said, "Thank you doctor. Nurse, do you agree with what the doctor has just said?"

"Thank you My Lord. Thank you The Duke. Thank you His Excellence. Thank you Doctor. Yes, yes, yes, My Lord, I agree with the doctor. Yes, yes, yes. Thank you My Lord." The poor nurse went on a thanking spree and that was all what she said. The judge thanked the nurse and then asked the doctor again, "Doctor, what do you think would happen if we took her off the hook today?" The doctor sneered and rumbled,

"Oh God, My Lord. Please don't put that idea into her feeble mind. I don't want even to think about it. Letting her loose on the streets to do her bush smearing? To cause havoc in people's lives? If you take her off her section, you will be putting people's lives at risk, My Lord. As for me, I will relocate. I will get on my horse and leave Bournemouth forever, My Lord. You have dark jokes indeed, My Lord." The judge nodded again and said, "Thank you Doctor." After writing something down, the judge continued, 'Now MH Solicitor, its your turn, please take us through the defence of your client." My solicitor went bla-bla-bla before I completely dosed off.

I can't recall exactly what was precisely said during the court. I kept nodding off and waking up to hear words like 'insanity' 'barking mad' 'satanic fetishes' and so forth. My solicitor had dragged me into that court. I didn't want to attend it as I didn't understand it and I thought it was a pointless exercise. But she insisted that I attended, telling me that the chances of my case being dropped and being discharged from hospital were higher if I availed myself to the court. I had no doubt that I wasn't in the right frame of mind and body to attend the court. I was confused and drowsy. My speech was slurred and I was drooling rivers of saliva. I didn't want to appear in that state before any court, let alone a Meerkat Court. I still wanted to preserve that little human dignity that was still left in my half-self. But my solicitor's insistence that I attend stripped me naked of any human value left.

I sat throughout the court against my will, my hair unkempt and dishevelled. My clothes dirty with food stains. I hadn't changed them since my admission, not for the lack of energy, but because I couldn't be bothered. My eyes had dark circles around them and they had large sacks hanging under them like a mad bull's scrotum. I found it difficult to move my eyelids, it was as if two overfed goblins were sitting on each eye lid, pressing them down with their mighty forces.

My thick lips had numerous cracks like the surface of a dried up dam, forming contours of different shapes and sizes. Humanity had deserted my face. Like a dam that had lost all its water through evaporation, I had lost my dignity through their forced injections.

My whole body shook like a leaf, it had been violated by drug companies' concoctions. Pumped deep into my muscles against my will. My blood vessels rebelled against the poison that had been illegally squeezed into my body. They aggressively shook and threatened to expel the poison. Threatening to ooze out the venom that had been deposited in them, leaving my whole body shaking like a dry leaf. I dribbled like a teething baby as a result of their injections. But still my solicitor had insisted that I attend the Meerkat Court in that state. For her pay cheque perhaps, or for my good, that I will never know.

I had hoped that the Meerkat Court chairperson would take one glance at me and order that I return to my room. That didn't happen. He allowed me to sit through the whole process that tore my life into shreds. I was discussed in my presence as if I was absent, like a child. I had hoped that I would not be put through verbal abuse just in order to assess the state of my mind. This is a first world country for God's sake, where Big Bang Theory is worshiped like a Goddess. I expected them to use the latest scientific head scans to find the missing link in my mind. The whole process lacked compassion. It was dehumanising and demeaning, even my worst enemies, I wouldn't wish them that.

My rights have been violated left, right and centre in this hospital. The side effects of the medication make me appear really mad. They make me look even madder than mad. Looking at myself in the mirror earlier on in the toilet, it was like coming face-to-face with my own great grandmother, with due respect. This isn't a face of a twenty something old woman. It's like my head has been chopped and replaced by a head of a goblin. The make-up, eye lashes, lip sticks have all gone, leaving me a stranger to myself. Stilettos, tight trousers, human hair and braids, which define who I am, my personality, have all vanished.

If I gather enough strength I could open my eyes, but the goblins sitting on my eyes lids wouldn't let go. Talking through my cracking lips the nurses accused me of speaking 'Neologism.' Neologism? What kind of language is that? I can't speak Neologism! I don't know a single country, anywhere in the world, that speaks it. My debates with the psychiatrist are always heated and sometimes violent. I missed the psychiatrist's broad forehead with my stiletto, the other day, the reason they have taken all my shoes away, and as a result, the nurses raped my behind with their extra-size needle. During these heated meetings with the psychiatrist, I sometimes use my mother tongue, to express myself clearly. To be heard properly. But, using my language during these confrontations, confirms my insanity to them, is considered a symptom of my illness in itself. Each time I'm accused of creating new words, I always receive an injection on my backside.

I don't agree with the psychiatrist's diagnoses of PTSD and PPD. My admission to this psychiatric hospital has nothing to do with any mental illness, it has got to do with so many things but none of them have anything to do with psychiatry.

I have been in this hospital for nearly two weeks now. My husband and his friends haven't visited me here. They have been shaken to their bones. All my other relatives, including my uncle, live in Zimbabwe. Therefore without the support of my husband and my childhood friend, Molly, in the United Kingdom, I am isolated and lonely, forget the population of over sixty-million people. Being more than five thousand miles away from my country of origin and detained in a psychiatric hospital makes me feel like I am the only person living on planet earth. Although my surroundings are littered with people of different races, colours, languages, and accents, they count for nothing in my island of aliens.

There are a number of psychiatric nurses from Zimbabwe working in this hospital, but to me it doesn't make my situation any better, if anything, it complicates it. These nurses will spread the word that a Zimbabwean has been admitted to a secure psychiatric hospital, and nasty stories, just as darkness is followed by light, will follow, with some touch of truth in some, but some with real fabrication made in hell. Made up so that they feel better. Like veld fire, stories will spread. Some would wonder why I flew all the way from Zimbabwe only to be detained in a psychiatric hospital. Some would say *ngiledlozi lobuyanga,* my ancestors want me to remain poor. Why should I get in the land of plenty and then lose my mind? Some will tell their relatives back home, that although their Home Office papers are not in order, at least their minds are in order. Some would quote my case to justify why they can't support their kith and kin back home. Some would want to make a point that although they are struggling in the diaspora, others, like me, *bayahlanya,* are insane. Whatever rumours they peddle, whatever lies they spread, whatever hatred they tell, they can't hurt me anymore. I'm beyond hurt. You can't hurt a stone, can you? I'm like a free spirit.

But my childhood friend Molly, keeps on visiting me and that makes a whole lot of a difference. She has been here several times already. The first day she brought me some roses and the nurses stopped her from handing them to me - they said roses' stems have thorns and I might self-harm with them. I'm a danger to myself, they concluded. I have not seen any visitors with roses, or any flowers, for that matter, in this psychiatric hospital. A mixture of stigma and prejudice stink worse than poo. In general hospitals, patients smell the scent of roses, the same flowers are lethal weapons here.

I enjoy Molly's visits despite the lack of roses. She brings me something that liberates my mind. Something that makes my brain tick. Something that keeps me alive in this hospital. Something that nurses and doctors cannot stop her from bringing in. Something, which even prison guards can't stop it from getting into their prisons. That is empathy. She's the only one who has walked every step in my shoes, with the same strength, vigour, determination and purpose. She feeds me with hope and purpose in this psychological torture chamber called a hospital.

How did my life take such a nasty turn? What caused my admission to a secure psychiatric hospital? Well, a few life events went pear shaped and then an avalanche of tribulations took over my life and turned it into an unrecognisable monster.

I am an asylum seeker in the UK from Zimbabwe. I have been granted temporary leave to remain. My temporary travelling document issued by the Home Office doesn't allow me to travel to Zimbabwe. I can visit any other country of my choice in the world but not to my home country. But when my mother fell ill, not for the first time, I was left with no option but to go and see her. I broke some immigration laws in the process. I believe these laws must be broken deliberately and repeatedly. Slavery, colonialism and apartheid had their own laws too that were broken deliberately and repeatedly until they were repealed. I'm convinced that these immigration laws must be broken until they are annulled. They're inhuman, cruel, savage and brutal. They have literally frozen my time in this country and returned my life into stone age. They have led me to insanity. They have created a rebel out of a conformist.

Chapter 2

BULAWAYO

When I arrived back in my home town Bulawayo nine months ago, I went straight to see my sick mother in hospital. It was a hot sunny day. The air was fresh and unpolluted. The sun roasted my skin and turned it from brown to coal black within an hour's exposure. I didn't know what I preferred at that moment. The biting British cold or the roasting sun of Zimbabwe. I was wearing my orange pencil skirt, which exposed most of my thighs to the fresh air. My floral sleeveless blouse did its best too, exposing most of my upper chest as well. Bulawayo was very hot that summer, one needed to expose a lot more than one would do in Bournemouth. I turned a few heads with my attire. With size 36DD breasts and natural, no boob job, I twisted a few necks that day. My breast and buttocks balanced my body quite nicely. I didn't look like I would fall on my face because of the size of my breasts overcoming the weight of my buttocks. Nor did I appear like I would fall backwards due to the size of my buttocks, too heavy for my breasts. I didn't look like those white girls in Bournemouth, *abangama-planka,* whose backs were as flat as planks, who went for a 40F boob jobs, leaving them leaning forward *njengabogogo,* like grannies.

Zimbabwe being quite a socially conservative country, I was careful with how much I exposed. But my uncle's wife, who accompanied me to the hospital every day, did not complain, so I assumed that I was within the realm of what was acceptable.

I was walking on a ten centimetre stiletto and my nails were painted red, I had to make an impression, after all I had just arrived in Zimbabwe from the United Kingdom. And I wanted my mother to see me looking at my best, so that she would concentrate all her energies on her own recovery and not worry about me.

I had not seen my mother for the past five years. I was stunned when I first saw her. She lay helplessly on her hospital bed, looking old, frail and wasted. She had suffered a heart attack, her second attack in the past two years. It had turned her from a bubbly woman to an almost lifeless body. I held her hand during each visit and said my best prayer. Her hands were cold.

"Mama I'm here, can you hear me? Can you see me?" She didn't respond. Life is cruel, I thought to myself, for reducing my mother to a cabbage at the back of a lorry. I visited her every day and said everything that I wanted to say, sometimes quietly in my heart sometimes aloud: "Mama, you are my life, my hope, my inspiration and you must not leave me alone. You have a heart of gold for bringing me and my brother to this life. If it wasn't for you, I wouldn't be living in the first world, my brother would not have been part of emancipation of our country. From nothing you brought us up to be God fearing and cherish freedom. You are my tower of strength.

"I'm sorry for not visiting you as often as I would have wanted mama. I am embarrassed because I have nothing to show for being in the land of plenty. But even those so called developed countries, are governed by heartless men. Men you would think *kabazalwanga babhotshwa,* they were not born but pooed. I tried to obey their rules mama, but when you became unwell for the second time, I thought *okungasikufa kuyini,* what is it that doesn't kill? I threw caution into the wind and that is the reason I'm here today.

"Please promise me that should you move onto another world, you will reserve a place for me. You must only leave me behind when you know where you are going and that you would be happy. You have fought many wars in your life mama, your own world wars, your own independence wars and your own NaKissmore wars and won many of them. One of those NaKissmore's battles you won, was educating me with absolutely nothing, selling vegetables and fruits in the streets until I graduated as a secondary school teacher. You are my life. If you decide to move on, I would be left to fight my own life wars too, which I have a good feeling that I would win them hands down now that I'm living in the world of everything. Through your unwavering love you have armed me for my life battles, better than you were equipped by your own parents.

"In my next life, should I be made to choose a mother, you will be my mother again, you are everything I want from a mother. You are my hero, a life giver and everything."

The day I said those words to my mother, I left the hospital in tears, as if I had lost her. My uncle's wife, Madawu, who always accompanied me to hospital, put her hands around my shoulders and said, "It's important that you take it out of your heart *mzukulu,* niece, otherwise it could turn into a tumour and eat you inside-out."

Something sitting on my shoulders lifted and left me feeling guilty because I sounded as if I was paying my last tribute to my mother that day. She was still alive, not dead. Maybe whatever was sitting on my shoulders was lifted by what I said, it lifted because if she died, I would have said all what I wanted to say while she was still alive. While she could still hear me. I treated each visit I made to hospital, most of the times twice a day, as the last time I would see her still breathing. My hope was running thin that she would survive the second heart attack, but I would assure myself that she was a fighter, that no one should count her out until she had exhaled her last breath.

I did not keep food in my stomach when I was in Zimbabwe during my last visit. I vomited most of the time when I ate something, especially in the morning. I blamed out-of-date food sold in shops. If you were fortunate to find food in the shops during my visit, you would not find any expiry date labels. Often they had been deliberately removed. No one was bothered about the out of date labels, one would just count themselves lucky to find food to buy in the shop in the first place. As a result, I decided to deliberately miss my breakfast to avoid feeling sick.

I was born and bred in Bulawayo. My earliest memories as a young girl, started at the age of four or five years. Before that age I don't remember anything about myself, life has a way of protecting you from the horrors of birth. Imagine seeing myself popping between my mother's legs, suffocated by the umbilical cord tying the two of us together. Bloodied and bellowing a battle cry. A shriek that is a must or risk a spank on the backside. A howl that announces the battle that has just been won and symbolises those that are yet to be fought.

At the age of nine, I was taller than average in my class, taller, even, than most boys. My mother was either called NaKissmore or MaNare. Kissmore was my brother's name. Older people were either called by their first born's names; NaKissmore or their maiden names; MaNare. Only a few people would call my mother, NaDolly, after me, doing it out of pity. I was told that many people stopped calling her NaKissmore and called her NaDolly, when my brother did not return from the liberation war and when I was born. I suppose it was a way of not reminding her of her darkest part of her life.

My teen years had their joys and tears of growing up. That was the time when I discovered myself. Created my own identity. When I moulded to who I am. My body played a bigger part in that. Sizeism played a major part, as I was described as tall and thin. At the age of fifteen I was taller than my mother, one hundred and fifty centimetres tall and on the slim side of the scale.

At the age of eleven or twelve, my breasts started to develop, at first appearing like two bees sitting on each side of my chest. Because those bees deposited honey into my young and innocent body, my chest responded by swelling up where they were sitting. My breasts continued to swell from the bee sting and faster in my teens. I was concerned about their rate of growth, I thought that if they continued at that rate, some people would think I did a boob job by the time I reached my late teens. I began to see myself not only as a young lady, but a beautiful one too.

At sixteen years my body started to take the shape of a real woman. My bottom began to beef up, becoming round like footballs, shaping up perfectly, to attract the right husband. My thighs thickened up to enable me to carry my baby and provide my husband with a homely and well-shaped environment to plant his seed. To propagate both of us. To enable us to live forever.

My face was as smooth as a baby's bottom at an age when most girls had faces like baby's bottoms littered with fragments of poo. Their faces as rough as the bark of mopane tree stems. Face and body wise, I was ahead of the pack, a leader.

Some girls at my school had been denied the gift of every woman, because they had flat backs. I felt sorry for them when they sat down on benches, with their bare bones rubbing against the hard harsh surfaces of the wood. At that age I reached all the mile stones. My mother said I was beautiful like her, but then who is ugly in the eyes of their own mother? I bloomed like a flower.

When I was thirteen or fourteen years old, two boys who were best friends took a shine on me. One day I saw them as I was crossing a bushy area between Phelandaba suburb, where my uncle lived, to Iminyela township, popularly known as Number One township, where we lived. The boys waved what appeared to be a white piece of paper in the air, put it on the ground and sprinted away. When I got to the spot, I saw an envelope with my name on it, so I picked it up and opened it. There were two letters, both addressed to me, one from Talkmore and the other from Bigboy. Both letters had the same message, word for word, but with different handwriting and signatures. I read one of the letters, which went like this,

Deer Dolly, I am written to you because I loved you. You are the flour of my hart. If you loved me two, wrote to me. I loved you with my every hart. I thoght of you all deyi and all nite. My hart is cried four you. You are beautyful and loveful. I want to held your hand and walked with you, hand and hand. Pliz love me second because I love you first. You are my tshokolate. You are sweetie like horny. babayi, Talkmore.

Oh, what a sweet letter I thought. The other one was exactly the same, but signed off by *babayi Bigboy*. I replied the letters and told both boys that I loved them too, that they would make good husbands and I would like them to share me between themselves. I said it would be an honour to be sandwiched in bed by two "loveful" boys every night. But only a few days after my responses, a rumour started to circulate that I was *umahotsha*, a prostitute for loving both of them "second." From that day Talkmore and Bigboy avoided me; if they saw me coming they would change direction. Our next door neighbour had two loving wives, so I didn't see anything wrong with me having two boyfriends who both loved me exactly the same way.

During that visit, nine months ago, I lived with my uncle in Phelandaba medium density suburb. My uncle was my mother's only sibling and with the help of his wife, they looked after her while in hospital. Both his sons were outside the country. His elder son lived in Australia and his last born lived in South Africa. Neither of them had been home since they left more than four years ago, promising to buy him a new house in low density suburbs, like Hillside or Khumalo. Promises, promises, promises. The same applied to me, I promised to buy my mother a house in low density suburbs too, but five years later, that was still just a promise.

We failed to fulfil the promises we made to our parents, who had stripped themselves of their possessions, like cows, houses, and cars to help fund our tickets to a better world because it was tough in the diaspora, money didn't grow from the trees as some people from Zimbabwe seemed to think. It's dog eat dog out there. Without the proper papers that allowed you to work, you were as good as dead wood. Ask Molly's niece, who bought a British passport from a Nigerian in London and when they caught her they put her in prison. As if that was not punishment enough, after her release, she was deported back to Comrade Moment of Madness's Zimbabwe.

You look over your shoulder all the time in the diaspora, one silly mistake, you are thrown back to wherever you came from. That you have friends, relatives and family in the diaspora matters nothing to the power hungry politicians. The more cruel, evil and inhuman they are, the more electable they become. Take London vans for instance. They guzzled diesel like thirsty lions, driving around London streets, further polluting the already polluted city, with inscriptions in big bold red letters that read, "In the UK illegally? Go home or face arrest." They might as well have read, "In the UK illegally? Go back home monkey, you are not wanted here." Or, "In the UK illegally? Go home or face arrest or torture or life imprisonment or the firing squad or all of the above." If your papers were not in order, and you came across one of those vans, you either wet yourself or wished the earth to open and swallow you up. That was diaspora's life in the twenty-first century modern Britain.

With my British blue passport, I was stuffed, I was not allowed to visit my country of origin. The reason, I assumed, was to protect me from Comrade Moment of Madness. But surely, if British white journalists, who were well known and obviously stood out in a black country, could sneak in and out of Zimbabwe undetected, I could do the same as I would blend better. I felt that those immigration laws were meant to punish asylum seekers, I was expected to live in the UK as if I didn't have relatives on the other side of the world.

My uncle had moved my mother from our relative's house in Lobengula West and took her under his wings, when she became unwell, that was what extended families were for. I will never thank my uncle's wife, Madawu, enough, for taking care of my mother. When nurses asked relatives to bring their own toiletries and bath their relatives in hospital, my uncle would have found it difficult to bath his own sister, but his wife was more than willing to bath my mother. During my visit, she helped me out. Words alone were never enough to thank her, I left it to God to thank her for me. As a token of appreciation, I bought my uncle and his wife large amounts of clothes from Highbury Park market in London and nice suits from Marks and Spencer. It was the only way I could show my appreciation, *ikhotha eyikhothayo*, one good turn deserves another.

My uncle's house in Pelandaba was next door to the late Joshua Nkomo's house. Joshua Nkomo was the founding father of Zimbabwe's politics and he was affectionately known as Father Zimbabwe or *umdala wethu, mudhara wedu,* our old timer. Soon after independence he escaped from Comrade Moment of Madness's Zimbabwe, tail between his legs, fearing for his life, running away from the independence he ushered to Zimbabwe. He found his way to Botswana before he flew to London. The rumour said that he deceived the immigration officers at Plumtree border post on his way to Botswana by dressing as a woman. He was huge and I found it difficult to imagine him in a dress. How he found his way to London without a passport, has always left me wondering how he managed to pull that one. Comrade Moment of Madness was left sitting on his passport, hoping that Nkomo won't find his way to Europe and tarnish his good name among his peers. Nkomo didn't only pave our way to independence, he also pointed us to where we could get help, should Comrade Moment of Madness relapses back to his old ways again. When the hen started eating its own eggs again, we all said United Kingdom, United States of America, Australia, Canada, South Africa, Botswana, even Venezuela, here we come.

When I last left Zimbabwe, way back in 2003, things were beginning to deteriorate politically and economically. By 2008 things had taken a turn for the worst. People were thin, tired and hungry. When the black skin is malnourished it becomes darker and glossy in appearance like a mummy. It appears as if it is losing the will to live. Preparing itself to feed the maggots. That was what I saw on the streets. Mummy, dark and glossy skeletons walking the streets. Bulawayo looked like a ghost city. Family and friends told me that women were using newspapers as tampons. Men had stopped going to work because their month's salaries were less than their fare to work. Inflation was running at hundreds of billions percent. Zimbabwe had changed from a breadbasket to a basket case.

Comrade Moment of Madness behaved like a soldier that went to war and lost both his legs and arms in a battle: he is alive but hopeless, dependent on everyone for everything, just like a baby, but still believes that he could call the shots, make decisions that affect those who carry him around. And he went on to kill those very people who carried him around, oblivious of their role in his own survival.

When their country couldn't feed them anymore, many Zimbabweans took the cue from their late dear leader Joshua Mqabuko Nkomo, who had sneaked out of the country many years ago. They left in droves, heading to the diaspora. They left their motherland overflowing with billions and trillions of dollars for greener pastures! At the same time Comrade Moment

17

of Madness told Tony Blair to keep his Britain and he would keep his Zimbabwe. He would tell those who cared to listen that the only blair he knew was a toilet! At the same time the opposition leader affectionately known as Chematama, fat cheeks, by his enemies, was calling for sanctions against Comrade Moment of Madness and his government for human rights abuses.

While Comrade Moment of Madness, who had seven university degrees on violence only, and Mr Chematama were exchanging verbal blows, sometimes physical blows, Zimbabweans suffered, where two bulls fight, it's the grass that suffers the most, so they say. On my numerous visits to the hospital to see my mother, I witnessed how the nurses and doctors treated their patients and relatives, it was beyond belief. They shouted and assaulted expecting mothers during their special moment of delivering life to the universe. They channelled their hunger, anger and frustrations towards their poor patients and relatives. Some people told me that doctors treated their patients humanly only in their private surgeries.

One of my uncle's neighbours told me how she was treated when she developed complication during childbirth in one of the government hospitals. The doctors and nurses performed a caesarean section under local anaesthetic without first gaining her consent or even letting her know. Imagine your belly being sliced open without your consent? The revelation staggered me since my mother was under the care of the same doctors and nurses. I feared that should she survive the heart attack, she might not survive their brutality.

Zimbabwe in 2008 was a hell hole, Satan's paradise. People selling tomatoes and vegetables in the streets were earning more money than teachers and nurses. Teachers who used to scare their students into taking their studies seriously by saying that they might end up selling tomatoes on the streets, were by then owing those same street vendors some serious money. How life had turned on its head, street vendors were treated like the Standard Banks and Santanders of Europe.

I had sufficient British pound sterling during the visit, but there was no medicine. Money is useless if you can't exchange it for goods. The lack of medicine plus uncaring nurses and doctors, equalled certain death. I turned my hope to God, but it was very difficult to find God in Satan's paradise. But not for starving Zimbabweans, most of the atheists I knew had found God in Satan's den - God is the only hope for the poor! I put my mother's life in God's hands. If He couldn't help her, so be it.

I left Zimbabwe with a heavy heart, as my mother had not uttered a single word or moved a finger in the whole two weeks I had been there. I had to go back to my new home, Britain, and leave sick Zimbabwe behind. I knew from the depth of my mind that I would never see her alive again. As I said goodbye to her for the last time, my eyes welled up but I had to go back to my new-found home. I had to go, hope was calling from Britain. Zimbabwe was in ruins.

I boarded a mini-bus affectionately known as a kombi in Zimbabwe, bound for South Africa via Beitbridge border post. The Limpopo River is Zimbabwe's southern divide, it separates South Africa and Zimbabwe. It was the white men's colonial divide, the white men's visual hallucinations of Africa, that gave birth to African countries. They gave each other portions of the continent without consulting the inhabitants. They gave those portions their surnames. Cecil John Rhodes gave Zimbabwe and Zambia double barrel surnames; Southern-Rhodesia, and Northern-Rhodesia, respectively. The colonialists believed that the Africans were too primitive, too stupid to give their own names to their own countries. They thought that the blacks had no capacity to make decisions. Because the partition of Africa was done by people who did not know the continent, but international bullies, same languages are spoken on both sides of the borders. On both sides of the Limpopo River, people speak Venda. And you wonder why there are perennial wars in Africa?

Our kombi left Bulawayo's City Hall, the city centre, at around two o'clock and drove onto Leopold Takawira Avenue, formerly Selbourne Avenue that led to Gwanda Road. The journey to Beitbridge usually takes four to five hours. Under normal circumstances my mother would have waved goodbye to me but not that day. Whether she would wave good bye to me in the future, I left that in our Creator's hands.

We drove through the Ascot traffic lights and entered the Khumalo suburb, a low density suburb, previously a white-only area. Black people were prohibited by law to walk or live in that suburb, unless they were garden boys. The so-called "garden boys" were married men with children, but they appeared never to grow up in the eyes of white settlers during the days of colonial abuse.

As we entered Khumalo suburb, a black cat attempted to cross the road. The kombi driver didn't give a hoot whether he ran it over or not. He didn't even attempt to apply the brakes; in fact, he accelerated. Most of the passengers were concerned about a black cat crossing the road in front of their kombi. Black cats are associated with bad luck in many other societies that included Zimbabwe. At first it turned back, but changed its mind and ran forward and then changed its mind again and it stopped. The kombi ran over it. From the rear mirror, I saw the blood stains on the road. The cat's indecision in the middle of the road had led to its untimely death. Life is a precious but hopeless commodity; one minute it's here and the next minute it turns to death.

Most of the passengers were happy that the black cat was run over. I hoped that bad luck would have nothing to do with me. As most of the passengers cheered the cat's death, I just looked on. The driver said nothing. He kept his eyes on the road ahead, as he was trained 'to keep your eyes on the road all the time.' I presumed he had run over many black cats than he cared to remember. Or he was worried about the bad luck too, but he could not afford to be seen either celebrating or mourning.

As we drove along Gwanda Road, past Chipangali Animal Orphanage, I wondered who was caring for the poor animal orphans now that Zimbabwe couldn't care for its own people? With Zimbabwe going down the drains who cared about animals? Living in the United Kingdom had led me to care about things I shouldn't care about. First the cat and now animal orphans! 'Forget about it Dolly, what's wrong with you,' I said quietly to myself. Soon we were zigzagging down the steep slopes in an area appropriately named Danger. I looked outside and marvelled at Mother Nature, at the beauty of Africa's landscape. When God made the world, he took his time to mould Africa. I was not surprised that other continents fought wars over its beautiful landscape and weather. But Zimbabwe, like most of the things that look so beautiful from outside yet are rotten inside, was haemorrhaging due to Comrade Moment of Madness.

We left Danger behind us and soon came face-to-face with a massive butte, a huge stone-like hill at the junction of Gwanda and Filabusi Roads. The huge stone-hill reminded me of a massive hill in Weymouth, in South West England. The Weymouth hill had a white horse sculpted onto it. It was beautiful to a certain extent. Compared to the Mbalabala boulder, the Weymouth one appeared superficial. It wasn't natural, it had been interfered with. It stood out. It was loud. It was attractive, good to the eye, good for tourism but it had lost its virginity. Man's hand had been all over it several times. It was actually shouting at you, 'Watch me, you dare ignore me!'

Mbalabala boulder versus Weymouth was like God versus man; for atheists, nature versus man. The Mbalabala one was still a virgin. No man's hand had ever touched it, except for one drunk white settler, who rode his horse to the top of the butte and jumped to the bottom and the horse landed on its feet. Both survived without a scratch. Since no one witnessed his stunt, he then went around and called his family, friends and neighbours to come and witness the stunt. Maybe he hoped to get into the Guinness Book of World Records. It was reported that people from all walks of life came to witness the stunt. Many people left their fields unattended in order to witness the miracle. He jumped but the horse landed on its back with him trapped beneath. They both died instantly and they were buried at the foot of the boulder on the same spot and in a single grave.

The kombi driver sped on in the ancient Toyota Hi-ace, imported into Zimbabwe from either Japan or UK as a panel van and then turned into a mini-bus. We were packed like sardines, eighteen of us, excluding the driver, so squeezed up to each other, that one couldn't let the wind out even if they wanted to. These kombis were human coffins on wheels, but the officers at the numerous police road blocks along the Bulawayo-Beitbridge highway were only interested in collecting bribes. Whatever they found wrong with our minibus, was put right by a bribe. The bribe was paid openly as if the police were collecting government taxes.

As we approached Gwanda mining town, a passenger with a missing front tooth who was sitting behind me said to the driver, "Do you know where the police officers in the next road block hide their bribe money?"

"Do they hide the bribe money? Hide it from whom?" asked the driver. I also wondered why they should hide their hard earned money collected in broad daylight in full view of the passengers.

"Hide it from their bosses," said the man with a missing tooth, showing it off.

"I thought their bosses were entitled to a cut."

"Ya, you're correct to some degree, but it's not always that simple. From time to time they receive surprise visits from the anti-corruption unit. To be safe, they don't keep money in their pockets, socks or shoes but keep it within the vicinity. At the next road block they hide it under two big stones in the nearby bush about twenty metres from the road. If you want to prove it, when they flag us down pretend that you want to use the bush and walk towards the two big stones before you pay them the bribe," suggested the man with a missing tooth. Most of the passengers in the kombi didn't believe him and they groaned as a result.

"How do you know that?" Enquired the driver, unbelieving the man too.

"Someone told me in a shebeen." Most passengers laughed.

"Ah, don't listen to shebeen patrons," said the driver, with a groan.

A passenger wearing a white shirt, sitting at the back of the kombi, joined in.

"Don't listen too much to the shebeen patrons, they are usually too drunk to remember their wives' names let alone their birthdays."

"If you don't believe me, try it *mfowethu,* my brother when we get to the road block," said the man with a missing tooth.

Soon, the road block appeared and the police waved us down, as we expected. If Comrade Moment of Madness travelled in a kombi they would wave him down too, I thought to myself. We stopped and as the police talked to the driver, the Doubting Thomas, the passenger in a white shirt slipped out of the kombi and headed towards the two big rocks.

"Mira ipapo! Stop right there" a police officer shouted at him. *"Urikuendepi,* where do you think you are going?"

"I just want to use the bush chef." The Zimbabwean police like to be addressed as chefs. That is how they address their superiors too. There's only one man in the whole of Zimbabwe who doesn't call any other man chef; take a guess, he's the top cock. The passenger made another step towards the two rocks.

"Ndati mira ipapo, I said stop right there. If you continue I will shoot you," barked the officer as he drew out his shotgun and pointed it at the passenger. "Do you know that it's against the law *kumamira musango,* to relieve yourself in the bush? Do you?" roared the officer, still pointing his gun at the passenger.

"I'm sorry chef, I'm really sorry," apologised the shell-shocked passenger as he returned to the kombi.

"Never ever try to relieve yourself at a road block again. Do you understand? Never ever. Get back to your kombi or I shoot you right now and you will caca for sure," shouted the officer, as he put his hand gun back to its sheath. No one was laughing any more. It was no longer a laughing matter. As soon as the kombi driver paid the bribe, we were allowed to proceed with our journey. As we pulled away the driver muttered, "They are prepared to kill to protect their stash *madoda,* men."

"I...I almost wet myself," stammered the passenger in a white shirt. "I've never had a gun pointed at me in my whole life. I was waiting for 'bang' and I'm gone, leaving my family behind,"

"Don't tempt the ZanuPF police, they're above the law. You dangerously encroached on their loot," said the man with a missing tooth, giggling.

To say that I was a bit shaken is an understatement, I almost wet my pants too. It's not every day that you see a police officer pointing a gun at a defenceless, unarmed passenger. What a police force! They behaved worse than thieves. If the police officers on those road blocks did just half of their job properly, Zimbabwean roads would be the safest in the world. A few minutes from the road block, we drove past Gwanda town and after a long journey we arrived at the Beitbridge Border Post.

Chapter 3

LIMPOPO RIVER

On my way into Zimbabwe, I avoided using my British blue passport by bribing the immigration officers at both borders. I could not risk showing them my blue passport, as they would have stamped it with a Zimbabwean immigration stamp and I would have been deported from the United Kingdom before I could finish saying my name. It was easy hitchhiking from South Africa. I found my way into Zimbabwe as if I was using a diplomat's passport. At the two border posts I remained seated in the kombi while the rest of the passengers and the driver went out for passport checks. My powerful British pound sterling blinded the corrupt immigration officers of the two countries.

But on my outward journey, things changed dramatically. As soon as we arrived at Beitbridge border post, two unkempt men approached our kombi. They whispered something to the kombi driver and he got out of the car and followed them to a distance of about ten metres away. I couldn't hear what they were saying, but our driver appeared surprised and shook his head so violently it could have snapped his neck. He was animated, talking to them using hand gestures, at times he pointed to our kombi, sometimes to his watch, sometimes to his head, as if he was saying that someone would shoot him for whatever reason. The two men talking to him appeared calm. Only one of the two seemed to say more. But whatever he was saying agitated our driver. For some reasons the driver's animation appeared to have a negative effect to me. You don't want to be driven by a man who was that agitated. I hoped whatever they were saying to him will not disrupt his driving concentration, although it was not one of the smoothest driving I had ever experienced. After a while our driver started to nod. At that point, I thought to myself, whatever they were disagreeing about had been resolved, so we could carry on with our journey.

The driver came back to the kombi and he demanded to see me and a few other passengers. Soon I learnt that those passengers either did not have or couldn't use their passports, for one reason or another, just like me. A bit of grumbling came from some of the men, but that soon died down as we quietly disembarked from the kombi and moved away from the rest of the passengers. The driver left us at the mercy of two scruffy men and went back to his vehicle. The first man was medium built, unkempt and wearing torn jeans. He appeared well fed for someone who was so dishevelled and dressed like a tramp. The second man was very tall and thin - whatever they ate, the first man clearly took bigger portions. He had protruding cheeks and he was wearing a red shirt scorched by the sun to its last cotton threads. They were both wearing heavy, weather-beaten boots as a sign that they trod the Limpopo River more than its inhabitant crocodiles.

"I'm Joe," said the first man, then pointing to his companion, he continued, "And this is Ben. Your kombi driver has asked us to help you cross the Limpopo River. The new immigration staff who have just arrived *abawubambi umtshina,* they are not taking bribes. The only way you can reach the South African side is by crossing the Limpopo River on foot. You will catch up with your kombi on the South African side, at Musina to be precise." His voice was commanding, expecting no arguments.

I found myself saying; "You can't be serious! I'm not walking to Musina. I paid the driver serious money to take me to South Africa in his kombi!"

"Shut up and listen British woman," shouted Joe, as if I had no rights to protest at the change of plans. So the driver had told them about my British blue passport. Everyone looked at me. Never had I been called a British woman before, I was a bit embarrassed. At that point and to my utter shock, our kombi pulled off and approached the immigration offices leaving us behind. It dawned to me that Joe meant business and he continued, "Don't try to be clever with us, we're only trying to help. We are only doing our job. You will still get to South Africa, but by different means. If you have any complaints, you will have time to talk to your driver when we have done our part and taken you across the border."

I had heard of many Zimbabweans who had perished at Limpopo River. It's a river with crocodiles that target Zimbabweans only. Their breakfast, lunch and dinner is made up of Zim fresh meat. If a South African and a Zimbabwean crossed the Limpopo River hand in hand, I could bet with my last penny that the crocodiles would pick the Zimbabwean.

I had to cross Limpopo River on foot that was a price to pay for not having proper documents in the diaspora. I took comfort from the fact that as a supposedly new British citizen the crocodiles might spare me, they might show me some respect.

There were six of us, the border jumpers, two women and four men. Ben threw an old pair of tekkies at my feet and another at the other woman, saying, "Put those shoes on women, you can't cross the Limpopo in your stilettos." They were dirty, smelly and oversized shoes. I hesitated but the other woman quickly changed into hers, leaving me with no option. She was obviously not a trouble-maker. She was short, not beautiful but pretty. She had a round face and puppy eyes, the kind of a face that you never forget. Slowly I put my new pair of shoes on too. It was clear that I had to learn to follow orders.

"You must walk quietly and in a file. You must obey all our orders all the time," said Joe, our chief minder, "This's not a picnic. Is there anyone who is sick here, or has nyctalopia, night blindness for those *abatshaya ababalisi ngerekeni,* who truanted? Anyone who can't walk fast or who has *umkhuhlane wamaphaphu kumbe inhliziyo*, lung or heart disease?" All other border jumpers shook their heads. I didn't. He wasn't a doctor, or nurse for that matter, he wasn't supposed to be asking us about our health problems. Our health problems were our privacy. 'Nyctalopia' my foot. He was certainly one of those *abatshaya ababalisi ngerekeni,* I thought to myself? He went on, "You must do as you are told or else there could be accidents, or even death along the way. I don't want that to happen under my watch. Get it?" He spoke without mincing his words. Again my fellow border jumpers nodded their heads, but I didn't.

"Get it?" Joe repeated himself, with his eyes, red as a tomato, fixed on me. What else besides cannabis could make a man's eyes so red, unless he had some eye infection? He deliberately put me on the spot. Perhaps he felt threatened by my being 'British.' In order to avoid unnecessary confrontations, I nodded too.

"Good," he said with a triumphant voice. "It's always best to cross the river at night, for obvious reasons. For a start, we don't want to be seen like *ondofa,* goblins. We are lucky tonight we have got a full moon and there are no clouds." He then ordered us to move on. "Ok, *asambeni,* let's go. Move people," he said using hand gestures too, like a herdsman driving his cattle into a slaughter house.

We started on a journey that I had not planned and we obeyed the orders. The vegetation varied considerably in the Limpopo area and there were huge baobab trees too, that appeared like elephant silhouette from a distance although bush shrubs dominated the grassland. Tall trees were far spaced, bushvelds and thorny shrubs covered most of the forest. Mopane trees also dominated that part of Beitbridge area. The thorny shrubs caused me some agony during our journey. Despite the bright light of the moon, I kept on catching my blouse on the thorny shrubs. I thought it would only be a matter of time before it was torn to shreds and I walked bare-breasted. I was wearing a thin nylon blouse and jean shorts, which turned out not be good for that journey. Luckily I had put a jean jacket in my hand bag and I debated whether to put it on or not as we slowly but surely made our way towards Limpopo River. The jeans shorts didn't offer much protection to my thighs and legs against thorny shrubs either. I kept reminding myself that that journey was not part of the deal I made with the driver, a week before my departure date.

In Beitbridge, it was hotter than in Bulawayo; sometimes it felt as if the moonlight was emitting the heat too. To say it was hot is an understatement, it was boiling, and I was sweating buckets. After a while it began to get darker and the sound of the Limpopo River grew closer and closer on our approach. I found myself thinking, 'I'm British - please get me out of here.'

Out of nowhere a voice thundered from the bush, "Who are you mother flippings? Talk to me or I shoot."

"Take cover bantwana babomazakhela," (children of single mothers) shouted Joe, showering us with insults as we dived onto the hard red earth, it was as good as diving into an empty swimming pool. It's an insult to be a single mother the world over. In the UK, single mothers are singled out, my apologies for the pun, for scamming the welfare system, because they receive preferential housing. Their maternity leave is said to be indefinite, their babies receive a weekly income from the moment they take in their first breath, as an icing on the cake. In Zimbabwe single mothers are called prostitutes, therefore a child of a single mother is a child of a prostitute, Joe had just called us exactly that!

We all took cover, not because we were *abantwana babomazakhela* - but who wouldn't if they heard someone threatening to shoot them in the middle of nowhere for no apparent reason. Joe shouted back, "We're Joshua Nkomo's orphans. The crocodile Crashers. The Limpopo Godfathers. *OmaGumaguma, beLimpopo,* the pirates of the Limpopo River. *VanaChinoz ve*Limpopo River. And who are you mother flipping?" He added more unprintable phrases. Two men emerged from the bush, carrying axes and knobkerries, one of them yelled insults at us,

"Where are you going without passports mother flippings? Leaving

behind *nyika yehuchi nemukaka,* land of milk and honey to enslave yourselves to other countries. What are you risking your lives for? *Simukai
mabhodajampa,* get up border jumpers! Get up cowards!"

We all got up and dusted ourselves down like proper losers. I didn't
know what to do, cry or laugh. The two men who emerged from the bush
had friendly handshakes as they chatted with our minders. I felt so abused.
I even felt more humiliated on behalf of the men in our company, who were
being subjected to this treatment by other men. They were being treated
like nonentities, like women, by school drop outs. If I were to be treated
like that by other women, *ngangizakhwica izidwaba ngifunga ngomama,*
I would fight back, I swear with my mother. It was obvious that the men
knew each other. It dawned on me later that it was all about control. Those
were well-orchestrated and rehearsed skirmishes with their friends planted
along the way to instil fear and obedience onto us. But most of all to make
sure that they don't get ambushed themselves.

Near the Limpopo River we met Zimbabwean soldiers guarding the
disused bridge, or it could have been the current one, everything appeared
broken in 2008. The soldiers were supposed to arrest anyone trying to cross to
South Africa by avoiding the official route. The soldiers, like the police before
them, they took the bribe, part of our money our money we paid the driver to
bribe the immigration officers not omaGumaguma and the soldiers. They were
paid in foreign currency and they let us continue with our journey. They even
supplied our minders with a rope, a necessary aid to crossing the river safely.
Who could blame them? If they arrested us, they would go without food for
days. Their salaries, in billions of Zimbabwean dollars, were not enough to last
them a day. Somehow they had to make a living outside their regular jobs, just
like the police, the nurses, doctors, the ministers and Comrade Moment of
Madness himself. Each man for himself and God for us all. That was Comrade
Moment of Madness's Zimbabwe, a basket case.

Joe explained to us the purpose of the rope: to lower us off the railway
bridge and into the shallow waters of the river. We couldn't walk to the
other end of the bridge because it was guarded by South African soldiers
who would not take our bribes, but would certainly take us prisoner.

Although the river was shallow at the shore, the bridge was too high to
jump into the water, so we needed a rope to lower ourselves into the river. We
could only hope that the crocodiles wouldn't be waiting for us, having picked
up our scent from the wind. We walked along slippery rails, high above water

28

infested with crocodiles below. My palpitations were breaking the speed limit of my heart's motorways. Beating at more than one thousand miles an hour. The fact that it was night time helped me a bit. My fellow travellers would have actually seen my heart peeping in my mouth with each heart bit. And in daylight I would have seen the actual height of the bridge and felt dizzy. As it was, I couldn't see the crocodiles watching me and drooling for my blood. The sound of the river was ferocious, hungry and powerful. My hair stood on end. That was not what I had bargained for. Just two weeks earlier, walking on a bridge of this height at night, could only have happened in a nightmare. But the nightmare had turned into reality.

At some point along the river, Joe stopped, tied the rope to the bridge and around his waist, and he inched downwards towards the water, telling us that we will all do the same. Ben would be the last one to climb down, he would lower himself to the water and they would leave the rope hanging there so that on their way back, before the sun rise, they could use it to climb up. We took it in turns, with Ben encouraging us and making sure the rope was tight and safe around our waists.

The short woman with puppy eyes was ahead of me. I only realised that she had been wetting her pants in fear when she slid round behind me to make sure that she would go down after me, to see that it can be done by a woman too, to get some encouragement. There was something that I did not like about this woman. During our Bulawayo-Beitbridge journey, she sat behind my seat and I could feel her piercing eyes at the back of my head, seeing through me. Her puppy eyes made me feel transparent. Twice, I caught her giving me the eye at the border post.

When my time came, Ben tied the rope around my waist and lowered me over the bridge, but halfway down the rope snapped and I went splashing into the water, screaming, "Mayibabooooooo!"

I said my last prayer as I disappeared beneath the surface of the water. The pain of the impact rippled through my whole body like a knife. The water felt ice cold on my skin despite the Limpopo heat. When I came to the surface, the flowing water tossed me about like a leaf, smashing me against a concrete pillar that supported part of the bridge. The pillar stopped me from being swept further down the river. I went back under the water but resurfaced again, gasping for more air. It was like someone was holding my nostrils tight because I had to hold my breath under the water. Despite the deafening sound of the Limpopo River, I could hear someone shouting, "Oh my God. Oh My God the British woman has fallen into the river." Each time I was above the water, I splattered franticly in an effort to stay afloat; it was like my lungs had sucked in all the Limpopo River water, making me heavy and pulling me downwards. I could swim but I didn't want to leave the sanctuary of the pillar that had turned God, as I would be swept away like a feather. I panicked and went under the water again but as I struggled to the surface again; suddenly something got hold of my left leg, with a crushing pain and pulled me back under. I clutched at anything: water, air and nothing as I was dragged down under. "Oh God! Oh God of all Gods! Mama lo! Mayi babo! Something has caught my left leg! Please help me! Please help...!" The creature hauled me under the water again, although I tried to stay afloat against its mighty strength, I eventually went under again. I swallowed some of the water. I was drowning. I came above the water again. I grabbed at the pillar for dear life and refused to go down, but the creature managed to drag me back under the water at will! When I came up to the surface again, Joe was hitting the creature with a weapon, as its teeth cut deep into my flesh. Joe became part of the struggle. He went under the water with us and came up to surface with us too. He shouted, "Let go crocodile, let her go animal!" And it dawned on me that I had been caught by a crocodile. That sent a chill down my spine and I wet myself. I had never heard of anyone who survived the Limpopo River crocodile attack before. I started saying my last prayers but stopped half way through, because I didn't want to die. If I had to die, I would die fighting, not praying. I had said many prayers in my life before, that would suffice, I thought to myself. After all I had already said, "Oh God" that was enough prayer that night, as more action was needed than words. It was time to try and save my life. I tried to wriggle out of the crocodile's grip in vain. Joe continued to thump the crocodile, hitting it repeatedly, shouting at it to let me go. I could see a dark stain spreading in the water. Was it my blood? Was I bleeding? Was I dying? There was a tearing pain in my calf, as though the crocodile was trying to chew my leg while it was still attached to my body. I gasped and screamed at the top of my voice. "Mama lo! Oh God! *Nkosiyami*! Help me! Please help me, I'm dying! *Ngadliwa yingwenya bo*, the crocodile is eating me!" I struggled and screamed, "The crocodile is chewing my leg. God of all Heavens help...!" The crocodile dragged me under the water again, but I knew that I had to fight back. I had to die fighting. I fought my way back to the surface of the water again. The crocodile sank its teeth deep into my calf, digging deeper with each blow the creature took from Joe. The pain was excruciating. I had read stories of people who fought and won battles against crocodiles, but they lost limbs, they left their hands and legs in the water (and they were not fighting the Limpopo River crocodiles, by the way). Those people talked about attacking the crocodile's palatal valve, nostrils and eyes. I began searching for its palatal valve feeling all over its rough, hard-skinned, slippery head, in an attempt to find its mouth and attack its palatal valve. Fight or flight was a luxury that day, as it gave a choice of escaping, but in my situation, it was fight or die. My fingers clutched the soft part of its mouth - the palatal valve? I clawed into the soft tissue with an eagle's claws, trying to rip it off with my bear fingers. Using all my mighty I tried to tear the palatal valve right out of the crocodile's mouth. Joe continued to pound its head, trying to damage its nostrils, I thought. It is a known fact that if you damage a crocodile's nostrils, it often let's go and I was reassured that Joe seemed to know what he was doing. The pain was indescribable. I was beginning to feel numbness in my left leg. The dark stain in the water spread on the water surface. The sensation in my left leg was going and it felt as if the crocodile had chopped off my leg and gone down the river with it. I screamed at the top of my voice, "The crocodile has swallowed my leg! Please help! The crocodile has gone with my leg. Help me please, please, please! I can't feel my leg! My leg's gone aaaa aa aa aa aa..."

I only stopped screaming when Joe slapped me saying, "Shut up British woman, the crocodile is still here! It's still holding onto your leg, you haven't lost your leg! So shut up!" Have you ever been slapped and felt good? Joe's slap reassured me that I was still in one piece and that he wasn't about to give up on me either. It brought me back to here and now. I reached for the crocodile's jaws again and frantically tried to pull what I hoped was the palatal valve out of the beast's mouth. In its response, the crocodile further clawed its teeth in my left leg's flesh. For a few seconds I felt I had got a good grip of the palatal valve, but then I thought that was only happening in my mind. Whether it was in my imagination or in reality, it didn't matter, I needed to feel that I was doing some damage to whatever part of the crocodile I could hold onto, but the crocodile held my leg like a vice.

I screamed and begged for life until Ben joined the struggle. "Joe, I've a knife! I'll gore its eyes out! I'll blind it!" He stabbed at the crocodile's head in a frenzy. "Stay strong British woman, stay strong!" He reassured me. I continued to pull the organ I clawed my fingers into, Ben and Joe continued with their blows, until the crocodile finally let go.

The two men lifted me out of the water and put me on the ground away from the river. They laid me down flat, but straight away I tried to sit up and check my wounds, but Joe shouted at me, "Lie down British woman. Lie down!" He added, "Your blood must flow to your brain, stay down. You have lost too much blood already," he turned to Ben, "What happened to the rope?"

"I don't know! I guess it just snapped," replied Ben. The rest of the group gathered around me, one man paced up and down, murmuring something under his breath. If that was my prayer, it had obviously been overtaken by events. The other man, just stood there dumfounded, holding his chin and as still as a mummy, as if he suffered from catatonic schizophrenia. The short woman with puppy eyes stood a distance from the rest of the group. Not interested, she was an on looker, not a participant. She was having none of it. It was like I had leprosy and she didn't want to catch it.

Joe paced up and down shaking his head like a possessed *isangoma,* witch-doctor . "I swear by my mother's life, that rope can hang all of us from this bridge without breaking! It can hang a thousand elephants. I can't believe that it just snapped like a piece of string. Like a piece of nothing. No, it can't just snap like that."

I had always viewed border jumping escorts as good for nothing, robbers, school drop outs, waste of space, money grabbers, but in a flash, Joe and Ben changed my view. They became true heroes. True bodyguards. My personal saviours. The two men acted like the masters of a passenger ship, only disembarking from the sinking vessel when no one else remained on board. Risked their lives to save mine like true bodyguards. They could have ignored my pleas and taken care of the rest of the group. As if acting from the teachings of the Bible, Joe and Ben left the rest of their flock, just to save my life. They could have ignored me and reassured themselves and the group that no-one would have been able to rescue me and then continued with their journey as if nothing had happened. When you are eaten by a crocodile, it gobbles up all the evidence - no DNA, nothing to turn their lives upside down at some point in the future. They could have easily drowned in the process of saving my life. They displayed the best of human nature.

A story is told that an experiment was carried out on a baboon, which had an infant, to compare human and animal protective instincts to one of their kind, in the experiment - their offsprings. To show the extent the baboon would go to save its infant. The baboon's feet were tied down onto an empty swimming pool floor, so that it would not escape with its infant as the water level rose. The pool was then gradually filled with water. As the level of the water rose to the baboon's chest, the baboon put its young one on its shoulders. As the water level reached its shoulders, the baboon put its infant over its head. As the water reached its head and the risk of drowning was real, the animal nature of the baboon came to the fore. It put its young one beneath its feet and stood on it to save its skin. That was animal nature not human nature. Joe and Ben showed that human beings will never behave like their cousins as they risked their own lives to my benefit.

Out of nowhere, the short woman with puppy eyes, who continued to stand furthest from the group, said, "Please let's go, the kombi will not wait for us forever!" She stood there, akimbo, uninterested in what had happened to me. I wondered if she was jealous of the attention I was receiving. Nobody responded to her. We all ignored her. She was obviously missing an organ. An organ that was supposed to separate her from a baboon. She was heartless, her body stature was so small that I was convinced it couldn't accommodate a heart.

As I continued to bleed, Joe took off his shirt and wrapped it around the wounds on my left leg, which was beginning to swell at a rate that was starting to alarm me. I feared that I might not be able to walk to Musina. If I couldn't make it to Musina, what would happen to me? Would these brave escorts leave me to die on the shores of the Limpopo River? Surely they would not have risked their lives only to let me die? Their hard labour would have gone for nothing. But would they have delayed the rest of the group to save one person? They had already risked their lives for mine. They wouldn't leave me behind to die. By that time I was sitting up with my legs stretched. Joe's shirt was soaking red with my blood. I felt a bit cold and took my jeans jacket from my handbag, which had my purse with my British passport in its inner jacket pocket, and put it on. Fortunately I had left my hand bag on the bridge for Ben to bring it down, as I could not multi-task the rope and my handbag at the same time. I trembled with both shock and cold. When I tried to stand up, the pain pierced my heart, I felt dizzy, collapsed to the floor and passed out.

Chapter 4

LAUGHING HYENA

I woke up in a lucid dreamlike state. Being in a dream that I could control. A condition between sleep and consciousness. I felt like I was being dragged along the ground and I was losing control of my dream. The surface was bumpy and bruising the back of my shoulders. When I finally woke up and opened my eyes, I stared directly into the eyes of a wild animal. I screamed and jumped up. My actions and screams shocked the animal and it let go and ran away at a tremendous speed. About fifty metres away it suddenly stopped, gathered itself up, turned and slowly walked back towards me, as if it was taking care not to alarm me again. 'Was it steadying itself to attack me?' Its eyes were fixed at me, but it stopped about twenty metres away, maintaining a safe distance for both of us.

Then I heard a giggling sound. The giggling sound again. 'Was the animal giggling? Did I hear it giggle or my ears were playing *umacatshe-lana*, hide and seek with my mind?' I heard it again and at that point I was convinced that the animal was really laughing. 'A laughing animal? Was it laughing at my swollen limb? Did it realise that my leg was swollen up to the size of a baobab tree stump? Did it think I had elephantiasis? Did it realise that I was injured? Was it laughing at my fear written all over my face? At my misery?'

When I woke up the shock of being dragged by an animal, forced my adrenaline to temporarily suspend the pain. But soon the pain returned in megabytes. Dawn was approaching, the moon was still giving very good light. The animal stared at me and I stared it back. I knew I must show some bravado; animals don't attack people who stand up to them and maintained eye contact. I had to stand my ground because I couldn't run, but the animal didn't know that, I thought to myself. Two cubs sidled up to their mother. So she was a mother, that experience had always eluded me as a woman.

As dawn appeared, the wild animal guarding me turned out to be *impisi,* a hyena. The ears were roundish in shape and the head and the jaws combined were longer than the ears. The front legs appeared longer and bigger than the back legs. At times I couldn't tell precisely, if it was

34

squatting or standing, because of the shorter back legs. It continued to giggle at me.

Folktales are pregnant with stories of hideous relationships between witches and hyenas. The witches are believed to ride on hyenas while on their witchcraft escapades, taking advantages of their stamina for long distance travelling and nocturnal tendencies. My hair stood on its end on realising what I was up against.

I assured myself that if I remained standing the hyena would not attack me. My left leg bore some small and artificial cuts, which were not the crocodile's imprints and I suspected that they were from the hyena's cubs, and it had swollen to twice the size of my right leg. It was heavy and painful.

I had no idea how long I had been dragged along and in which direction, but it was clear that wherever I was being dragged to, I was presumed dead and I was being taken to be the cubs' supper.

It also dawned on me that my escorts left me for dead. They thought I was dead and dumped me in the forest, despite saving me from the jaws of *ingwenya,* the crocodile. They wasted their labour saving me from the crocodile attack, only to dump me at the feet of a hyena. That was exactly what the baboon did to its young one, when faced with the real prospects of drowning. It was me under the feet of my escorts that night. They sacrificed me to save their journey.

My hand bag was gone, but I could feel my purse in the inside pocket of my jean jacket. When I moved my left leg, which was difficult because of its size, the pain was like being stabbed by a thousand spears at the same time. I have heard that the hyenas have attacked human beings before but my companion appeared content to watch and laugh at me. She was waiting for me to drop dead. Hyenas are scavengers. They eat leftovers - in my case; the crocodile's leftover. I knew that they hunted alongside bigger and stronger animals; that thought left me shaking with fear. There could have been lions or leopards in that forest waiting to pounce on me. I couldn't run, I couldn't fight back, I was hopeless.

When I took a few steps towards the hyena, it took a few steps backwards. When I stopped, it stopped. A few steps away from it, it took a few steps towards me. It was like a dance, a human-animal death-dance, where the human was the hunted and the animal was the hunter. And a thought crossed my mind that some animal rights groups have lost their lives trying to save the animals. They should have seen how *impisi* treated

35

me that morning - the way I treat my own food. Waiting for it to cool down before taking a bite. The animal was patient. It continued to giggle. It could tell that I'd been injured. That I was sick, it wasn't stupid. It would keep on singing its lullaby until I dropped dead literally, and then it would feed its cubs.

I remembered seeing animal documentaries where human beings wouldn't intervene when animals attacked and mercilessly killed each other, the commentators would say that they didn't want to interfere with the laws of the jungle, with nature, with the ecosystem. The law of the jungle was at play that night and I was fully part of it. I was forced to adapt, to be part of it and play the game to the very end: real end, end end. My plan was to keep standing, keep upright until sunrise and hope for the best.

To keep myself awake, my mind wondered into my childhood. I had an unadventurous childhood, a happy childhood despite growing up without a father and in pure poverty. Not the British poverty, where poor people are fat. Mine was real thin poverty. Put simply, we had nothing. My mother worked hard selling chicken feet and heads at a local beer hall to keep a roof above our heads; she also sold vegetables in front of our house in order to put food on the table and pay my school fees. She told me that she once lived in a township called Old Lobengula and then moved to another township called Magwegwe North, where my brother was born. They then moved to Makhokhoba, where they lived until my brother left to join the liberation war before I was born. I was born in Makhokhoba, each time she only managed to pay for one room. After Makhokhoba we were a bit lucky, because we moved to a distant relative's house, in Lobengula West, where we stayed until I left for the United Kingdom. It was a bigger house with three bedrooms and my mother managed to sublet two bedrooms and we shared the other bedroom, the two lodgers supplemented our income. She was a very clever woman, very resourceful, she would not let an opportunity pass her by.

My brother, Kissmore, was seventeen years old when he went to join the liberation war. Although I never saw him, I knew him very well from what my mother told me. He didn't return at the end of the war in 1979. We didn't know what happened to him. With my eyes welling up that night, I found myself thinking, 'Wherever you are brother, if you're alive, you have to know this; you are still loved by your sick mother and a sister you never met. If you have moved on, may your soul rest in peace.'

36

There were rumours that he went for his military training in Cuba from neighbouring Zambia, then deserted the army and eloped with a South American woman. I never believed that story an ounce. How could a teenager desert the army for a woman? At that age boys want to show off their masculinity in war, not in women. The war gave them the best opportunity to show off their bravery and fighting skills. Women came later in their lives when they needed a shoulder to cry on, when their mothers have long gone or didn't understand them anymore. I was convinced that he didn't desert the war. My mother used to tell me that he was the kind of a boy to die with his gun in his hand. He was very passionate about politics, he believed in majority rule and that no race was superior to another, he reasoned well beyond his age.

Other rumours said that he died in Mkushi, in Zambia, when their camp was bombed by the then Rhodesian forces. The white regime made several raids into Zambia and Mozambique, where they killed thousands of black Zimbabweans who were training to liberate themselves from the clutches of colonialism. I believed that story line because it resonated with what my mother used to tell me about my brother's ideals. He was young and willing to die for his country. He was very passionate about people's freedoms and he cherished the idea of one man, one vote, so he wouldn't have deserted the struggle.

But if he really died for Zimbabwe indeed, that was a tragic death. A wasted life. A well-meant sacrifice that had since been hijacked by Comrade Moment of Madness. There I was, his sister, fighting crocodiles and hyenas. Running away from independent Zimbabwe, the Zimbabwe he died for. I had to make a conscious decision to live in foreign lands in order to survive, to put food on my table and to be able to express my views without fear or favour; to be free from harm and ridicule. The irony was that I was running away from my fellow black man, from a black ruled Zimbabwe. At least my brother ran away from a white man, a white ruled Rhodesia. Neither of us were happy with our motherland.

Maybe it was for a good reason that my brother didn't return from the war. Would he have witnessed the suffering of the people he liberated and kept quiet, did nothing about it? Or would he have joined the new breed of oppressors? Would he have denied the people he liberated the freedoms he risked his life for? Would he have said that the gun was mightier than the pen, when on the verge of losing an election? I wouldn't know, people

37

change. Who would have thought that our current rulers would have said and done exactly that? At least he died with hope. I hope when he exhaled his last breath, he had a picture of a prosperous Zimbabwe. If I had exhaled my last breath that day, I would have had a picture of Zimbabwe Ruins. I would certainly have been animal food - that would have been how his sister's life ended, in foreign land, away from the country he liberated.

I never knew or saw my father too. My mother never talked about him, it was as if he never existed. None of my relatives mentioned my father and I never asked my mother about him because I thought she would have thought that I was ungrateful for what she had done for me. She would have volunteered who my father was if she wanted me to know him. Who knows, in the process of searching for my father, I could have stumbled into disturbing information about him that would have haunted me forever. My mother used to say, *ungabokuya entabeni ubone indwangu, ubususithi ziyakuhlolela,* you must not go to the mountains and see the baboons, and then say they are a bad omen. Don't go there in the first place.

All I knew was my mother and my uncle, my mother's brother, and they were very close. But his children, my cousins, were never close to me; perhaps they felt I was too poor to be befriended. Against all the odds my mother managed to educate me to a secondary education level. After that I got a loan from the government, which I used to pay for tuition fee as I trained as a secondary teacher at Gweru Teachers' College and she was very proud of me when I graduated with a Diploma in Higher Education. But would she have been proud of me that morning, if she had seen me fending off wild animals with my teacher's certificate? Doing what the school dropouts always did, risking their lives by crossing the Limpopo River on bare feet.

I used to urge my students to work hard on their school work in order to avoid being crocodile's food one day on their way to find employment in neighbouring South Africa. It used to be those youths who didn't take their studies seriously who searched for employment in South Africa. But in 2008 it looked as if every Zimbabwean, young or old, healthy or sick, educated or uneducated, from the south or north, was a school dropout who never took their studies seriously. The failing economy forced people to leave their loved ones behind and head for the diaspora. People were falling over each other in a scramble to get out of the country, as if they were leaving a burning building. Zimbabweans had been reduced to school dropouts. It was no longer a matter of finding jobs in neighbouring South Africa, it was a question of searching for jobs all over the world. On my way into Zimbabwe, there was a Zimbabwean in our kombi who had a Honduras passport. And I thought to myself, she must have been the first Zimbabwean ever to hold that country's passport. She was our Zimbabwean Vasco da Gama. We took the term 'global village' literally and made every country our home. A teacher that night was being threatened by hyena, a witch's motorbike.

That early morning, I knew I had to keep alert until sunrise in order to survive. Keeping upright in my condition was difficult. Dragging myself in a particular direction could have been a futile exercise, as I could easily move away from help and deeper into the jungle, perhaps into worse trouble. I could hear the sound of Limpopo River, but funny enough, I heard it all around me. So I could not purposely move in a particular direction, as I could move towards lions or leopards. But staying put would only convince the hyena that I was on my last legs. And I was on my last leg literally.

As dawn gave in to more light, I felt very tired. The pain was getting numb. I had to stand supported by a tree. I couldn't stand up without support any longer, I couldn't climb the tree, I couldn't do anything at all. I felt useless. I began to feel dizzy and sleepy. I was losing the battle. The group gave up on me for a reason. I started to have stolen naps - the kind of sleep that comes to you no matter what, the kind of sleep that steals over you whether you are behind the wheel or manoeuvring a plane through a violent storm. I knew that I couldn't be supported by the tree forever and that at some point I would fall asleep and collapse, which would certainly give the hyena a good reason to attack. I searched for a mopane tree, pulled its bark from the tree and made a rope out of it. The mopane tree has a very strong kind of bark that is used as a rope in remote villages. I then stood very close to the tree and tied myself to it, wrapping my body and the tree together using the man-made rope. I made many knots so that if I fell asleep the weight of my body wouldn't break the rope. After every circle around my body and the tree, I made a knot. I was fully aware of the consequences of a broken rope. When the rope broke the first time, I ended up being dumped for dead by my escorts. If it broke for the second time, I'd be a hyena's supper, I had no doubt about it.

My plan was that if I fell asleep, the rope would keep me upright, and fool the hyena to think that I was still awake and not attack me.

Soon after tying myself to the tree, so tightly with many knots, I saw a snake coming my way. It was sidewinding slowly through the soft grass towards my tree. The moon was giving enough light for me to see clearly. The snake was slowly but surely approaching the tree I had just befriended. To avoid its path I needed to untie myself fast, but with the number of knots I had made, it was going to take a while. If the snake held its course, it would pass through where the hyena and its cubs were crouching. They were all watching me with interest, to them I was not a human being, I was their next meal.

The snake slickly made its way towards my tormentors and captors who were watching me with their eyes wide open but with their backside shut. They couldn't hear the smooth serpent approaching. I'd never witnessed the meeting of these bush cousins before. I hoped that the snake would bite the mother hyena first, but before the mother hyena dies, she bites the snake back and kills it immediately. Both animals would die and I would be free. Set free by a snake. I could easily chase the cubs away with one leg. But I didn't trust that belly moving serpent. Remember what it did to Eve?

I tried to free myself from the tree before the drama started, but it was a slow process because of the number of knots I had done, intending them to save my life although at that moment they were quickening its demise. All of a sudden the mother hyena sprang up, when the snake was only a metre or so away, as if her shut backside had suddenly developed eyes. If only I had had the hyena's seventh sense, I wouldn't have been there witnessing that charade. I would have refused to use the rope, refused to cross the Limpopo River on foot and refused to board that kombi.

The cubs scattered in different directions like headless chickens. The frightened snake raised its front and head to the height of the hyena. It flattened its head too, wow! I knew right away that it was a black mamba, a very quick snake with toxic venom, well known for defending itself when under attack. The belly-dancing creature had suddenly grown feet. Welcome to my territory it appeared to be saying. The hyena tried to claw or bite the black mamba, but the snake avoided the claws and the teeth by twisting and wriggling to the hyena's other side. The mamba's somersault left the hyena not so sure of where to put its feet next. I was surprised by the strength of its hindquarters, those deceivingly weakling back legs, had springs in them.

That was not the type of dance the hyena put me through when we first met. That animal-human death dance was like a waltz, but the dance

I was witnessing between the black mamba and the hyena easily qualified as *tsabatsaba,* saltation. In this kind of dance the dancer hardly put a full foot on the ground. It's as if the ground is red hot. The dancer keeps on jumping, leaping, one footed, two footed, zero footed, writhing, wriggling and twisting. The mamba kept the hyena busy, jumping up and down as if it had lost its marbles. It appeared in control of the fight in the initial stages. The hyena was kept guessing. That wasn't a giggling matter anymore. It was a do or die encounter. Its shorter, smaller and springy back legs kept it alive though.

With a surprise move that took me by surprise too, the hyena standing on its back legs, falsely jabbed the snake's head, the mamba fell for the false move and suddenly its head disappeared into the hyena's mouth and it chewed it as if it was chewing gum. The black mamba writhed, twisted and wriggled on the ground, but its toxic realising part, had been turned into mincemeat by its ever laughing neighbour. Soon the mother hyena shared the starter with her cubs, but the main meal was still on its legs, although on its last leg by then. She looked at me giggling as if to say, *I know what you were hoping for, it's not gonna happen. I have lived in the bush for all of my life, you have just arrived. You are still green. I and my ancestors have ruled this forest for centuries. I'm not a scavenger for nothing, I will bide my time and my kids need something solid to eat before sunrise, hee hee hee.*

I didn't even have time to completely untie myself from the tree before the drama was over. I was back to square one. I then made the final addition to how I tied myself to the tree. Using the branch of the tree that was almost horizontal to the ground, at my shoulder level, I tied my left arm, making some kind of a three quarter cross. Just like Jesus Christ, but with his right arm missing. I only left my right arm free in case I had to defend myself against *impisi*. But the truth of the matter was, my right arm couldn't tie itself to the branch as well, I had run out of arms. For the first time in my life, I wished I had more than two arms. I believed that when I fell asleep, with my face facing down, the hyena might take my horizontal tied arm, still outstretched, as a sign that I was still awake and a threat to it. I knew that I had to stay awake, and preferably stay up. My only consolation though, was that, if I didn't stay up, or stay awake, or both, I would never know about it.

41

Chapter 5

MUSINA

When I opened my eyes again I lay on what appeared to be a hospital bed and one of my husband's friends called Beans gazed over me. He was tall, bald-headed, with a missing front tooth. Ice my husband called it a 'missing striker' and it had been missing since he was born. Ice suspected that the tooth rebelled against the slap of life at his birth. He said the missing striker was behind Beans' single status at his mid-thirties. He was Ice's best friend and they were of the same age.

When it comes to giving names to their children Zimbabwean parents are very creative. The names, especially the English ones, come in all shapes and sizes: Smile, Moregoats, Overtake, Talkmore, Rollover, Tellmore and many more. My husband's name was a short version of his full name, which is Icecoldbeer, but he preferred to be called just Ice. He was given his name by his late maternal grandfather, who used to admire this big white man, who came to this pub at a golf course, where Ice's grandfather worked as a cleaner, and he would just say to the bar tender, 'Icecoldbeer' this was never followed by 'please,' otherwise his name could have been Icecoldbeerplease. White Rhodesian colonialists never used the word 'please,' when talking to black people, they just commanded them, saying that the black inhabitants should be grateful that the whites came and settled in their countries, otherwise they would have remained in the dark ages forever. Ice's friend, Beans, who towered over me, was called Beans because he was born when there was a bumper harvest of beans. To remember and cherish that year his parents called him Beans.

Zimbabwean surnames or totems are not exempt either. If some of them were to be translated into English, many people would never be given visitors' visas into the United Kingdom. Some could even be deported back to Zimbabwe. Take for example, *Manyengavana* - the one who proposes love to children or *Chinanzvavana* - the one who licks children or kidslicker. Such surnames could be deemed politically incorrect. Some people might ask what is in a name? I would say that there's a story behind every name.

The first thing I asked Beans was "Where am I?"

"Musina hospital."

"Musina Hospital?"

"Yes, you're in hospital in South Africa."

"How did I get here?"

"South African soldiers brought you here."

"I was brought here by South African soldiers? How did they find me? Did the hyena attack me? Did they hear my screams? Did they know that I was attacked by a croco..."

"Shh..." Beans placed his finger over my mouth and whispered, "They don't know that here."

"They don't know what?" I was confused.

"That you were attacked by a croco...crocodile." He whispered as his words choked him. I got more confused.

"How could they have known that I was attacked by a crocodile?" I asked Beans. I didn't expect them to know that I was also attacked by a crocodile. My worry about the crocodile attack was based on my fear of being seen as border jumper by South Africans. I didn't expect Beans to know that either. But his response left my mind muddled up for sure.

"You told me earlier," he said, forcing a smile.

"I told you earlier? Beans, what are talking about? I have just woken up, or should I say I've just come back from the dead. I have been unconscious all along, how could I have told you that?"

"About thirty minutes ago, you opened your eyes and you saw me and you said, '"Beans I have been attacked by a crocodile,"' and I said to you, "Shh...they don't know that you have been attacked by a crocodile here," and you said "Oh" and immediately went back to sleep. You also spoke to nurses as well before falling back to sleep."

"Have I? I honestly don't remember talking to any of the nurses or to you." Why would Beans lie to me, I thought? He certainly had no reason to.

"Do you remember how you came here?"

"No, I don't."

"There are many things you might not remember Dolly. You have been unconscious for a while. Your brain might still be in shock. You need time to relax and take in things easy and slowly. The brain is a very clever organ you know, it might decide to put what you went through in the subconscious mind to spare you the agony of what you went through. That way it protects you from reliving your trauma too early for it to deal with it."

43

I had thought that I hadn't woken up since my standoff with the hyena. It appeared I was wrong.

"So, Beans, what else have I told you - or them - while I have been unconscious? This is frightening me, you know. Am I losing my mind or what?"

"Fortunately enough, you have not told them much. You didn't tell me much either. You didn't mention the crocodile attack to the nurses and doctors. They think you were attacked by wild animals. Being attacked by a hyena would do for now Dolly."

"But did that hyena attack me?"

"What hyena? I don't know, but what I know is that you were found unconscious by an army unit patrolling Limpopo River banks. They searched you and found your British passport in your purse and they assumed that you were a tourist who fell victim to Africa's notorious wildlife. They transported you to this hospital. Are they treating you well?"

"How would I know, since I have been unconscious?" I said sarcastically.

"This isn't the first time you have been conscious. As I said before you have already spoken to the doctors and nurses," he said and continued, "Whatever happened Dolly, you are very lucky to be alive I'm sure you know that?"

"It's a miracle that I survived, two attacks, Beans."

"Two attacks?"

"Yes," I said whispering, "The crocodile attack and the hyena attack."

"Oh, so it's true that you were really attacked by the hyena too? You are not making that up, are you?"

"I thought I told you that I was attacked by a hyena earlier? You think I'm lying?"

"You're serious then? I thought you were just making it up."

"No, I was really attacked by the hyena too. What would I make it up for?"

"So you survived both the hyena and the..." Whispering, he continued, "crocodile attacks? That's incredible. You're lucky, your life must have a reason."

"Oh, what a revelation! I didn't know that my life had a reason all along, Hallelujah!" We both laughed and I continued, "Do you remember the song 'Mr DJ saved my life?' From now I'll be singing it as 'the British passport saved my life.'" He smiled and I asked him, "How did you know that I was here?" Leaning forward, he replied, "Someone contacted Ice in

England and told him about the accident and that you were here. And as it turned out, I was in Johannesburg on my personal business and Ice asked me to help and make sure you were safe."

"Someone contacted Ice? Something does not add up here Beans. Just someone? I thought it was the British Embassy or...

"Oh yes...it was someone from the British Embassy that contacted Ice," Beans interrupted me. "They got your details from your passport and then got hold of Ice who then contacted me, since I was already in South Africa."

"What a relief. I thought Ice had me followed or you are a stalker." We both laughed. Beans then said,

"You are a lucky woman Dolly." He was on about my 'luck' as if he didn't believe that I had survived two animal attacks. I smiled and examined my left leg, which wasn't in good shape, maybe that was the reason he kept saying I was lucky. I couldn't see the wounds as I had the dressings on.

Later a nurse approached us and asked to check me on what she called "hourly observations." She checked my pulse, blood pressure, breaths, temperature and any other observables. She went on to redress my wounds. She asked me if I knew what happened and my answer was "I don't remember" to all her questions. She told me that I would have to be seen by a psychiatrist to assess my mental state. She didn't tell me why I needed to be assessed by a psychiatrist before she left my bed area and I didn't ask. The way she approached and spoke to me, it showed that that was not the first time I was conscious.

"Nurses are nice in here," said Beans, beaming, as his eyes followed and undressed the nurse with his lust look. "If only they knew that you were a '*Mukwerekwere*" - a derogatory term used by the black South Africans to describe black foreigners. He grinned before he continued, "But unsurprisingly, the black South Africans don't have derogatory names for white foreigners, except *toyitoying* and shouting 'kill the Boer.' That explains what colonisation did to the black man's mind. Brain washed to a point of hating fellow blacks. Totally white washed. Colonisation deliberately exaggerated tribal differences. That is the reason why Rwanda happened. Tell me, what can make people from the same country butcher each other like that? That kind of deep-seated hatred was planted during colonisation." He paused for a moment to give himself a breather from his political lecture before he went on, "If the nurses here knew that you were a Zimbabwean, they would not even have touched you. They would avoid you like a leper.

South Africans are xenophobic as you know. They burn alive fellow black foreigners for seeking sanctuary in their country. These are the same people who sought sanctuary in every country during apartheid. The same people who were being burnt alive by the white South Africans for the wrong skin colour, in their own country. Those who escaped white persecution, were given sanctuary by the very people they are killing today. They have very short memories indeed. The irony above all this, is that, here you are, as black as soot, like the majority of them and they are treating you very well because you hold a British passport. They have a very long way to go to totally eradicate the white supremacy mentality that was planted by apartheid and colonialism." When Beans started talking about discrimination, colonisation and racism, just like my husband Ice, the lecture was endless.

I sometimes wondered whether living in white countries made black Africans more radical. Does the discrimination and racism they experience in their adopted countries radicalise them? Or does living in foreign territories teach them wisdom that they use to analyse issues differently and form new perspectives? A new approach born from a new brain? Then I said to Beans,

"At least the nurses are nice to me here."

"I'm not saying they shouldn't be nice to you per se, don't get me wrong, Dolly. I'm just saying they have a long way to discard the 'master-servant mentality.' I remember when I first arrived in the UK and saw a white man digging a trench with a pick. I just thought 'wow these guys can do manual jobs too. A real man's job.' I almost took the pick away from him and apologised, *Please bass (boss), let me do it for you. Just watch me work, with one hand in your pocket and the other on your ciggy. You don't have to embarrass yourself with manual work sir,*" said Beans with tongue in cheek and continued, "Look at South Africa - so many years after attainment of independence they're setting fellow Africans on fire like a pile of rubbish. The irony is that they still live in tin houses themselves. They live in shacks and they call that independence. Surely their comrades didn't die so that they would continue living in shacks. Did they? They allow whites to occupy vast tracks of land, allow them to live in splashy suburbs, with walls as high as hell walls, to keep the majority of them out, but they have the guts to kill their fellow blacks."

"But they say that their fellow Africans are stealing their jobs, Beans." I was being a devil's advocate.

46

"Eastern Europeans are taking the British jobs, but have you ever seen the British burning them alive? Instead, the British tighten their visa regulations against Africans, and not against their fellow Europeans who are taking most jobs, but against those who are taking the least jobs. In fact, the British have relaxed the visa regulations to the Chinese, Arabs and Americans, but tightened them against black Africans. But black South Africans target their fellow black Africans whilst the white South African university students are forcing their mothers, wives and sisters to perform degrading sexual acts. Forcing them to eat food mixed with the white students' urine, Dolly. Those very white students put the videos on YouTube to share and enjoy them with the whole world. And they call that independence. If that is what independence means to them, then God forbid what else they will tolerate!" Knowing Beans, the way I did, his Martin Luther kind of speech could go on forever. I tried to change the subject by saying to him,

"The nurse said I should be seen by a psychiatrist, what for? Do you think it's necessary?" Smiling, Beans said,

"You've heard enough of black South Africans xenophobic nostalgia. I hate discrimination and racism with my life, Dolly. With a passion." He made sure that he concluded his speech and then in a gentler and measured tone, he answered my question, "I think it's because to all their questions about what happened to you, your response was the same, 'I can't remember,' they think you might have lost a few of your marbles during the attack," he said jokingly.

"I'm worried that I might say things that are contrary to the picture they have already painted of me. Or say something contrary to what I would have already said, just as I did to you, which might raise some suspicions as a result. I will stick to 'I can't remember' mode."

Beans agreed with me, nodding his head.

When the psychiatrist saw me, I stuck to my 'I can't remember' mode like a scratched record.

"Were you alone when you were attacked?"

"I can't remember"

"Did anyone help you?"

"I can't remember?"

"Is your full name Dolly Sibanda"

"I can't remember." That was how the assessment went, not the last bit of course. I risked being presumed unfit to fly by the psychiatrist than be found guilty of illegally crossing the Limpopo River. That would have had worse repercussions and severe consequences. When the psychiatrist was satisfied with my mental state, he gave me a clean bill of health and he recommended that I should be discharged from hospital and continue with my rehabilitation in the United Kingdom. As I left his office he said to me,

"Whoever tied you to the tree is a genius, they might have saved your life. Most animals don't attack people who are upright."

I limped out of the psychiatrist's office on crutches, thinking to myself, 'I saved my own life sir. You are not a mind reader, please don't fool yourself.' Eventually, I was discharged from hospital in order to catch my flight back to the United Kingdom on time.

Beans came to pick me up in a hired BMW X5; leather seats all round, it drove like a dream. Travelling in that beautiful car, with spacious windows that allowed me to see the gracious veld and terrain of Africa, made me feel proud to be an African. The N1 motorway between Musina and Johannesburg felt like driving on carpet. Looking down the mountain, as Beans manoeuvred an extremely responsive vehicle, the trees at the foot of the mountain appeared like tennis balls scattered on a grass court in Wimbledon. I am aware that I am doing a disservice to those beautiful views along those roads meandering, swaggering around and sometimes piercing right through the foot of the mountains. In my language we say, *ukutshelwa yikuncitshwa,* by being told a story you are being denied the experience. To truly experience the tranquillity of Africa and enjoy its marvellous scenery, you have to be there in person.

During the journey to Johannesburg, Beans let slip something that left me puzzled about my accident. He told me that Ice, my husband, first heard that I had died at the Limpopo River prior to the embassy's call. When I asked him how he would have known about my attack before the embassy called him, he was vague. He said that there might have been someone who knew me within the group. Surely, if there was someone who knew me, they should have introduced themselves or talked to me at least? Or I should also have recognised them? How could they recognise me when I couldn't recognise them? I was not a celebrity.

Firstly, while I was unconscious, I told Beans that I was attacked by a crocodile, and then later someone among the group of passengers might have known me. Both Beans and Ice didn't know the person who was letting out bits of information about my accident. Either they knew more about my attack than they were telling me, or someone was playing with my mind. It felt creepy to me and my thoughts became more muddled as a result. Something didn't add up and it was not good for my mind especially after what I had just gone through. It felt as if someone was playing with my mind like a joystick. Or was I just having much to do about nothing?

Chapter 6

JOHANNESBURG

When we arrived in Johannesburg, Beans drove to a fuel service garage. As soon as he got out of the car, a red BMW saloon that was behind us accelerated and missed hitting him by millimetres, as he jumped out of its way. The BMW then suddenly halted with a screech of tyres. Three hooded men jumped out of the car brandishing guns, leaving only the driver in their car. One of them shouted at Beans, "Give me your car keys mother flipping! Give me the keys, son of a bitch!" Beans handed the car keys to the first carjacker, who got into our driver's side. At the same time the second carjacker jumped into the back of our car and the third carjacker came to the passenger side of our BMW shouting at me, "Get out of the car mother of all bitches!" I struggled to get out of the car because of my injuries and the man ran out of patience. He grabbed my arm and literally threw me out of the car as if I was a piece of rubbish. I tumbled, lost balance as I was sent flying hitting my head against the wall. I screamed as I lay helpless on the ground. Beans looked helpless too, as the three carjackers got into our car. When the first carjacker turned the ignition key, the car went up in flames. It was engulfed by a ferocious fire. The three carjackers panicked, jumped out of our car and dived into their getaway car, taking off with a screech of tyres.

Beans rushed to pick me up and shoved me in the passenger seat. Fortunately I only received bruises on my back and on my right thigh. They were not life threatening injuries. They were not comparable to the crocodile wounds. He hurriedly got into the car and quickly drove off, mumbling, "This's caca city! Welcome to Johannesburg, Dolly."

"What happened? How come the car is undamaged? Why don't you call the police?" I fired those questions at Beans as he sped off.

"The police don't react quickly when there's action, in this city, Dolly. They come later, well after the action is finished to pick up the pieces. Are you okay?"

"I'm fine. But you should have called the police."

"You don't understand Johannesburg Dolly. Police in this city are allowed by law to shoot first and ask questions later, but they still don't attend the scenes of robbery quick enough in order to do what they have been mandated. What does that tell you? You would be very unlucky if someone called the police and they quickly arrived at the scene of crime only to find out that you're a Mukwerekwere, because they would direct all their attention to you and let the robbers off the hook."

"Sure?"

"Firstly, they would demand your passport and confiscate it. Secondly they would threaten to arrest you for entering their beloved South Africa illegally, despite the valid visa on your passport. Thirdly, if you're lucky they would take a bribe and hand back your passport. If you're unlucky, they would leave you stranded in the street without your passport. The next thing you know is that their girlfriend is flying to the United Kingdom using your passport." The words shot out of Bean's mouth at the same speed he was doing on his car.

"You're joking."

"I'm serious *umama sibili.*" Swearing by his mother. "I can't joke a few seconds after having a gun pointed at my head." He wasn't smiling. I could feel the tension through the way he was driving - too fast and erratic on roads that were too heavy with traffic.

"How come the car is okay, why didn't it catch fire?" I asked him, trying to distract him from his speedy and erratic driving, so that he could slow down as he tried to construct a response.

"This car has an antitheft device with another set of car keys that are kept separately from the main keys, which when pressed produces a false fire that engulfs the car. It automatically locks in the ignition key and the steering. That is the only way you can keep your car safe in Johannesburg." He rumbled his response and he continued to speed.

"It sounds a clever idea, but won't the carjackers learn about the device and then ignore the fire in time?"

"But still the car won't start."

"Then they demand the antitheft device or threaten to shoot."

"When someone is carjacking their adrenaline is already running high, the fake fire tips it over the edge. At that stage it's fight or flight. In most of the cases, as you have just witnessed, it's flight. Even those who want to fight choose flight, because the fake fire invites a lot of unnecessary attention to the robbers, the last thing they need. Who would want that level of attention in the middle of committing a crime? Also, they can't be so sure that it's not the real fire." Beans talked as if he invented the antitheft device himself.

"That was a close shave, Beans."

"My friend warned me against hiring a BMW X5 in Johannesburg. He told me it's a carjacker's darling. I didn't notice that we were being tailed by another BMW. It's likely to be stolen too. I just wanted to refuel the car and return it with the same amount of petrol I got it with, thus why I stopped at that garage. I expected to be blown with a loud bang when that carjacker pointed his gun at my head," he said as he drove into the premises of the car hire company.

While waiting to catch my flight back to London, I stayed with Beans in Johannesburg, in a sixth floor flat, which he shared with a wide range of people. Black South Africans never cease to amaze me. Only a tiny minority live in massive houses with Olympic-sized swimming pools, in satanic, filthy luxury with high walls as if to keep fellow liberation heroes out. Not willing to share the independence spoils with them. But the majority live in tin houses and poo in tins. Some live in filthy or overpopulated flats, sometimes with as many as ten people sharing one bedroom.

Our flat had two bedrooms. Beans and I shared one bedroom. Although it was a bit unsettling, I always regarded Beans as my brother. He wouldn't try anything on with me unless I encouraged him. The arrangement was much preferable to sharing a bedroom with three married couples. Three men and three women shared the other bedroom. God forbids how they fornicated. It would be like a race, a race in which the winner comes last.

One day, I sat on the balcony admiring Johannesburg's skyscrapers, a few days before I was due to return to the United Kingdom. All other flat occupants were out. You would never know whether they would return from work or not. They could easily be picked up by the corrupt South African police. If they failed to pay the bribe they would be detained at the Lindela Repatriation Centre. If their relatives failed to raise the bribe too, in a few days later they would be loaded like coal into *imbombela,* train, and deported back to Comrade Moment of Madness's hell hole.

I became wrapped in my thoughts as I admired the rainbow city from my vantage point. I just thought that when the white man built this city, he thought he would rule this country, *amatshe aze antswebeke*, till the stones were soft enough to be pinched. He wouldn't invest so much money, sweat, diligence and above all, his blood, only to walk away at the first sound of *toyitoying*.

South Africa was the last country to gain its independence in Africa. The Boers were tough nuts to crack, they resisted to the bitter end. But the black South Africans were resolute in their fight too, just like their God Father Mandela. They didn't give up until apartheid fell on its face as Mandela walked majestically free from Robin Island to become the first black president of the Republic of South Africa.

Hillbrow is dominated by skyscrapers. Sitting on the balcony of a sixth floor flat was like perching on top of a tree like a bird. Originally, that part of Johannesburg was whites-only, but when the whites started to move out to the outskirts of the city before the end of apartheid, the black immigrant workers moved in. Johannesburg reminded me of big cities like London and Birmingham in England. In most parts of Birmingham and in the east and north London areas, when the indigenous whites moved out, to the outskirts, the black immigrants moved in. In Tottenham and Edmonton in particular, if you threw a stone in the air I could bet with my last penny that on its way down it would hit a black person or a foreigner. But during Tottenham FC's home matches, the High Road from Seven Sisters tube station, which leads to White Hart Lane, would be as white as snow. Blacks evaporated from the streets during those games. British white hooligan football fans would be out in full force, retaking the streets. The blacks would melt away into their houses or churches. Especially churches. I remember a newspaper title 'Teaching the teacher' which was about black African priests being invited into the UK to spread the word of God to white atheists. How history had turned upside down. Missionaries that spread the word in Africa coming back home, but in black faces and thick lips. At first it was forced slavery but later it was slavery mentality, blacks continue to freely enslave ourselves. Some might argue that it is slavery of choice.

Out of the blue I witnessed a drama across the street. A man talking on his mobile was approached by two men. And in what looked to be unprovoked attack, one of the men appeared to punch the man with the mobile in the neck, while the other snatched his mobile. The man fell to the ground as his attackers ran away. Soon the police arrived, unlike what Beans had told me soon after the attempted carjack about police delays.

The victim lay on the street and some passers-by held their mouths as they passed him. Those in the company of children placed their hands over their children's eyes. Soon the police covered him with a blanket. He was dead. He had been stabbed, not punched, as I first thought. Without any forensic work being involved, the police removed his body from the streets. He had lost his life over a mobile phone. *Welcome to Johannesburg*, Beans would have said. It was like in East and North London, witnessing gang violence, in those under resourced and poor areas! Black against black. Gangster multiculturalism. Duelling over the control of the market.

I was still in pain as I sat on the balcony. Being tossed like a bag of potatoes a few days earlier had not helped either. The crocodile wounds still had stitches in, although the swelling had gone down immensely to what it was on the night of the attack. It was my delight that the trained man of uniform mistook the crocodile's teeth for a lion's teeth; although Joe did mention that it was a young one, it was not the biggest he has ever seen.

As I still sat on the balcony, to my surprise, I thought I caught the glimpse of the short woman with a round face with puppy eyes. Was it the real short Limpopo River woman? The woman who could have hurried my demise. She came out of a car wearing a wedding dress and entered the foyer of the flat opposite. Her face was veiled but I was convinced that it was her. I couldn't see the face of the groom but he was tall, over six feet. Was it her, or my eyes? That sight troubled my mind. It was like she got into my head, spread-eagled her small frame in my scull, and feasted on my grey matter like a maggot, and left me with missing parts of my brains. The result: paranoia?

I began to fear the state of my mind. I thought to myself how does insanity develop? Does one go to bed as usual and work up the following morning a raving lunatic. Or does one experience what I was experiencing - paranoia, which grows like a tumour and spreads to the rest of the brains, destroying all the common sense, leaving one mad? The fear of what was happening in my mind reminded me of the visit to Engutsheni, Zimbabwe's biggest psychiatric hospital and the conversation I had with a psychiatric nurse and Molly's brother, while I was in Zimbabwe. The image of the short woman with puppy eyes frightened and reminded me of that visit.

Molly, my friend in the United Kingdom, had asked me to pay a visit to her brother who had been admitted to Engutsheni, while I was in Zimbabwe. My uncle's wife accompanied me to Engutsheni hospital, and a male nurse led us to Molly's brother's dormitory. As we walked along the hospital's corridors my uncle's wife and I witnessed the restraining of a patient who was shouting all sorts of obscenities to the nurses. He was obviously quite upset about something, or very unwell. He was frothing around his mouth. One male nurse played decoy by threatening to hit him with a stick, attracting his attention while the other male nurse sneaked behind him holding a blanket and he pounced on the patient, covering him up with it. The two nurses managed to bring the patient to the ground and they restrained him with a blanket. The hospital was called Engutsheni (Blanket) as that was their restraining method. I turned and asked our nurse escort, "Don't you think goading a patient with a stick is unethical? Don't you think it disturbs the patient making him more paranoid and aggressive?"

"What do you want them to do, my sister? Plead with him to calm down?" boomed our escort.

"Yes, calm him down. Talk to him nicely and find out the cause of his aggression. De-escalation and engagement might even reduce seclusion."

Our escort suddenly stopped, looked at me from head to toe and shook his head and said, "You have no idea what mad men do my sister. These people see what the rest of us don't see. They can kill you, while laughing! One of them here killed his father and ate his liver. And you talk of *calm him, talk to him nicely and find out the cause of his aggression. Deescalation and engagement might even reduce seclusion.*' He mimicked me and continued, "The rule is don't try and engage a mad man my sister." As he walked on, he asked, "I understand you are visiting from the United Kingdom, is it true that mad people there are treated like normal people?" He laughed.

"I have never worked in a psychiatry hospital, but my husband, who is a student nurse, told me that patients are treated humanely. They are treated *'like normal people.'*" Mimicking him.

"Ah, you are one of the few Zimbabweans I have met who have not cleaned a white man's bottom. Most of Zimbabweans I know are BMWs?

"BMWs"

"Yes my sister, they are employed as Bum Management Wipers in the United Kingdom. How did you manage to avoid that my sister?" The nurse was definitely getting on my nerves. With such awful views against people suffering from mental illness, I hated the thought of him nursing my friend's brother.

"Mad people don't think like you and I," he continued. "All they understand is the stick. My advice to you is don't try to understand a mad man. Just hit him with a stick or surprise him with the blanket; that is the only language he understands."

We entered the dormitories. On one side there was a line of toilets, and none of them had doors. I said to our nurse escort, "Why were the toilets doors taken off?"

"These people are dangerous my sister, not only to others but to themselves too. Before the doors were removed, they used to kill themselves in there. Some would relieve themselves and then smear their caca all over the walls. Sometimes they would write nurses and doctors' names with their caca and also insult us with their caca. Insulting us with their caca my sister. Do you think that is normal, my sister?"

"Who is mad here, the patient or the staff?" I could not resist the question.

"What do you mean?" he asked sharply, omitting his favourable phrase 'my sister.' I liked the thought that I could be getting under his skin too.

"I mean who is mad? The patient who relieved himself in the open or the nurse or doctor who sanctioned the removal of the doors? Who needs psychiatric help here, the patients or the staff?"

"Which is better my sister: relieving oneself in the open or death? Ye my sister? What would you choose?"

"Dignity. I would choose dignity. I would choose respect and fair treatment. I would choose death over humiliation. I'm not surprised that your patients kill themselves in this hospital. They are choosing death over humiliation and disrespect. I would do the same if I were in their position, honestly."

"My sister you speak with highly expressed emotions, which appear to cloud your thinking process. Too many emotions dilute your thinking. You're wasting your emotions advocating for these people. These patients don't thinks clearly like you do. They hardly know what they are doing right now; they live in their own world. They're as good as children. Their bodies might be here but their minds are in the moon. Do you know the connection between the moon and insanity? But when they get well, they will take their medication, having got the message loud and clear that if they stopped taking their medication they would end up in hospital where *vachamama pachena,* they poo in the open as you would say in England." He smiled.

56

"So you use humiliation as punishment? You use humiliation as a teaching tool? You humiliate them so that they will not stop taking medication? You should sit down with them and tell them the importance of their medication and explain how it works."

"He he he, *seka zvako mwana waChimbimbino*, allow Chimbimbino's son to laugh. You can't teach a mad man, my sister. You can't explain anything to a madman, you mean you don't know that? *Ingawani Engirand yacho yatokuitatofo*, England has made you dull." He paused to enjoy his own joke before he continued, "Explain how medication works? Explain to a mad man why his brains are not working? What would he use to understand what you are teaching him since his brains are not working? There's a sign on his forehead written 'out of order' and you try to explain science to him. The toilet is blocked and you flush it my sister? Honestly, who is mad here?" He asked, attempting to stab me with my own knife. I ignored his question and explained,

"When they get better and they are about to be discharged, you should teach them about their medication and symptoms of their illness. Ask them what usually happens before they breakdown, their early warning signs, their relapse signatures, so that they would learn how to manage their illness in future and avoid hospital admissions. So that they take control of their illness. Some of these patients are more intelligent than you, if you don't know? Civilised societies don't resort to humiliation to reduce suicide by mentally ill people." There was a short silence and then I asked him, "Are you married?" He remained quiet and walked on. I asked him again, "Do you have children?"

"I have been married for twenty years my sister and I have two boys, the oldest is nineteen and the youngest is thirteen."

"Would you want them to be treated in this hospital if they developed a mental illness? Would you want your brother or father to be treated here? Would you?"

He stopped again and looked fixedly in my eyes. I kept my gaze, I didn't blink. He shook his head and said,

"You are insulting me? What has my family got to do with these people? Don't involve my family in this. Do you want to jinx my family?" He strode on. I pursued him and said,

"These unfortunate patients are other people's sons, brothers and fathers. Please show them some respect, my brother."

My uncle's wife was quiet throughout our conversation. Maybe she thought I was too opinionated. Maybe she thought Miss UK was living in my head. Maybe I took her words out of her mouth. We soon reached Molly's brother's bedside.

I knew Molly's brother before I went to the United Kingdom and he was well then. I could see scars on his wrist and ankles. He was frail and bony, but all Zimbabweans looked like skeletons in any case. If a country couldn't look after its well citizens, what would it do with the sick? The vulnerable? Those who have lost their minds? He didn't even look at us as we stood beside his bed.

"Ndodana you have visitors today," said our nurse escort. He turned his head and just gazed at us mute. Uninterested. I then said to him,

"Hallo Ndo, do you remember me?" That was how Molly used to call him. At the mention of his shortened name, he took a good look at me and said,

"Do I know you? You seem to know me?"

"I'm Dolly, your sister Molly's friend. Have you forgotten me?"

"Oh, I remember you now. You were Molly's best friend, Dolly?" He said with a smile and reaching for my hand. He gave me a firm handshake, his grip was very strong because he was literally squeezing my hand with his bare bones. He was so thin that there was no flesh left on his fingers, it was a handshake with a skeleton.

"We're still best friends, Ndo."

"No you can't be, she went to England years ago."

"We are neighbours in England, in Bournemouth, Ndo. We are stuck to each other like Siamese twins," I said laughing.

"You look well, you're round like a real woman. You are eating all the England's left overs, are you?" He laughed exposing one front missing canine, I suspected that it was knocked off by our nurse escort, he continued, "The British are keeping you well, Dolly. So what have you brought me? I hope Molly hasn't stolen my money again."

"I thought it was her money she was sending to you Ndo."

Laughing, he said, "That's what she tells everybody. It's not her money, it's my money from the Queen." I smiled and said,

"Your money from the Queen? You're joking, right?"

"I'm not joking Dolly. The Queen owes me some stupid money for working for her under Ian Smith's Secret Service. She gives my money to

Molly, as my sister, and she sends it to me. But what she has been doing is stealing some of it. Some months she doesn't send me even a penny. No wonder why she goes around telling people that it's her money."

"I thought you trained as a teacher? When did you join Ian Smith's Secret Service, Ndo?" I challenged his train of thought.

"That's why it's called Secret Service, Dolly! Nobody should know that you are working for them! That's why you thought I was a teacher. That was the camouflage, Dolly." His response unsettled me a bit as his argument carried some water.

"All I know is that Molly works hard in order to earn the money that she sends to you, she's..."

"She tells that to everybody, Dolly. And who do you think people will believe, Molly in London or I at Engutsheni?" When I realised that I couldn't win that one, I changed the subject.

"What happened to you?" I asked, my eyes settling on his arms and ankles, "I can see scars on your wrists and ankles." For the first time he looked at our nurse escort as if to say, '*You answer that one.*'

There was a pause before he answered.

"When I was admitted here I was very ill, Dolly. My grandfather's voice was telling me to kill myself to save my soul. To protect me from myself, the staff chained me to my bed." Again he glanced towards the nurse, as if to seek approval and he continued, "They didn't mean to harm me Dolly, all they wanted was to keep me safe. But I feel much better now. My grandfather's voice is gone with the wind. I don't want to kill myself anymore. I am taking my medication and I am a good boy." That sounded rehearsed to me. I was sure that if the nurse wasn't present he would not have worded his responses that way. Good boy? That was the language of that hospital, not Ndo's language. How could a grown up man call himself a boy? Looking at my uncle's wife he suddenly asked,

"This's not your mother Dolly, is she?"

"No Ndo. This's my uncle's wife."

"Your uncle who lives in Phelandaba?" He extended his hand to greet her.

"Yes, you've got a very sharp memory Ndo."

"You can't work for the Secret Service if you don't have a sharp mind, Dolly," he said, laughing. I thought he suffered from some form of fixed delusional beliefs, I had picked a few psychiatric terms from my husband.

59

He continued, "I would have bought my own house in Pelandaba by now, if Molly wasn't stealing part of my money. Where's my money from the Queen, Dolly? Did you think I would forget?" We both laughed and I said,

"Molly gave me two hundred pounds from her money, not from the Queen, as well as these clothes," I reached for my travel bag and handed him the clothes I'd brought.

"She tells the whole world that, she wants to appear as if she's caring while stealing my money at the same time. I worked hard for that money, Dolly. I risked my life as an informer." When I tried to hand him his money from his sister, the nurse attempted to snatch the money from my hand as he explained to me that it would be handed back to Ndo on his discharge. I expected Ndo to contest, but he didn't. I reluctantly handed the money to the nurse, I didn't want to cause a scene. My right brain told me that Ndo was not going to get that money, that those were hard times in Zimbabwe and the nurse would, without feeling guilty, spend the money on his wife's tampons, since they were out of reach for most families, especially for government workers. The nurse would use the British sterling to put some food on his table. My right brain was being creative and artistic with what would happen to the money. But my left brain tried to be analytical and logical. The nurse would put the money in the hospital safe, record it down, so that it would be given to Ndo on his discharge. I left it at that.

On our way back to the main reception, I noticed that all the patients were wearing hospital clothes except for one patient, the only white patient I could see and I enquired from our escort;

"Why is it that the only white patient in the grounds is not wearing the patient uniform?"

He smiled and said; "You're too observant my sister. You see too much."

"I'm just wondering, all the black patients are wearing dirty hospital gowns but the only white patient isn't."

"It is for the same reason my sister that our fingers are not of the same size, but we love and treat them equally. You can't say that it's unfair that your thumb is shorter than your forefinger. Or it is wrong that the fore-finger is thinner than the thumb. They are both ours, they are all equal in our eyes. Their differences are for a purpose, if they were the same they would be of no good use to us, would they?" He said, cogitating.

"Are you saying the patient uniform is for those who can't afford their own clothing? Or you're saying that blacks can't afford and whites can afford that's why they are wearing different attire, but they are equal in your eyes?"

"Yes to both your questions my sister. The white patient has rich relatives and friends, who bring him a lot of clothes and they sometimes bring us some lunch and give us lifts to town. They keep us fed; that allows us to look after the black sick. If it wasn't for the their contribution, all these black patients would be running lose in the streets killing and raping everyone, as the government doesn't pay us decent salaries to look after our families. In return the white man's relatives ask for a small favour that we allow him to wear whatever he wants. One good turn deserves another. In any case, most of the black patients' relatives do not even visit their relatives, let alone buy them clothes or buy us some lunch. The black majority patients keep us employed and the white patient keeps us fed. They play different roles, but are both useful to us."

"Are you going to allow Ndodana to wear his new clothes?"

"My sister you didn't bring me some lunch. You need to motivate us to allow him to wear whatever he wants."

"You want me to bribe you? That's corruption."

"No my sister, corruption is a dirty and discriminatory word. It's mainly used by losers, to disguise their failures. It's not corruption my sister, it's called networking. It's about who you know."

"But I think that white supremacy is still running deep in this hospital, despite having no white doctors and nurses. It's easy to change the people but it's very difficult to change the system."

"You can't say that my sister. We are running the show here. We're also truly independent in our country, we have even taken back our land."

"But you're adopting other nations' currencies. Is that what you call truly independent?" I left him agape.

As we bade farewell to our nurse escort, I just thought to myself that a system that allows one percent to wear what they want and ninety-nine percent not to, needs changing because it is discriminatory to say the least. But, that day in Johannesburg, the fear of getting mentally unwell and getting treated like patients at Engutsheni made inroads into my mind.

Chapter 7

IMMIGRATION OFFICERS

I checked in at Oliver Tambo International airport with Beans, when my time came to leave Johannesburg. I was on crutches. When I first landed at this airport two weeks ago, I could not have imagined myself on four legs on my return trip. I was bubbly, strong and healthy. My mind was wholly on my mother's poorly health. I didn't expect so much change of opportunity on my way back. I was a different woman. It showed how much clueless I was about my future. My experiences of the previous two weeks, would certainly shape my future, I had no doubt. Life doesn't throw you in at the deep end and then return you to normality again, or does it?

The immigration officer scanned me from head to toe with suspicious eyes. Eyes that were seeing a different human being. Eyes that didn't believe my crutches were real. It was only "hallo" from the immigration officer and that was it. He left the rest to his talking eyes. Eyes that have seen all and sundry. Eyes that have taken human trafficking by its horns and tamed it at this airport. Eyes that could have stopped 9/11 in America. I could tell that he felt his job was very important, that he saved lives. He went through my passport with a fine-tooth comb. He took his time. He owned the airport. I didn't shrink faced with his inquisitive eyes. I looked right into his eyes. I fought fire with fire. There was nothing wrong with my passport. I wouldn't be intimidated. That was a real passport. If he wanted a bribe he could try his own mother, not me, I was squeaky clean. A little bird in my mind said, '*This is Johannesburg airport, many people have stories to tell about it.*' The little bird deliberately refrained from calling this airport Oliver Tambo airport because it would be soiling the name of a great man, who fought gallantly and selflessly for black emancipation in South Africa. A man who could be turning in his grave day and night, every time the immigration officers took a bribe.

The daughter of one of my friends, who was in transit to Zimbabwe, was once forced to buy another air ticket to Bulawayo, because her original air ticket had her surname and first name transposed. She had travelled from Heathrow airport in London, via Charles de Gaulle airport in France without problems and her difficulties only started and ended at Johannesburg airport. On her way back to the UK she used her original ticket that was initially refused by corrupt officials on a South African airline and there was no problem. Was I about to have my own story to tell?

Eventually the passport officer ordered me to follow him to a private office. I was aghast. There was nothing wrong with my passport, I assured myself. Why should he call me into an office instead of discussing it with me right there? In the open. Beans tried to follow me but the officer ordered him not to. He watched helplessly as the officer escorted me into a very tiny office, so small that I doubted that it was officially used as an office at all. If it wasn't for the two tiny windows it could have qualified as a bribe room. There was only one chair in the tiny room. Once inside, the officer said to me,

"There's no need for me to ask you to sit down, with your crutches you might not get up." I didn't know how to take his comment. Was it a joke or he was just rude? I just gazed at him and he continued, "How are your crocodile wounds healing?" To say I was shocked and dumbfounded would be a big lie. I was staggered. It was a knock-out punch. How did the immigration officer come to possess such privy information? Where did he get it from? Who gave it to him? Why? Why was this information not available in hospital? Why? Why? Why? There was no way he should be in possession of that information. Only Beans knew it. What was happening? Was Beans selling me out? I forced a smile and said,

"I was attacked by a hyen…"

"Don't give me that crap mama," the immigration officer interrupted me. He was wearing a serious face, the face of a man in authority, who did his job to the best of his abilities. He had obviously sensed something unusual about my wounds. Did he sniff at them like a dog to know that they were not hyena but crocodile inflicted? What was he angling for? He looked me straight in the eye, and I blinked first. He didn't blink. He knew the truth and trusted his informer. He went on, "They might have bought your hyena story and *'I can't remember'* approach in hospital, but not here! I have no time for liars. How much did you pay the doctors to accept your lies?" He paused. I was stunned and started panicking. I was confused too. I thought to myself, *'But I was also attacked by a hyena, wasn't I?'* It seemed he didn't know or acknowledge it. If it was Beans telling, he would have told him that information. "But I was attacked by a hyen…"

63

"Are you sure you want to play games with me mama? Never play games that you know you would lose. That's my free advice to you."

I was satisfied that he didn't know about the hyena attack. If it was Beans who sold me out, why didn't he tell him about it? Was he trying to cover his tracks, by leaving that bit out? Was he a sell out? Was he the informant? But what for? What would he gain? My paranoia went into overdrive.

The officer continued, "If you want to catch your flight start talking now. It's your choice. Don't forget I know everything about how you sustained your injuries. You hold a passport that does not allow you to enter Zimbabwe, to circumvent that you illegally crossed the Limpopo River and you were attacked by a crocodile, so stop lying. You were attacked by a crocodile and rescued by your escorts. When you passed out they dumped you for dead a few kilometres from the Limpopo River."

I thought to myself '*Oh good Lord I am like an open Bible now. This man knows a lot of what happened, arguing with him is waste of time.*' At that point my suspicions hit the roof! Was Beans really working with this man? What was going on? There were a few things that Beans let loose that did not exactly add up. Was there someone who knew me at the airport, like in the kombi, at the Limpopo River and everywhere else? Yet Beans wanted to come with me and the immigration officer barred him. None of it added up. The way things were going, he would tell me the design and the colour of my pants! I had to tell him the truth. But I was fighting within myself about how much I should tell. What did he want, a bribe or the truth? How much truth? How much bribe? Why would he need the truth? What would he do with it? He knew it in any case. Since he knew how I got the injuries, why doesn't he turn me to the police? Questions flooded my poor mind? Any slip my return to UK would be doomed. He couldn't deport me back to Zimbabwe. I couldn't survive in Moment of Madness's Sodom and Gomorra.

The immigration officer made himself comfortable in the only chair in the room. He had no manners, he didn't even respect women, let alone my injuries. He was too fat to stand longer than five minutes. A corrupt, fat, lazy man. When Beans finally entered the cubicle, I was on the verge of a breakdown, mentally. I looked him straight in the eye and he didn't blink. I explained to him what the officer was accusing me of. He sighed, shook his head and immediately offered the officer five hundred British pounds. The officer smiled and said to him, "You might be carrying a British passport *mtakwethu,* mate, but you still remember the African way of life. You can take the boy out of Africa but you cannot take Africa out of the boy. Give me two thousand pounds, and save this poor woman."

"I don't have that kind of money with me right now, sir." Beans pleaded with the officer. The officer said, "Do you see that building with fancy brickwork, you will find an international bank." He pointed in the direction of the departure lounge. But as I cast my eyes towards the departure lounge through the tiny office window, they rested on the short woman with puppy eyes. I couldn't believe it! I was stunned, rooted to the spot, as Beans left the office to get the officer's money, which he had negotiated down to one thousand pounds. It was as if the officer was selling a goat, and they argued over its price. I couldn't help Beans to raise part of the money because I didn't have any. My purse was emptied in Limpopo when they left me for dead.

I was not allowed to leave the office until Beans had returned and greased the officer's palms. I sweated from the apparition I had just seen. The short woman with puppy eyes was at the airport too. Did I really see her or was it someone who looked similar to her? Could my eyes be trusted anymore? Were they playing games with my mind? Or was my mind playing games with my eyes? Or was I on my way to Engutsheni?

Beans eventually returned and paid the officer his bribe. We were finally allowed to leave the room to complete our check-in. Beans didn't bring up the subject of the bribe nor discuss how I was going to pay him back. I left it to him to discuss it with Ice. I suspected that it was not the only expense he had covered on behalf of his friend. Eventually, we boarded our plane back to London, back to hope and safety.

I was on board a Virgin Airline plane and because of my condition and the crutches, my seat was upgraded to business class without me paying a penny. The crocodile attack had put me into business class. The service was first class. There was more leg room and the seats were sofa beds too. That was what I called *ukuphapha ngeqolo,* flying on my back. Not economy traveling, where you're so squashed; as if you're travelling in a flying kombi. Beans and I boarded the same plane, but he kept his kombi seat despite being offered a business class too as my helper. I didn't understand his actions. I remembered him telling me on our way to the airport that those black South Africans who were living *emkhukhwini,* in tin houses, some of them were given brick and mortar houses, and they either sold or rented

65

them out and kept their tin houses. He did exactly that that day, turning down a business seat for a kombi seat, it didn't make sense in any way or form you tried to look at it.

During the night flight I thought I caught a glimpse of the short woman with puppy eyes again. I saw her when the door separating the business and the economy classes briefly opened. I was convinced that I saw her as she stood between business and economy classes. Was it my eyes? Was I visually hallucinating? Was I seeing things? The woman seemed to appear everywhere. Was it my mind? The appearance and disappearance of the short woman with puppy eyes started to make me doubt my own mind. Did crocodile saliva have hallucinogenic properties? I knew that the crocodile liver was poisonous, according to what I heard when I was growing up, many people used it to settle old scores by mixing it with their victims' food. The victims would die writhing, slithering and squirming like the Limpopo snake. I wasn't sure of what the crocodile saliva could do to a human being. But I thought it surely made me to see visions. The vision of the short woman with puppy eyes popped up everywhere.

Once I got comfortable in business class, my mind wandered before I fell asleep. Ice would be waiting for me at Heathrow airport and I had asked him to bring with him my childhood friend Molly. But she had turned down my request, according to Ice, because she had a shift. In Zimbabwe our relatives demand money from us as if we picked it from the trees; if that was the case most of the diasporians would be married to monkeys. In the UK we put in shifts to get the money. No one knew how to turn shifts into money better than Molly. One time when she still lived in London, after working ten nights in a row, she told me that she fell asleep on the tube at around nine o'clock in the morning and only woke up at around four o'clock in the afternoon and she didn't bother going home for a bath and change of clothes, but went straight back to her eleventh night shift in a row. The dropping in and out of the tube passengers left no dent on her slumber. She slept like a baby. What made her laugh at herself most was the fact that tube cleaners, who were mainly immigrants themselves, did their cleaning and left her to rest because they understood what shifts could do to your body. But how many times have you received a telephone call from a relative in Zimbabwe, asking you to buy them the latest iPhone, when you don't have one yourself. Where did they think we got the money from? Some, including Comrade Moment of Madness, had said it loud and clear that we dug it out of the old man or woman's backside and that we should be ashamed of ourselves for doing those demeaning jobs.

I first met Molly at Gweru Teachers' College in Zimbabwe. We lived in the campus and we were both training to be secondary school teachers. We spoke the same language and that brought us together. Most of the students at college spoke Shona and we both spoke Ndebele. She came from a fairly rich family. In those days, when you were driven to college by your father in his own car, battered or not, you were considered to come from a fairly rich family.

In my case my mother would have wanted to get into a kombi with me to take me to *Erenkini,* the main bus terminus to catch a chicken bus that would take me to Gweru town. Those buses were called chicken buses because they were used mostly by rural people, who travelled with their chickens to give them to their relatives in town as gifts. To soften and pacify their urban relatives for those few days while they lived with them. They had their pride to maintain too. They wouldn't want themselves to be seen as taking their relatives generosity for granted. Coming to the city to live for free, *hay'bo*, no.

But I would kindly ask my mother not to worry herself in taking me to the chicken buses. I would assure her that I would be fine, but mainly because Ice would be accompanying me. But poor Molly, her father would drive and drop her at the doorstep of her dormitory. So she wouldn't meet her boyfriend until her father had left the college campus.

My mother did not meet Ice until I graduated from college. That was after he sent his people to meet my family and ask for my hand in marriage. My mother and relatives were not expected to meet my boyfriend until he was ready to marry me. Boyfriends were exactly that, boyfriends. What would they meet a boyfriend for? Boyfriends should be changed like panties if they don't suit the purpose. But as a parent you might end up asking a few questions about your daughter's choices. Was she that bad at choosing boys? Doesn't she know that she should pick them as if she was picking *amaganu*, marula fruits from the ground? Some would look appetising from the top, but rotten to the core down below? Picking boyfriends and showing them to parents and then dropping them later, was tantamount to picking and putting a marula fruit in your mouth before thoroughly checking it. Parents would only meet someone who was serious enough to marry you, not a boyfriend, not a half rotten marula fruit.

Molly met her husband Dollar at college. He spoke Shona and most of their conversation was in English until she learnt how to speak Shona. Dollar didn't even attempt to learn to speak Ndebele, just like most Shona speakers, they find Ndebele difficult to speak. To speak Ndebele one has to click, that put off most Shona speakers from even trying to speak Ndebele as they feared to accidentally bite off part of their tongues in an effort to click.

Molly's parents were not happy at all about their daughter marrying him because Dollar was a Shona. There was a general belief in Matabeleland that Shona men didn't marry Ndebele wives for life. Young Ndebele girls, intent on marrying Shona men, were warned that retired Shona men who live in urban areas, would go back to their rural homes to live with their Shona young wives. Ask Sally Mugabe, if you happen to doubt this assertion.

Molly and I often laughed at how Ndebele-Shona marriages were viewed back home. It was similar to how white-black marriages were viewed in the United Kingdom. Both sides felt that the other side was up to no good. White-black marriages more often than not fall apart. Many of them are sham marriages in any case, meant to regularise Home Office papers, and gain permanent residence in the United Kingdom. The problem with those marriages though, is that they end up with victims, *abantwana bamaphepha,* paper children, when their parents divorce some years later. Beside these marriages of convenience, black-white marriages seem to fail for other reasons, just check how many single white mothers are left fending for their offspring when the black man had done a Bolt.

When Molly first moved to the United Kingdom, she lived in London and once we met up again, she moved down south to Bournemouth. It was easy to attract her down to Bournemouth. I invited her over to come and visit me in Dorset and took her to places like Bournemouth beach, Old Harry Rocks in Purbeck, Dancing Ledge in Swanage, Hengistbury Head in Christchurch and many more attractions and she fell head over heels in love with beautiful Dorset. We soon became neighbours again and supported each other in a country of shifts.

When I woke up it was light outside and we were being served business breakfast. For the first time in a plane I was asked what I would like to have for breakfast. Not the usual choice between two junk breakfasts in the kombi class. I chose what I wanted for breakfast and it was cooked according to my preferences, half-done eggs, half-done coffee, half-done organic tomatoes and half-done the rest. Life in business class was like in a five star hotel and in the kombi class it was like in a bread and breakfast in Boscombe in Bournemouth.

Beans visited me only once during the whole flight, when we were about to land. He approached my seat and sat next to me and said, smiling, "I will land in business class to feel if there is any difference from economy class landing." I smiled back and said to him,

"You should have sat here the whole flight to really feel the difference, instead of sitting on those kombi seats with no legroom as if they are made for legless people." I shifted a bit in my seat, took a deep breath and said, "There is something that really worries me Beans. I keep on seeing a short woman with puppy eyes who was with me when the accident happened at Limpopo River. She is very short and pretty. I've seen her three times so far, once in Johannesburg, once at the airport and again during this flight."

"Are you sure that you saw the same woman? It could be someone similar to her. Are you sure you saw the same person, Dolly?" asked Beans, but before I could respond, our flight started to make those landing tingling humps, that made my stomach cringe and tickle and I smiled. Beans smiled back, perhaps he was feeling the same thing, perhaps he wondered about the short woman who kept appearing and disappearing and thought that I was going mad. Finally we landed safely at Heathrow airport in London. There were no prayers and ululation when we touched down, as it would have been the case if we were in Air Zimbabwe. Apparently, Zimbabweans prayed and ululated each time Air Zimbabwe landed safely, as though they believed that it was flying on urine and only managed the whole journey on God's mercy.

Beans helped me with my hand luggage as we disembarked from the plane and we went through the check-out without the Johannesburg adventures. Many people have tales to tell about Heathrow airport too, I included. When I first landed in that airport, five years ago, the immigration officer refused to grant me a visitor's visa on the grounds that I did not have enough money on me and he doubted if I had a host in the United Kingdom. He therefore suspected that my purpose of my visit was to find work or work illegally. Immigration officers all over the world always think the worst of anyone before they even utter a single word. The guys joined the wrong profession, they should have been FBIs CIAs, CIOs or M5s of this world.

69

I told the immigration officer that my husband was a student nurse at a local university and had enough money to support me, but the officer did not believe me because, "Your husband is by British immigration law only allowed to work a maximum of twenty hours a week ma'am" he said arrogantly. I had deliberately chosen to be attended to by someone with a skin colour that was very close to mine. Someone whose first generation would have been immigrants. I thought that an Asian immigration officer would understand me. How wrong I was as it turned out. I honestly believed that he would understand my situation, *kanti angibuzanga elangeni,* I didn't enquire from those who knew better. I then said to him,

"My husband told me that he works more than forty hours a week and there was a lot of work in the United Kingdom."

Smiling and shaking his head he said, "If he's working those hours and he has a student visa, he's breaking the law ma'am. As a foreign student he should know better. The jobs he told you about are for British people not for foreigners like him and you." At that point I thought to myself, *'but Ice told me that he works more than forty hours a week, or am I confused? But why would he lie to me?'* The immigration officer continued, "Do you have his contact details?"

"Yes I do," I said searching my purse and at the same time thinking; *what does this man take me for? Coming all the way from Zimbabwe without the contact details of the person I'm visiting. What do these British people take foreigners for? He thinks I'm stupid.* "Here," I said shoving the piece of paper with Ice's details into his hand, confidently adding, "He should be waiting for me at the arrivals. His name is Ice Sibanda." The immigration officer announced Ice's name on the airport's tannoy,

"Mr Ice Sibanda please come to immigration desk 98. Mr Ice Sibanda please come to immigration desk number 98. Thank you."

I expected Ice to come forward but he didn't. Tick tock went the time. No Ice.

The officer repeated his call, "Mr Ice Sibanda your wife is waiting for you at immigration desk 98, please come forward. Mr Ice Sibanda please come forward to immigration desk number 98, your wife's waiting." He spoke with untainted British accent. He might have been born here, *wayetshila ulimi njengomlungu,* for twisting his tongue like a white man, I thought to myself. He didn't understand the trials and tribulations of being an immigrant.

But again my husband didn't turn up. The officer then rang Ice's mobile number and he said to me, "It's switched off ma'am."

Had my loving husband deserted me? Had he chickened out? Had he developed cold feet and decided to leave me at the mercy of the immigration officers? I couldn't believe that Ice could do that to me. He later explained to me that he was not at the airport, because he had overslept. He told me that when he got up late, he panicked, quickly freshened up and left his flat. He told me that he only discovered that he had forgotten his mobile, when he got onto the tube, which he had switched off and put on the charge the previous night, but he decided to continue with his journey since he was running late. I believed his plausible explanation, I had no reason not to.

The officer then excused himself and went into an office with my passport. When he returned he said, "I'm sorry ma'am I can't grant you a visitor's visa because I'm not sure of your purpose of visit. I will therefore send you back to Zimbabwe on the next available flight."

'Back to Comrade Moment of Madness's Zimbabwe?' I thought to myself.

He went on to say, "I think you're an economic refugee." The word 'refugee' planted an idea into my mind. Some people told me back in Zimbabwe that their relatives claimed refugee status and had been allowed to live in the United Kingdom permanently. I immediately said to the officer,

"I would like to claim a political refugee status."

He looked me straight in the eye and said, "Don't play games with me ma'am."

I looked him right back in the eye and said, "I'm running away from Zimbabwe because my life's in danger."

"Please don't try and play games with me. Why didn't you say that from the start? Why did you create a husband that didn't exist? Stop your games, they won't stick with me ma'am." He was adamant, he didn't want to listen to my story.

"If you had allowed me entry, I would have entered the country and found out how to go about claiming asylum. But by threatening to put me in the next available flight back to Zimbabwe you gave me no option but to claim asylum right here and right now." My voice was rising with each word I said but he continued to threaten me with deportation. I then said to him, "Can I see a lawyer please?"

71

"What?"

"You heard me." I got a bit confident when I detected some bit of hesitancy in his tone. I declared again, "Can I see a lawyer please."

All of a sudden he was getting deaf or developing problems with my accent. On the other hand I was smelling his blood and going for a kill.

"You can't see a solicitor. Please ma'am stop playing games with me."

"You can't stop me from seeing a lawyer, can you? The United Kingdom is the mother of all human rights. The mother of all black or white or yellow human rights. You have no right to deny me the right to see a lawyer." At that time English words sounded like Ndebele words, the frustrations behind my pronunciation made my accent as heavy as a baobab tree.

He stuck to his guns, "You can't see a solicitor ma'am. There's no credible reason why you should see one. I have made my decision to deport you back to Zimbabwe."

I looked at him with a talking eye. I told him with my mouth shut that I was going nowhere. I was staying put.

"Excuse me ma'am, let me consult my manager." He turned and left. I knew my God had intervened. His manager would tell him off for wanting to send a poor woman into Comrade Moment of Madness's den. He would order him to allow me to see a lawyer.

But when he returned he delivered the same old message, "I'm sorry ma'am, my manager agrees with my decision. You will board the next available plane back to Zimbabwe."

I began to get worked up. I couldn't go back to Zimbabwe. What would the people who came to my leaving party say? What would my mother say? Having tried to claim asylum, the CIOs would be on my case like wolves. How would I pay for the ticket I bought on a *fly now, pay later* scheme? "I would like to see a lawyer right now or I show you what Mugabe's Gukurahundi did on my back side."

"Stop it," the immigration officer said.

"Do you really want to see for yourself what they did to my back side sir?"

"Stop that," he said.

"Do you really want to see for yourself then sir?"

"Please stop acting ma'am."

"We have a way of dealing with rogue men in authority, in my country, sir. We show them our backside. We show them our buttocks," I said as I started to pull my skirt up.

"Stop, stop, please stop," he pleaded with me. I ignored him, turned my back to him and up went my skirt, revealing my back and my bum. He covered his face with one hand as if he was being blinded by the eclectic bright colours of my panties and he used the other to beckon security to take me away. "Security, security please take her to the seclusion room," he ordered them.

"You are a Doubting Thomas sir, do you believe me now?" I said to the immigration officer as the security men dragged me away.

Three months after my arrival I was granted refugee status for five years, given a blue passport, but I was not allowed to visit Zimbabwe.

Chapter 8

BOURNEMOUTH

Ice met us at Arrivals, as I was on crutches, poor Beans had the pleasure to push all the luggage. When Ice and I met at the airport we kissed and hugged for a long time until Beans cleared his throat as a sign that we should move on, then Ice said, "Thank Heavens you survived the croc's attack Dolly. Many people have not been that lucky in that river." Ice and Beans greeted each with a fist bump. Beans took his luggage and said he had arranged his own transport. He bid us farewell and off he went. I found that a bit surprising and I said to Ice, "Isn't it a bit strange that Beans has arranged his own transport, why not travel with us since we all live in Bournemouth?"

"Maybe he felt that the suitcases would not fit in the same car."

"He refused to travel on business class with me in the plane. I found that strange too."

"Oh, you travelled on business class? I hope you had a comfortable journey in the class of businessmen, Dolly."

"Oh it was for sure. I would like to fly business class in future. You feel you are living *impilo-mpilo*, real life," I said as we left the Arrivals building. But as we waited to cross the road I saw the short woman with puppy eyes again, pushing her suitcase trolley on the other side. She was wearing the same clothes she was wearing at Oliver Tambo International airport and on the plane. I stood, there, transfixed. Her appearance had had the same effect to me - it stupefied me. "It's her," I said, pointing in her direction. "That woman was there when I was attacked by the crocodile," I said excitedly and added, "She was there. It's her. It's her, my eyes are not deceiving me." By the time Ice looked her way, she had been swallowed up by the swarming traffic and disappeared behind the buildings.

"Which one? I can't see her. Is she black or white?" He asked.

"She is obviously black, Ice. What would a white woman be doing crossing Limpopo River illegally at night?"

"You never know, *amakhiwa athand'izinto,* white people like the adventure." He responded without looking at me. We crossed the road got into another building and then took a lift that left us at a level where he had parked his car. We were both quiet by the time we got to the car. I was struggling with the sight of the woman with puppy eyes. If it was her, why didn't she say that she was on her way to the UK too, when Joe called me a British woman? Or did she think it was my nickname? Maybe it wasn't her, I thought to myself as we got into the car and drove off.

I was relieved that I'd seen her at good distance and I believed that it was definitely her. My eyes had not been playing games with me. What if she was stalking me? But I dismissed the idea. Why would she stalk me? She couldn't stalk a stranger from Africa to Europe, it was impossible.

"But what if she is stalking me?" The question popped out of my mouth involuntarily.

"Stalking you? Who's stalking you? Are you talking to yourself, Dolly?"

"That short woman with puppy eyes."

"The Limpopo River woman?" He asked as he frowned and continued, "So you've got a stalker now? Are you OK Dolly?" He glanced at me before his eyes went back to the road. "Maybe the croc's saliva poisoned your mind!"

I didn't like his body language and his words, whether he was joking or not. I had thought about the properties of the crocodile's saliva in the plane. But for Ice to repeat that to me as if he read my mind, infuriated me. I had to be careful of what I said. He appeared able to read my mind. At that instance he had read it brilliantly, which made me further doubt myself. I chose to keep quiet. We drove quietly for some time.

As we turned onto the M25 South, I thought to myself, 'This man will never understand what I went through in the Limpopo River in his entire lifetime even if he were given the chance to live it three times over. Although, so far he appears to be taking it lightly, what he doesn't understand is that only a few people have survived my ordeal with the kind of wounds I have. Some people who survived crocodile attacks like I did, part of their limbs were either swept away by the water or were left rotting in the crocodiles' stomachs. I would not have survived the crocodile attack had it not been for brave Joe and Ben. I was left for dead and he has the guts to doubt my mind.'

After a while I asked him, "Are you OK Ice, you seem a bit quiet and irritable?" I deliberately threw back to him what he had earlier thrown at me. If it was sarcasm, I threw back sarcasm. If it was false empathy, I threw back false empathy. All in an effort to disarm him before he fully understood how weakened my mind had been affected by the appearance and disappearance of the short woman with puppy eyes. My eyes and mind appeared incongruent. The short woman with puppy eyes played games with both of them and left them baffled, not trusting each other. Her sight left me thinking of Engutsheni, frightened and unsure. What if I was going mad? What if...? What if...?

He responded without looking at me, "I should be the one worried about you Dolly. You seem paranoid about people following you. Honestly, how could someone stalk you from South Africa to the United Kingdom? From Zimbabwe to Britain? From the Limpopo River to Heathrow airport? For what? That stalker would deserve an Olympic gold medal and an entry in the Guinness Book Of World Records. I'm just worried that your croc's experience might have traumatised you..."

"Please stop referring to the crocodile as 'croc' Ice. Are you trying to make fun of my attack? Are you trying to trivialise my attack? What kind of a husband behaves like you? You should be putting your arm around my shoulder and trying to understand what I went through. Instead you make me feel ridiculed and inferior." In spite of myself, I laid my emotions bare to him. The more I tried to hide to him what was happening to my mind the more I exposed it and the more vulnerable I became, not only to his jibes, but to my mind too.

"Wow, I didn't see that one coming," he prophesied innocence and both of his hands momentarily left the steering, "Never in a million years would I make fun of your crocodile attack Dolly. What you went through was a matter of life or death. I'm sorry that you feel this way. I'm not trying to trivialise your experience. I'm very, very sorry, if that's how you feel. That is not my intention at all. I'm in shock too. Your experience is mine too, Dolly." He drove quietly until we turned onto the M3, "How is your mother?" He asked.

I deliberately avoided eye contact, turned my head and looked outside the passenger window, but I couldn't hold back what was in my mind anymore, "And it took you more than thirty minutes to ask me about my mother's condition. More than thirty minutes? The very reason that I went to Zimbabwe, putting my residence in this country in jeopardy. Risking my life in the Limpopo River. Being attacked by wild animals and robbed of my money? Thrown out of a car like a piece of caca. Forced to pay a bribe..." I stopped and wiped off the tears that were rolling down my cheeks. He remained quiet, so I rumbled on, "Thirty minutes to ask me about my mother? She could be dead by now. Thirty minutes to ask me about my mother? You just don't care. Do you?" Tears were rolling down my face like the Limpopo River water. They rolled down my cheeks, my chin, they jumped from my chin onto the space between my breasts, but were too strong and fast for the bra's material to absorb them all, they flowed over part of my stomach, in and out of my navel, over the rest of my stomach and disappeared into the dark bushy area. I could feel them wetting that area. An area where, if he was *indoda emadodeni*, a real man, he would have wetted with his baby. Not only a baby but babies. Instead he watered the area with my tears.

"I'm sorry Dolly, it appears I can't say anything right today. You seem to be extremely sensitive and volatile. In all honesty, I understand that you have been through a life-changing experience." After another long pause he asked again, "How is your mother?" He didn't give up. He doesn't give up. He was a stubborn man.

"She was still breathing when I left her."

"I'm sorry Dolly. We can only hope that she gets better."

There was something not right with me that day. I was not usually that irritable and teary with him. That day I was fluctuating between being myself and someone else. I had another person residing in me. Maybe Ice detected the new me, the new person that he didn't know. A stranger he didn't know how to deal with. The new me he didn't like. The new me that didn't mince words. That he couldn't placate and manipulate. Trying to get grips with her? To tame her on my behalf, because I couldn't? She frightened me too.

Ice has twenty four siblings, fourteen boys and ten girls. His father was polygamous, he had three wives. His mother had one girl and nine boys, Ice was the last born from his mother but he was the twentieth from his father. He was the only one who managed to come to the UK, he has three brothers in Canada, one sister and four brothers in Australia and one brother in the United States of America. He didn't know where his half siblings were and he wasn't keen to talk about them. Despite having so many siblings he failed to make me pregnant. He fired blanks. Maybe his father fired live rounds on his behalf and left him with guns loaded with rubber bullets, as his father used all the live ammunition to satisfy all his wives. I suspected that he was born infertile, but he blamed me for being infertile.

"You are a sitting duck, he should take aim, not you. If he misses it's his problem, not yours Dolly," my friend Molly would counsel.

Ice once cheated on me in Zimbabwe. I found a woman's picture in his shirt pocket. When I confronted him about it, he said that it was a picture of his distant cousin. Only when I threatened to take the picture to his mother to confirm the relationship, he confessed his cheating. He apologised profusely, promising not to do it again. My husband behaved like a teenage boy sometimes. How could a grown up, married man, carry a picture of his prostitute in his shirt pocket? How low could he go? I tore the picture of the prostitute and threw it in the bin. His mistress was just a face, which I deliberately wiped out of my mind in order to save my marriage. But still, in the process of apologising, he somehow managed to blame me for not giving him children. He wrongly and repeatedly blamed me for failing to bear children, and, eventually, I blamed myself too. A good wife was expected to bear her husband children, but I failed dismally on the basic female function. I was good for nothing. I believed that I failed him, therefore I wasn't a good wife. He told me that he cheated on me as he tried to father children with someone. He said that he didn't cheat on me because he didn't love me, far from it.

I began to wonder whether Ice inherited cheating genes from his father. I read it somewhere that some researchers have proved that cheating genes may be inherited. I concluded that Ice's grandfather passed polygamy genes to his father, who in turn passed them to him, but because modern society does not entertain that nonsense, his polygamy genes turned to cheating genes. Men with cheating genes are not satisfied by one woman, so they cheat their beloved. My friend from the church was just blunt about it and said that men who marry many wives or cheat are just greedy, they didn't realise that it's the same soup in different shaped bowls.

I was still thinking about Ice's cheating genes when we went past Ringwood, a small market town, and turned onto A338 leading home. I was relieved when the neon lit sign 'Welcome to Bournemouth' met my eyes on the walkover bridge. We finally got home after one and a half hours' drive. Home sweet home, I sighed with relief.

Whilst Ice prepared something to eat I took a shower. I couldn't take a bath, because I wasn't sure I would be able to get out of the tub. I calmly took off the bandages as the nurses had taught me in Musina hospital. My left calf was in a mess. The swelling had come down though. The crocodile just planted its teeth there and refused to let go. My leg had dropped into the Limpopo River like manna from Heaven. But two brave men denied it its dinner. If it were not for them, I would be rotting in the crocodile's belly by then.

As I carefully washed my leg, Ice sneaked in and said, "Hey *madoda,* men, that's some damage. The croc...crocodile, hurt you Dolly." He remembered my outburst and he continued, "You are brave, I'm proud of you darling. What's important though is that you came out with your life. Can I help at all?"

"No Ice, thanks, just make sure you prepare good nutritious food that will help to heal my leg quickly," I said as he made his way back to the kitchen downstairs and I continued with my long shower.

Ice came to UK in early 2003 and it was quite easy for him because he had an uncle who was already a UK resident. Our plan was that as soon as he arrived in the UK, he would borrow some money from his relative, buy and send a ticket to me. We didn't want to be apart for too long, as we knew couples who had never had problems in Zimbabwe, getting divorced in the UK. But six months down the line, he failed to send me the ticket and he told me that his relative didn't have enough money to lend him, so he couldn't send me the ticket. Despite telling me that he was working many hours, he insisted that he wasn't making enough to buy my air ticket. After waiting for more than six months the alarm bells started to ring. That was the man who had cheated me before. Was he at it again, knowing that I might never come to the United Kingdom and prove it? When I started to hear rumours that he was seen with some white girls having a good time, the bells rang even louder than the Big Ben. *Ukubona kanye yikubona kabili,* once bitten, twice shy. That was why I took the 'fly now and pay later' scheme from a travel company, and flew to the UK, denied the visitors' visa and the rest is history.

I first dated Ice, while at Gweru Teachers' College in my late teens. Not that he was my first love. He was my love number...let me not embarrass him lest he read this note. I would never forget how I first met him.

When my love affair with this other young man, whom I was seeing at the time, was wobbling, a friend of mine told me that he was seeing a girl, whose only advantage over me was that he wore mini-skirts. To outbid the girl and keep him, I started to wear min-skirts too, although I knew that wearing a mini-skirt wasn't the best way to attract a future husband. I knew for sure that I would attract those who would chew me up and spit me away like a chewing gum and pretend that I never existed.

So I started to wear mini-skirts only while in the city centre. I would leave the house with my mini-skirt in my hand bag and when I got into town I would go to the toilet and change into the mini-skirt. I would walk the streets, visit the places my boyfriend was likely to visit in the hope of meeting him and make him jealous at what he was missing. Missing this beautiful face, sitting perfectly on a long and appetising neck, attached to a chest with two beautiful rounded original breasts, (not fake ones like the English ones), dangling appealingly to a four pack stomach, well supported by deliciously rounded original buttocks, (real ones not the fake Nigerians ones), sitting on to die for thighs, connected to long legs, like that of a long distance runner. That was what that loser was missing.

But one day while I was walking towards the main bus station, on my way to the toilet to change into my decent clothes and catch a bus to Lobengula West, I saw a group of boy-men, boys in their mid-twenties who didn't know whether they were boys or men, who exhibited traits of both, so I preferred to call them boy-men. The boy-men started to whistle and shout at me because of my mini-skirt, calling me all sorts of unprintable names. I was shocked and embarrassed, and wondered what my boyfriend would say if he saw me being hounded and harassed for dressing like a whore? Would he join the crowd or fight my corner since he loved girls in mini-skirts? I looked down in fear and walked on. The mob charged towards me. I wished the ground to open up and swallow me. Suddenly someone put their hand on my shoulder. I turned startled and saw this handsome, smiling tall man, who said, "Keep calm and keep on walking. Ignore them. Don't worry they are hooligans. Pretend you know me and keep walking." The group stopped shouting and the stranger saved my dignity. As it turned out he boarded the same bus as I did. When I got onto the bus, I searched for a seat for two. I made sure that the handsome and well-muscled stranger sat next to me.

Sitting next to me and smiling, he introduced himself, "I'm Ice," showing off his milk white teeth.

"I'm Dolly." By the time I said these words, I had already fallen in love with him. He swept me off my feet instantly. In my eyes he was the man of my dreams. He was not only tall, imposing and handsome, but brave too as he took on the mob and won, few men would have dared.

He said, "Isn't it a shame that girls are treated like that for wearing mini-skirts, in this day and age."

I was not listening to him. How would I? I was dying to insert my tongue through those white teeth. It was love at first sight. He oozed confidence and he was definitely caring and brave, as he had just silenced a pack of boy-men. He was mad too, very few other men would have come to the rescue of a stranger at that point. I chose him before he could say that he loved me. I was ready to say yes before he completed asking. Men believe that they choose the women they want, but they are liars, for how can they be choosers, when the right to accept or refuse their proposal lies with the women? Men and boys only chose their wives and girlfriends in their dreams, in reality, women choose them. Men also deceive themselves that they make the first moves, women make the first silent effective moves, just like heart attacks, every time.

During the bus journey, Ice told me that he had videoed the mob using his state of the art mobile phone, which had a camera. Few people had such gadgets during those days and he got it from his uncle who was studying in the United Kingdom. As he played back the video to me, I could not believe my eyes when I saw my boyfriend with the mob. He was one of the leaders of the pack, one of the hunting dogs, boy-man, frothing and shouting, ready to pounce, given any chance.

It was then that I realised that my boyfriend was two faced. Not only was he two timing me, he was double crossing me with a girl who wore mini-skirts, yet he hated girls who wore mini-skirts. Anyway, *ukuwa kwendoda yikuvuka kwenye,* one's man loss is another man's gain. His fall was certainly the rise of Ice. Again, as they say in my language, *impethu ingena ngenxeba,* a maggot only find its way into the flesh through a wound. My cheating boyfriend created a scar in my heart and Ice, like a maggot, took full advantage to find his way right into its core, where he has feasted since then. That was how I met the man who went on to be my loving husband.

Chapter 9

DAYMARES

On my first night back in Bournemouth, I experienced nightmares. I woke up more than three times, screaming and sweating, with my heart racing. The same nightmares happened each time I fell asleep. I dreamt swimming in the sea near Bournemouth Pier and all of a sudden I would be surrounded by crocodiles with human bodies and crocodile heads, and each humcrocodile would bite off part of my body: fingers chopped off, hands chopped off, arms chopped off, in that order; toes severed, feet severed, legs severed, in that order; ears cut off, mouth cut off, the chin cut off, in that order; intestines ripped off, liver ripped off, the lungs ripped off, in that order. All my body parts were severed and swallowed by the humcrocodiles except my eyes and my heart, which were left to float on the beach. Those parts were avoided as if they were leprous, they didn't touch them. Each time, I woke up screaming, sweating and my heart racing.

The nightmares were quite frightening. My experience in the Limpopo River was tormenting me day and night in Bournemouth. I had thought that once I returned to the United Kingdom, my predicament would be over. The Limpopo River misfortunes would be behind me. I was wrong.

I continued to suffer from the Limpopo River experiences. The terrible experiences stuck to my skin and scalp like lice. They sucked my blood day and night. Each time they took a bite, I screamed, but nobody would know and see why I was screaming. They began to question my mind. But the fact that they didn't see the lice, didn't mean that I hadn't been bitten by them. It didn't mean that they were not there. Only I experienced the bite.

The nightmares gave me no time to relax and reflect on my Limpopo River experiences. To look at what I could have done differently on that fateful night, when the kombi driver changed the plans. To question if I should have been more assertive and refused to cross the Limpopo River on foot.

I was left to deal with the aftermath. With the consequences. I had to get up, dust myself off and move on. But how could I move on with a diseased mind? Something serious had happened to it. It didn't allow me to sleep in peace. Why did it betray me that way? It relived the attacks. I had expected my mind to bury the horrible experiences in its subconscious and set me free. Let me live my life as before. My brain betrayed me. It was weak, clueless and useless organ that didn't protect its owner. Only fit to be fed to the dogs.

After six weeks, my crocodile wounds healed very well. I stopped using the crutches and I was able to walk unaided. My life was improving physically, although I would sometimes wake up with both of my feet swollen, but that would not last. I also observed that my breasts were more tender than usual. But if the swelling of my feet in the morning and the tenderness of my breast, was caused by the crocodile attack, it appeared like a small price to pay for coming out of the crocodile's mouth with my life.

I was like a woman being raped by goblins, screaming, kicking and shouting all night. Experiencing no peace at night. During the day, I couldn't walk the streets without seeing a short woman with puppy eyes. Experiencing no peace during the day either. I feared that God must have been very angry with me when he filled the water melon sitting on my neck and shoulders with nightmares and goblins. I hated the nightmares. I hated the short woman with puppy eyes. And I hated my brain.

In the coming weeks and months, the nightmares alternated with another one, where I was swallowed by a crocodile. I would shout to Ice to save me, but he would turn and walk away. Sometimes he would give me two fingers. Two fingers, smile and walk away. Inside the crocodile's stomach I would meet my mother, who would look at me and not utter a single word. She would point towards the mouth of the crocodile, from where I came from, as if she was pointing me to the door. My weak and useless mind would not figure out what she meant. Was she pointing me out of the crocodile and out of the situation I was in? Again I had that dream repeatedly and woke up screaming, sweating and with my heart racing faster than Hamilton's racing car.

I didn't tell Ice about my second dream, I feared that he would take offence and think that I was creating it in order to blame him for failing to control my weak mind. That I was trying to use him as a scapegoat. Making him part of my problems.

The crocodile dream appeared to have more relevance to me than the humcrocodile one. The fact that I saw my mother was comforting. The fact that she was able to move her limbs, something she couldn't do for the two weeks while I was in Zimbabwe, gave me hope. The second dream gave me the desire and strength to get out of my situation. A situation of horrible nightmares and a short woman with puppy eyes who kept appearing and disappearing.

One day I saw the short woman with puppy eyes at Castlepoint bus stop sitting alone at the back seat of the bus. As I approached the bus, it pulled off. Less than forty metres away the bus stopped at the pedestrian traffic lights, I took that opportunity to run after it. As I got closer, the short woman with puppy eyes, sitting at the back seat, looked towards me. I gestured at her by pointing a finger at her and she gestured back, giving me the finger. I had a good look at her. I was pretty sure that it was her and she dared to give me the finger. But as I got closer, the bus pulled off again. I continued to chase the bus and the short woman with puppy eyes had a field day with me at the back window of the bus. She indicated to me with her hands to run faster. She laughed as I tried to run faster but couldn't catch the bus. She pointed her forefinger to her head and made a circle with it, a gesture that I was mad. She gave me two fingers and that really infuriated me. She followed me everywhere and she dared to do that to me? Did she know that she was playing with my mind like a toy?

I knew the bus route, it would take first exit at the Broadway round-about and make a few stops before it came to Queen's Park Academy bus stop. I took a short cut, I ran up the hill like a woman possessed. By the time I got to the academy bus stop I was breathless. I didn't know where I got the energy from. I experienced some kind of thrill and suspense whenever the short woman with puppy eyes appeared. Soon the same bus approached, I waved it down and it stopped. I got into the bus, paid the fare went to the back of the bus but the short woman with puppy eyes had gone. She must have got off at an earlier bus stop. She had disappeared as usual. I sat at the back seat of the bus and cried with rage, saying to myself, 'This woman is playing games with my mind. She is playing hide and seek with my brain. When I get hold of her, she will rue the day she first came to the United Kingdom. I will make her pay for every appearance and disappearance she had put me through. I will hit the hell out of her. That is my promise to her and I usually keep my promises.' Humiliated, I dropped off at Charmnister shops and took another bus going the opposite direction. It was clear that she lived between Castlepoint and the Academy bus stop. 'One day I would hunt her down. I hope she wouldn't be as lucky as today.' I thought to myself.

At first Ice was supportive, but as the nightmares increased per night and their intensity double folded, waking me up twice or thrice a night, nearly every night, sometimes waking up under the bed, he couldn't handle it any longer. He had had enough. He left the bedroom and went to sleep downstairs in the lounge on the sofa. What made matters worse was the fact that he doubted that I was seeing a real person. He believed that the short woman with puppy eyes I saw everywhere, didn't exist. He thought that my experiences were mere flashbacks, something that I should accept and move on. I therefore decided not to tell him some of the experiences I had with the short woman with puppy eyes.

He had no clue on what I was going through. I was on a twenty-four seven shift, one that even my friend Molly couldn't do. Savaged by the nightmares at night and chasing the short woman with puppy eyes by the day.

Each day that passed, sent my mind spinning out of control. It was like watching a beautiful flower, beginning to lose its petals, one by one, day by day, the wind would blow each petal away, leaving behind an ordinary and ugly stem, with no future or hope. Day and night my mind lost meaning. I dreaded the nights. I didn't want to fall asleep. I dreaded the days too. I didn't want to chase the shadows, as that made people to doubt my mind.

One time I decided to reverse my sleeping pattern, I stayed awake all night and slept during the day, in order to avoid nightmares. I thought that since they were called nightmares, they would only happen at night. The reversal of sleep didn't stop the mares, instead I experienced the daymares, which further distressed me. I was a slave to the mares. I was a prisoner of my own mind. A prisoner of my own eyes. *Ngangipika ngigqoke ezami,* I served a prison sentence wearing my own attire.

Sleeping in separate rooms made me feel quite unsupported, to some extent I understood Ice's argument. He went to college during the day and worked most nights in order to support us. He said that he needed to sleep with no disturbance on his nights off. But sometimes I felt that he was deliberately denying me my conjugal rights. Admittedly, I experienced nightmares and I might have displayed some symptoms of insanity, but I still needed to be loved, to be touched and to be appreciated. I was still human. I was still a woman, his wedded wife. Where had the vows, 'till death do us part' gone? Were his 'till the nightmares' do us part or till 'the short woman with puppy eyes do us part?' Sometimes I wanted

Ice to touch me, to reassure me, just to show that I was his wife. Trying for a baby was no longer an option by that time, we had been trying for a baby for the past ten years and it seemed that we had both given up. We never agreed that we did not want the baby anymore. When he went to sleep down stairs, the message was loud and clear - 'no-more baby trying, Dolly.'

Ice reduced to zero my love for him. I felt humiliated. I would lie awake for hours, pondering on how my life had changed. The cuddles and 'love yous' had disappeared? After hours of being awake, I would fall asleep only to be the victim of the nightmares. He didn't only deny me my conjugal rights, he took my affection for him downstairs with him. He took everything that made us a married couple downstairs with him. He left me empty and unloved. It appeared our feelings for each other died at the same time. We didn't tell each other that we felt nothing, that the spark had gone. We just lived our separate lives under the same roof. When our friends visited we pretended that everything was fine, we were both told when we got married, "don't wash your linen in public."

Both the nightmares and the appearing and disappearing of this short woman with puppy eyes were relentless. They were never ending. I needed help and my GP was the obvious first choice. When I saw him I told him that I was attacked by a hyena while on holiday in Uganda. I did not want to mention to him that I was in South Africa, which was too close to Zimbabwe for my comfort. I didn't trust the GPs anymore. They were being used and encouraged by politicians to check their patients' Home Office statuses. I didn't trust my GP because of that, so I didn't disclose to him the truth about my injuries. He told me that he suspected that I could be suffering from Post Traumatic Stress Disorder (PTSD), following the animal attack in Uganda. He also suggested that I see a psychiatrist. I told him without mincing my words that I didn't want to see a psychiatrist and Ice supported me initially.

When I googled what PTSD meant, I found that people who experience PTSD suffered from nightmares and flashbacks, often came from war zone areas. I had not been in a war zone area. Zimbabwe was not a war zone, although economically it qualified as one. I was just unlucky to be attacked by a crocodile. I felt that my GP was just trying to give me a label. He wanted to make me think *ukuthi ngiyahlanya,* that I was mad. *Yay'bo,* no. His limited psychiatric knowledge was not supposed to be used

86

as the reason that I see *udokotela wengqondo,* a psychiatrist. I wasn't going to 'Engutsheni' to be treated like rubbish. Not in my lifetime.

During the same visit, my GP also did some physical check-ups on me. He took my bloods and urine and told me that he wanted to make sure that I didn't catch any transferable diseases like rabies during the attack. As soon as I got home from the surgery, I checked the symptoms of rabies from the internet. The minor symptoms included sleeping problems, but they did not mention, nightmares, so I ruled that out. On the major symptoms, delusions and hallucinations were mentioned. On delusions, that is believing in things that are not real, I wasn't sure, therefore I ruled that out too. But hallucinations, meaning seeing or hearing things that are not real, left me concerned. If I was suffering from any rabies, the short woman with puppy eyes might not be real as I could be hallucinating. But I didn't agree with that. The short woman with puppy eyes did exist, it was impossible that I was seeing things that were unreal. I first met her in the kombi from Bulawayo to Beitbridge. She was present when I was attacked by a crocodile at the Limpopo River. The woman I was seeing existed. I wasn't visually hallucinating. I wasn't suffering from rabies, I reassured myself and I ruled out that too.

But soon after visiting my GP, I received a letter from him saying I should make an urgent appointment to see him at his surgery. His letter left me with a lot of unanswered questions. Had he found out that I was actually attacked by a crocodile in South Africa, not by a hyena in Uganda? Had he told the Home Office about his finding? Was I going to be deported? Had he found that I have rabies? If so, was it treatable after all this time? If I had rabies then Ice was right, nobody stalked me from Zimbabwe to the United Kingdom. It was all in my rabies infected mind. If that was the case, it would be a relief, I would do nothing if I saw someone who appeared like the short woman with puppy eyes. There was nothing to prove. Perhaps he had found that I have cancer, which was at an advanced stage. My mind went into overdrive with all the possibilities. When I showed Ice the letter, he offered to accompany me to the surgery.

While we were waiting for our turn at the surgery, I checked out any suspiciously looking people, who might be immigration officers in plain clothes waiting to pounce on me as soon as I went into the GP's clinic room. I looked out for the UK Border agents. I scrutinised everyone who came into or left the surgery. Those who were coming in and out of my

GP's clinic room received my special attention too. I frequently pretended to go to the toilet just to check for immigration officers. Ice tried to calm me down but to no avail. I deliberately sat next to the door, ready to run out of the surgery should my suspicions become a reality. My adrenaline was overflowing, I was ready for a flight. We waited for less than fifteen minutes to be seen by the GP, but it appeared like several hours to me.

Finally, we were invited into the GP's clinic room. My GP was calm and relaxed. He greeted us with a smile and a handshake and even started a small conversation, something which he had not done before. I thought to myself, 'is he buying time to allow the immigration officers to arrive?' Ice on the other hand was very relaxed too, but I was in panic mode. We obviously had different things in our minds. Smiling the GP said, "I should start by congratulating you Mrs Sibanda, you are eleven weeks pregnant." I was shocked and dumfounded. Ice and I looked at each other, both pleasantly surprised. We both smiled and hugged for some time. We had not touched each other for many weeks. It felt indifferent, it felt like hugging a tree. It reminded me when I tied myself to a tree that saved my life in the Limpopo. There was no connection with the tree, except the rope, with Ice it was the marriage, and that day, it was the baby.

The GP continued, "The other good news is that you did not get rabies during the hyena attack." He asked me to lie on his clinic table and placed the stethoscope on different parts of my stomach and he said, "The baby's fine too." Ice came over and we kissed and hugged again. We couldn't help it. I don't know how Ice felt about hugging me. Was it like hugging a croc for him? But we both warmly hugged anywhere. That was something we had been trying since we got married ten years ago. The baby had eluded us *njengomkhobo,* like a goblin. There have been accusations and counter accusations in the journey of baby making. Some people get babies by mistake and abort them the following day, but it took us ten years to be blessed with one. There have been tears along the way, but finally, the mission had been accomplished.

We both thanked the GP for his fertility pills, support and advice while we were trying for the baby. That meant that I was two or three weeks pregnant when I was attacked by the crocodile.

My lack of conceiving had made me feel very insecure in my marriage. It even made me suspect that Ice was seeing other women. 'Who would blame him,' I could hear people saying behind my back. We shook the GP's hand when we left his clinic room.

We were obviously both shocked but happy. We were shockingly happy. When we got home Ice phoned his friends and relatives and told them about my pregnancy. I phoned Molly and told her the good news. Failing to fall pregnant had always played in my mind. It made me feel like a half woman and insecure. I used to discuss it with Molly and she would counsel by saying, "Dolly, you are the target and Ice is the shooter. If he misses, it's not your fault. Blame the striker not the goal."

When I got pregnant, I said to her, "Here I am pregnant but not fit to be a mother. Pregnant but mad. Ice has finally taken a proper aim and what does he hit? A lame duck."

"You are a fit mother, Dolly. Don't worry everything will be fine," she would reassure me.

Even after learning that I was pregnant, my nightmares and the appearances and disappearances of the short woman with puppy eyes didn't abate, if anything they intensified. Each time I saw my GP, he would tell me that he was more than happy to refer me to a psychiatrist. I would tell him that I wouldn't see a psychiatrist in my condition. Ice and I were both worried that the psychiatrist would advise an abortion. It wouldn't make sense to try for a baby for ten years and as soon as we got it, we dumped it in the bin like dog caca. In any case, we felt that there was nothing the psychiatrist could do, since he couldn't prescribe psychotropic medication to a pregnant woman as it would affect our unborn baby. Privately, I was worried that Ice might not be able to bring up the child by himself, if I was locked in a mental hospital. I didn't tell him or my GP about my private worries, though.

Chapter 10

THE LUTON WITCHDOCTOR

As the nightmares and sightings of the short woman with puppy eyes continued unabated, Beans advised us to see an *inyanga or isangoma,* traditional healer or witchdoctor from Luton, since we were reluctant to see a psychiatrist. At first Ice and I laughed off his suggestion. My Christian beliefs were not in tandem with witchdoctors. Ice ridiculed the idea, saying that he didn't trust traditional healers in the diaspora, as they were looking for money to support their relatives back home, just like the rest of us, so they were likely to be dishonest and overcharge for their work. He also wondered where the witchdoctors got the right concoction and the nitty-gritty that come with traditional medicine. When the concoctions have been sent from overseas he wondered how the witchdoctor would ascertain that they came from the right trees and shrubs? For how long would they have been kept and stored? There were so many things that he didn't like about Beans' suggestion that we both refused to entertain the idea outright.

But as the nightmares and the appearing and disappearing of the short woman with puppy eyes continued to haunt me, making our lives a living hell, Ice changed his mind. He summersaulted like the Limpopo River snake. He started to sing a song with a completely different tune. I couldn't say that it was a discord, but it was certainly a different tune. He said that we should try everything and anything to help ourselves, saying, *umtwana ongakhaliyo ufela embelekweni,* if one doesn't actively seek for help, they don't get it. Since we didn't want to see the psychiatrists because we didn't trust them, he said we should try *inyanga* - better the devil you know, he would add. Although I resisted seeing the witchdoctors for some time, I eventually gave in. There are so many battles to be fought in marriages, many of which you must lose just because you are an African woman. You're not expected to stand toe-to-toe with your husband, as if *ulengisa amaphambili,* you have testicles dangling between your thighs. The man is the head of the house, says the Bible. Some battles are not worth engaging in. With my mind going on holiday so often, one way or the other, I needed to do something to bring it home. I had to sacrifice my Christian beliefs to keep my husband happy and to save my marriage.

My pregnancy initially had a positive impact on our marriage. We made love on the day we learnt that I was pregnant. That was as if Ice wanted to be very close to his baby, to feel its pulse. But even then, the man kept running on flat tyres, one flat tyre after another during his baby cuddling. I kept inflating his flat tyres, which kept going flat, which was a bit strange, since we hadn't made love for a long time. I thought to myself, 'Could he be experiencing flat tyres because he is running them on another car?' I always had the paranoia of him seeing other women since he cheated on me. We had last made love on the first week of my return from Zimbabwe, before my nightmares took over our lives. After the laboured love making process, where he came out of panting and sweating as if he was digging his own grave, I hoped that my pregnancy would bring us together. But before I could even finish blinking, the light went off. Ice went back to his old ways. He went back to spending most of his time with his friends, coming home late at night and sometimes I would not even hear him coming home. I would only see him in the morning.

The baby was supposed to bring us closer, but it did the opposite. The short woman with puppy eyes kept appearing and disappearing, separating us further. We lived like strangers, no love, no affection and no feelings for each other. I felt my marriage crumbling around me. The fear of my marriage failure took over and I agreed to see *isangoma*. For the sake of my baby, my marriage and my sanity, I agreed to see a witchdoctor.

So, one Friday night, Ice, Beans and I drove from Bournemouth to Luton to see the witchdoctor. Ice drove, Beans sat at the passenger seat and I sat at the back seat. When men travel, especially African men, they like to talk to each other. I opted to take the back seat to save Ice from straining his neck as he talked to Beans during the journey. They talked about various subjects as we drove to Luton, Beans liked politics, but he called himself a social commentator rather than a politician. Maybe he feared stepping on the toes of Comrade Moment of Madness. Ice was the jack of all trades, he could engage anyone on any subject. During the journey, Beans said to Ice, "You know what Ice, Midlands cities like Birmingham and Leicester, and up-north cities like Bradford and Blackburn, remind me of apartheid. Indigenous and immigrant people in these areas live separate lives. Do you remember the BBC documentary that showed Asians and Whites living in separate communities separated by a single road?"

91

"Where a school in the Asian area had black children only and the other one in the white area had white children only?" asked Ice.

'Yes, but be careful of calling Asian children 'black'. To them is like using an n...word. But that's the debate for another day," said Beans and he continued. "Did you know that it's the result of a policy called Multiculturalism, created by black people for black people. Ironically, the policy has successfully landed immigrants in squalors."

"You mean it has failed?" Ice asked.

"Yes, multiculturalism is a failed policy. The policy only succeeded on separating people not integrating them. Black and white people keep their separate cultures, beliefs, ideas, values, areas, knowledge and even local shops. The policy is discriminatory to say the least. Simply put, it encourages immigrants to come to Britain and form cultural cliques under the disguise of multiculturalism. So Zimbabweans come to the UK to live in their little Mashonaland or Matebeleland in the midst of England. This denies them the opportunity to integrate into the main society? But the question is, why did they leave their own country in the first place, if their culture mattered so much to them?"

"You're right social commentator. Keep your Britain and I will keep my Zimbabwe, as Comrade Moment of Madness would say." They both laughed and I only smiled. Beans added,

"Keep your Bournemouth I will keep my Bradford." They both laughed even louder. At that point I thought to myself, 'If it wasn't for multiculturalism, we wouldn't be going to Luton at this time of the night to consult a witchdoctor. Their witchdoctor would have been integrated into the main society and he would have had no time and space to practice his witchcraft. He would have thrown away all his skins and clothes during the integration. He might have studied proper medicine instead, and became a proper healer, not a stunt healer. As things stand right now, most of Zimbabweans are cramped in Luton, practicing their culture and traditions including witchcraft, thanks to multiculturalism.' I couldn't say that to them as they would certainly be offended. They would have doubted my sincerity of seeing the witchdoctor, whilst holding onto such views. By what they were saying, they were biting the hand that feeds them, making a joke of the system that allows them to practice their tradition, their witchcraft. They were a joke. I agreed entirely with what they were saying, but the irony lay with what they were practising.

They were benefiting from multiculturalism but they appeared oblivious to that fact.

"Multiculturalism has created "little apartheids" in the middle of England!" Beans emphasised his observation. I found myself thinking, 'Beans does not call himself a social commentator for nothing. He has made a brilliant observation here too. But his problem is that he can't see the other side. He has one dimensional view of this situation.'

He continued, "The problem is that when immigrants live in tight groups in certain areas of the country they become easy targets of discrimination. They can easily be denied resources or be deliberately under-resourced. You don't need a magic wand to realise why some areas in east and north London, Leicester, Birmingham, Blackburn and Bradford are poor! Do you remember the Bradford riots?"

"Oh yes, who could forget them? It was what you expected to happen in hell. It was as if hell had descended down on earth," replied Ice. I remembered them too, I thought to myself.

"They were reported to have been caused by heightened tensions between growing ethnic minorities against the white majority. Nobody dared to mention that the riots marked the demise of the multiculturalism policy. When blacks live in under-resourced areas and whites in over-resourced areas in the name of keeping one's culture, what do you expect? I'm sure the British National Party celebrates the birth of the multiculturalism policy every year! If they can't have the whole country to themselves at least they have some 'little apartheid' white only states in their filthy minds!"

I couldn't help it, but express my own observation in addition to what Beans was saying. "Did you know that there are Asian women who have lived in this country for more than twenty, thirty or even forty years who can't speak English? To those cultures that oppress women, multiculturalism provides them with the platform to do it in the middle of the UK. In addition, Beans, multiculturalism unintentionally supports forced marriages. Young girls are forced into marriages in these groups created and protected by multiculturalism."

"These are some of the major failures of multiculturalism. 'Keep liberating your women, we will keep oppressing ours under your long nose,' Comrade Moment of Madness would love to say this," added Beans.

"Women circumcision continues unabated within these communities in a country that gave birth to women rights." I felt I had to say it.

93

"You're right Dolly, *pasi nemulticulturarism*, down with multiculturalism," said Beans.

"On the other hand," said Ice, "The Home Office spends resources on forcing immigrant nurses and doctors who possess degrees and PHDs obtained in English in this country's universities, to write English tests."

"Resources that could be well spent on policing immigrants from maiming each other's private parts," added Beans.

"It's like speaking good English is more important than female circumcision," said Ice. The conversation really kept me interested, distracting me from thinking about the purpose of our evil journey.

When we finally arrived at the witchdoctor's Luton house at midnight, we had to follow orders. The witchdoctors gave orders just like Limpopo River escorts, there're no discussions entertained. 'You come at midnight or the goblins continue to make love to you under the darkness of the night.' The other reason I agreed to see a witchdoctor than a psychiatrist was that I would see the witchdoctor in the middle of the night, without any strings attached. Nobody would see me and set tongues wagging. Psychiatrists are seen in broad daylight and too much unnecessary details get recorded: "the date of birth, place of birth, number and names of siblings or children, ethnicity, libido levels, history of mental illness in the family, history of sexual or physical abuse, thoughts of harm to self or others," Ice would warn me. When such questions are directed at a person considered to be mentally feeble, they could trigger their complete breakdown. People shouldn't be bombarded with so many unusual questions, when their minds are at their weakest point - as if it was an attempt to read their minds and trick them into insanity. The questions, in some cases, could even be tricky to a supposedly normal person into showing symptoms of madness. Too much private and irrelevant information is kept in psychiatrists' laptops and ipads. With the witchdoctor nothing gets recorded, it's like the consultation never happened.

On arrival at the witchdoctor's house, we stood at his gate as it was the tradition. Ice called the witchdoctor on his mobile to alert him of our presence. We could not just get down to our knees at the witchdoctor's gate and start shouting at the top of our voices to alert him or his runners of our presence, as the tradition would demand. Times have changed, there are mobile phone witchdoctors who could prescribe to you over the phone. When Ice finished talking to the witchdoctor he instructed us to kneel at

94

the gate as per tradition. I was amused by all of it. Kneeling at the gate of a house in Luton, in England, in the middle of the night! Thank heavens it was the middle of the night, maybe that was the reason the witchdoctor instructed us to arrive at that time, to avoid prying eyes. Imagine if we had arrived during the daytime, kneeling at the gate with school children passing by. They could certainly mocked us. We could have found ourselves on YouTube, but who could have blame them? If there was a tradition that should never be practiced out of your home country, that was the one to remember.

Eventually, the witchdoctor's runner approached the gate and handed us a wooden plate. Ice took it and put some money in it and handed it back to him. The runner told us to follow him into the lounge of a terraced council house. He offered us seats but we passed up the offer in case we offended the ancestors or the witchdoctor. After a while the man led us into the witchdoctor's private clinic room. The witchdoctor was sitting on *icansi,* a reed mat, on the floor, with his legs folded as if he was meditating. There were no chairs. He pointed us to an open space in the room and we sat down exactly in his posture. He was wearing his traditional attire, dressed in animal skins with beads decorating his head, his bull-like neck and horse-like wrists. He wore *umsisi,* an animal skin skirt-like material that had been cut into threads, around his waist. He had *izambia,* chequered cotton material that is shaped like a flag that went over his left shoulder and under his right armpit. His manhood was covered by an *umncwado,* a cone-shaped skin, lying there calmly, which meant that the beast inside was calm too. The witchdoctor came from the Ndebele tribe, but he also spoke Shona and English fluently too. Ice and Beans called him *ukhulu,* grandfather but I called him a witchdoctor, but not to his face of course.

The room was decorated with bones and skulls hanging over the walls and from the roof. The bones and skulls came from all types of animals you could imagine. There were skins of different animals decorating the walls and the ceiling; lion, baboon, leopard, lizard, frog; you name any animal skin the *sangoma* had it. A python's skin zigzagged around the walls of his little clinic room. I wouldn't have been surprised if he had human skulls in his closets too. I wondered how he managed to bring all these skulls, skins and bones to the United Kingdom. But it was an open secret in the Zimbabwean diaspora that DHL was the main culprit for delivering the witchdoctors' animal and snake skins, skulls, bones and *umuthi,* concoctions from Zimbabwe. Some people smuggled in drugs to make a quick buck and this witchdoctor smuggled in skulls, skins and bones of dead animals and creatures for what? Oh, wait a minute, to make a quick buck too. Ice put one hundred pounds into the traditional wooden plate and it wasn't the last money he would pay.

The nightmares and the short woman with puppy eyes turned my life upside down. I wouldn't have thought that one day I would be found in a witchdoctor's paradise, worshiping idols instead of praising my Lord Jesus Christ in Church. I painfully sat in front of a Satan worshiping serpent. My body was there but my mind was miles away. In front of *isangoma,* there were bones of animal vertebrates, shells of snails and every other creature that has got shells. I suspected that he picked some of the shells from the nearest beach. I wondered if shells from Southend-on-Sea would really work too. On his left side there were a number of bottles of different sizes and shapes. Each bottle had some *umuthi* inside, roots and barks, some crushed some not, all of them were of different colours : black, orange, khaki, grey; name it, the *inyanga* had it in his *juju* collection.

At the beginning of my treatment, the witchdoctor held the bones and the shells in both hands, he shook them, groaning like a wild pig, and threw them on the floor and they scattered about like sand. He scrutinised them closely, pointing at some of them with his stick, a stick glittering with some animal fat. He shook his head and picked them up and scattered them again. It is believed that although *isangoma* throws the bones and shells, the ancestors control how they lie on the floor. It is only him who can interpret how they lie. Ice, Beans and I couldn't, we didn't have that gift, that's why Ice paid his money to see the genius of Luton. He had the gift that few other men had. He gathered and scattered them. He gathered and scattered them. He gathered and scattered them. Groaning louder and louder as he failed to find the cause of my problems. His walls must have had the thickest sound proofing in the United Kingdom. His windows must have had quadruped instead of double glazing, to keep in his groans, especially at that time of the night. His neighbours might have wondered if he kept wild animals. Or they might have reported him to the council and ended up with an anti-social behaviour order (ASBO). He could turn out to be the only doctor with an ASBO in the country. Each time he scattered the shells, he poked them with his stick- as if to make them lie the way he wanted them to, to make meaning, I thought. He repeated that again and again groaning and groaning until he found both the cause and the solution to my problems. And guess what! Apparently when I went to Zimbabwe someone cast a bad spell on me and that was the reason I had been very unlucky. That was the reason I was attacked by a crocodile. It was also the reason why I was experiencing nightmares and flashbacks and seeing things that were not there. So a bad spell was cast on me - that witch-doctor was a genius. And you know what? He even had the concoction right there to make my troubles disappear. All along I had been chasing the shadows of a goblin woman with puppy eyes in Bournemouth, while my medicine lay untouched at a terraced council house in Luton.

He handed me some concoction, a mixture of roots and some soot, in two small bottles. He also gave me some white ashes in a transparent plastic bag. He went on to advise me to mix the concoction with ashes and smear my whole body with it in the bush. At that point I almost burst out laughing but Ice and Beans remained serious so they put me off. His advice was that I should smear my whole body with his concoction mixed with ashes in the bush in Bournemouth? That witchdoctor should have been knighted by the Queen for his excellent work. He deserved a medal. Great Britain was very lucky to have such a talented man in her midst. More immigrants of his talent should be encouraged into the country in order to save the NHS some serious money. With his gift and talent, who needed NHS?

Wet ashes smeared all over the body and allowed to dry on the skin would quickly turn white. I imagined myself pregnant, standing naked, white as snow in the bush in Bournemouth. If I waited for the ashes to dry on my skin, as the witchdoctor had advised, that would take ages, that would increase the chances of me being seen by dog walkers, who patrolled Bournemouth bushes with those enslaved animals, always on the leashes.

The witchdoctor went on to advise Ice that after the smearing, he should drive me home, still naked, but covered by a white sheet, which he handed to Ice. I was also advised not to bathe for two days. I told myself that I would never have body ash smearing in the bush in my life time. Not in the United Kingdom, not in Zimbabwe and not even on Jupiter. I had gone there to solve my problems and all he came up with was ridiculous, foolish and outdated treatment. The way things were going I thought of seeing a psychiatrist in broad daylight, and tell him that I was born on Mars in the fifteenth century and my libido levels were so high and uncontrollable that

97

I could make love to a monkey, than have a body ash smearing in the bush in Bournemouth!

But he had not finished with me yet. The ancestors also told him that I should receive two forms of treatment before I left his house that night. He picked a bottle with black stuff in it and mixed it with Vaseline. He didn't tell us the ingredients of his concoction. Witchdoctors don't divulge the ingredients of their wonder medicines, lest someone steals their formula and replicates it and they lose their magic business. Could that be the reason behind the non-availability of inyanga/isangoma training institutions in Zimbabwe? The fact was that even if the kind witchdoctor had told us the ingredients of his concoction, we had no way we of verifying it. We were being fooled. Duped. Bamboozled. Didn't Ice play *amadlwane*, child's play game' called *'bantwana bantwana wozani ekhaya*, children, children come home,' as a child? The first group of children would hide their 'so called lions' after calling the second group of children to come home.

The second group of children would respond, *'siyesaba*, we are afraid.'

The first group would ask, *'lesabani*, what are you afraid of ?'

The second group would answer, *'izilwane*, lions.'

The first group would reassure them, *'izilwane kudala zafa zaphela zathi du du*, the lions have long died.' The second group would then 'come home' only to be caught and be eaten by hidden lions. Ice was being fooled by that witchdoctor. He was being cheated with his eyes open like *amatemba*, tiny fish. The witchdoctor wasn't playing science, but fiction, and he wasn't good at it.

He told us that he needed to apply some concoction on my shoulders and buttocks. He would use a sharp razor blade to make two minor cuts on each shoulder's deltoid and buttocks' cheeks. He would then rub his concoction into those cuts. He would also put some of his *muthi*, medicine on the red hot charcoal and cover me with a blanket in order for me to inhale the smoke of the concoction. I shook my head so violently that it sent a clear message to Ice, who excused us from the witchdoctor's clinic room for consultation outside. We stood near the fence, next to the road, and in a hush-hush voice I said to him,

"I'm not having a witchdoctor fondling my bottom. I'm not inhaling his dog poo, I'm..."

"Don't be so disrespectful Dolly. This man is trying to help you. To help us."

98

"Do you know the number of people he has cut with his razor? Do you?"

"Well, I don't know, but does it matter?"

"As a student nurse, you must know better. Yes it matters, Ice. He might infect me with HIV?"

"Come on Dolly, HIV lasts a few minutes outside the body. The chances of the razor blade passing HIV to you are very slim indeed. An old razor blade that has been used on an HIV positive person a few minutes ago wouldn't pass the virus to the next person. We will ask him to use a new razor blade instead."

"I'm not having him scarring my body Ice." I was almost in tears. In the first place, I didn't believe in witchdoctors, but at that time he wanted to apply his filthy stuff on my body. "I'm not inhaling his charred *muthi*. I would rath..."

"Please Dolly, this could be the best thing to happen to you. This could solve all your problems, our problems, once and for all. Please if you can't do it for the baby, do it for me." He was serious about all the witchdoctor thing. He was really serious that I should allow an unqualified stranger, because he was known and trusted by Beans, to slash and smear me with whatever and to inhale it too. What had entered his head? Just a few months ago we were mocking these witchdoctors and now he was a convert. How did he manage to change his beliefs so quickly and so recklessly? I was caught between a rock and a hard surface. I'd be damned if I did and damned if I didn't. Ice pleaded with me, "Please Dolly, let's do this and move on with our lives. Our lives have been held back since your return from Zimbabwe. Who knows, this could be our only chance. It could be the turning point. Why did you agree to this if you still had doubts, Dolly? Why did you come all the way if you didn't believe in this? Why?" But at that moment, a short woman, wearing a burka, with her eyes the only part of her body that was not covered, glanced at me as she went past on the road. Her eyes sent a chilling feeling down my spine. Was she the short woman with puppy eyes, in Luton, at midnight? I said to Ice,

"Did you see the short woman wearing a burka?"

"You mean the woman who just walked past?"

"Yes."

"What about her?"

"I don't know. She reminded me of the short woman with puppy eyes."

"Thus why you have to do as the healer says, Dolly. He will stop all this nonsense."

"Okay, okay, Ice, I will do it."

When we returned to the witchdoctor's clinic room, Beans and the witchdoctor were having a hush-hush conversation. The witchdoctor might have been thanking Beans and promising him a bigger cut in future if he kept bringing lucrative clients like Ice, *ikhotha eyikhothayo*, one good turn deserves another.

I wasn't sure anymore whether trying to appease Ice would save our marriage or destroy it. How could showing another man my bum in the presence of my husband and his friend save my marriage? I was confused and I hated what I was being forced to do. As soon as we returned to the clinic room, I told the witchdoctor that I was ready. I started by pulling my maternity dress's sleeves to expose my shoulder muscles and the witchdoctor made two cuts on each shoulder and rubbed in his concoction and it stung a bit. I lifted up my maternity dress and pulled down my panties to expose my behind in full. If I had known that I would need to undress in front of a stranger I would have come prepared. I would have put on a two piece maternity dress. The witchdoctor would not have seen too much, but as it was, he was thunderstruck by the size of my boot. Beans had left the room but Ice was there and he was watching. I wondered what was going through his head. Was he enjoying it, or did he hate it too? I was facing him and the witchdoctor was behind me, fondling my boot. Ice was standing there like the Limpopo hyena watching over me while the witchdoctor was watching a free movie. That was how he earned a living, salivating on the boots of other men's wives. I felt pity for his wife. He was performing *mbobobo* frottaging on me and I felt a slight sharp pain similar to the shoulder one, some rubbing and some stinging. It was a humiliating experience. It was like being forced by my husband to make love to another man while he was watching. I was making love to that man for him, not for me. I believed that he enjoyed every cut he made on my bum, the sorry sadist.

As soon as he finished cutting and pasting my bottom, his runner brought a small metal plate with glowing charcoal in it and he put it on the floor in the centre of the clinic room. The witchdoctor put his concoction on the charcoal and the smoke rose up. He instructed me to kneel down near the plate, put my head over the fumes and he covered it with a blanket. I inhaled the chocking stuff. It was sharp in the throat and it made me cough. It was bitter in the eyes and tears poured out. I couldn't tell whether the tears were caused by the concoction or by my frustration at what was being done to me. I was choking and crying, it was like being trapped in a hell house. I pulled the blanket off my head when I realised that I couldn't breathe properly. I was panting, sweating and angry. I didn't wait for him to take it off, I had heard of accidents where lives had been lost while undergoing that kind of treatment in Zimbabwe. I didn't want to be the first in the statistics to be killed while undergoing that treatment in the United Kingdom. The witchdoctor said it was OK, it was enough for that night. It would work. Under my breath I said that I hoped it would or else I would be back, not only demanding our money, but his head too.

Seeing the witchdoctor showed that desperate situations required desperate measures. Measures that could be as disgusting as they are despicable. Only God and the witchdoctor knew what I had inhaled. It was like inhaling smoke mixed with sin. The fact that God knew what I inhaled too, gave me the solace that He will render it useless and save me.

Ice paid his witchdoctor and we left Luton in the early hours of the morning and drove back to Bournemouth. Before we left the witchdoctor emphasised to Ice that he should make sure that he guarded me while bush ash smearing as it should be at twilight. We discussed the whole scenario on our way back and Ice was adamant that I should do as the witchdoctor had prescribed. I didn't understand what was going on in my husband's head. He was forcing me to do things that were unGodly. That were against my beliefs. Beans supported him. Ice told me that he had not paid five hundred pounds for nothing, *kabhotshi mali yena,* he doesn't poo money, he reminded me, as if he wanted reassurance from me that he didn't. It became clearer to me that in order to save my marriage, I should do whatever he and his witchdoctor wanted.

Chapter 11

BUSH ASH SMEARING

A few weeks after our journey to Luton, Ice found some bin bags in our loft and started shouting,

"Dolly what are these bags doing here? One, two, three..." counting them, "...eight, nine ten..." and more. "What the hell's going on here Dolly?"

I knew at once what he had just discovered. He had found my stash before I could search it through. He came down from the loft carrying some of the bags and threw them on the floor in the lounge and barked, "What are these bags for Dolly? What are they doing in the loft? What are they doing in our flat?"

I was dumbfounded, the words refused to come out of my mouth. It was like someone had remotely locked my jaws. Because of what I had gone through with the appearances and disappearances of the short woman with puppy eyes, I had trained my mouth not to betray my mind, especially in the presence of Ice. With my mouth shut, nobody, not even a psychiatrist or a witchdoctor, would know what my mind was thinking. Only God knew.

Ice was quick to blame. Quick to put his boot through my mind and blame it for everything that my mouth said. He went back up into the loft to bring some more bags. He came down with both his hands full and went back again. When he brought the rest of them down he said, "What's going on here Dolly? What are these bags for? Who put them up there? Please answer me. What is in them anyway?" He opened one of them and he found a load of papers, people's old bills, used bus tickets and old shopping receipts. "Dolly what's going on here?"

I didn't know what to tell him. Tell him the truth or lies. Did he deserve to know the truth? Would it help me? Would telling Ice that I have been raiding people's bins early in the morning, before they were collected in an effort to track down the short woman with puppy eyes, set me free? Make him sympathise with my situation? No. I doubted that. Whatever I told him, it would be my fault. He would turn it against me and stab me with it. He wouldn't believe me, so I felt liberated to tell him whatever I wanted. To lie, lie and lie again. That was a liberating thought to have at the time.

He frantically searched one bag after the other and he found similar contents. "Please Dolly what are these bags of rubbish doing in our flat?" He said slowly and emphasising on each word he said, like a British tourist when talking to foreigners who don't speak English.

"I'm trying to track down the short woman with puppy eyes Ice," I bleated out my response. With both his hands over his head and looking up as if asking God to save him from the clutches of a lunatic he married, he said,

"Oh my God. Oh my God," he said that so loud and with so much conviction that I thought he had seen a real God. I looked up and I only saw the ceiling. If he could see a God on the ceiling then he must be seeing things too, I thought to myself. He paced up and down in the lounge like a dog with rabies. I decided to defend my actions and said to him,

"Who knows, some of those old bills, tickets and receipts, and whatever, might have some information about her. Might have answers to my problems." As if he didn't hear me he went on,

"Now I'm really living with a real mad woman. God have mercy on me. I married an insane woman. A woman who goes picking dirt from people's bins on the streets. Dolly, you need help. Where did you pick them from? Whose bins did you pick them from?"

"From the houses between Castlepoint bus stop and Queens' Park Academy, along Castle Lane West and Charminister Road."

"I can't believe that you deliberately targeted certain people's bins when searching for this dirt? People saw you between these bus stops picking rubbish from their bins and staffing it into black bags, and they thought, 'she's mad and from abroad, from where she comes from they eat papers.' And you had the guts to bring that dirt into the flat and hid it from me? *Owakuloyayo sewafa, ngabusaphila ngabe uyakuzwela,* whoever bewitched you is dead, if they were still alive they would have mercy on you. Why did you pick them between Castlepoint and Queen's Park school? Why along those roads, Dolly?" After a pause, he slowly continued,

"Dolly, you are not right in your head. I have told you that several times. But today you have proved that you don't have one screw missing but several of them. A thousand of them. But why target the bins along that route Dolly? Why that route? Why not pick them from somewhere? From anywhere?"

"I'm convinced that the short woman with puppy eyes lives between the two bus stops, along the..."

"You don't stop to amaze me, do you? There's nothing you can say or do without mentioning your imaginary friend, Dolly." Those words were shaper than a knife. No knife would have hurt me more than that. How dare he referred to the short woman with puppy eyes, my day and night tormentor, my number one foe, as my 'imaginary friend?' He continued, "How do you know that for God's sake? How do you know that she lives between those two bus stops?" He was shouting and not listening to me. He didn't know that the quieter you become the more you hear and the more empathetic you become.

"I saw her on a bus and I chased it and when I finally got on the bus at Queen's Park school bus stop she had already got off. So I concluded that she lives between the two bus stops," I said calmly.

"Am I hearing you properly Dolly? Did I hear you properly? Did you hear what you said? You chased a bus and overtook it? A pregnant woman chased and overtook a bus and waited for it at the next bus stop? How did you manage that? How did you?"

"It was easy Ice. The..."

"It was easy, only a mad pregnant woman would find chasing and over-taking a bus easy. Onl..."

"Please allow me to finish my point. Stop talking over me and listen. It was easy because there was heavy traffic between the two bus stops so I took a short cut. Common sense tells you that since she got off before the Queen's Park school, she lives between these two bus stops - between Castlepoint and Queen's Park School. I didn't even know that I was pregnant."

"Don't talk about common sense Dolly. Anyone who chases a bus is bereft of common sense. Anyone who picks rubbish from the bins on the streets and brings it home is foreign to common sense. You use uncommon sense when you do strange things, Dolly. How did you know that it was the real short woman with puppy eyes for a fact? How did you know how far she lived along that road in order to target the bins on those roads? How did you know that she got off before Queen's Park School to fool you? How did you know?" I kept repeating his words in my head, *'how did you know'* when he went into questioning frenzy. Who was mad? It was impossible to put in a word. He was like a talking machine, a 'how do you know' talking machine.

"She gave me the finger when I chased the bus."

"Good. You deserved it." After a brief pause, he continued, "Dolly, it could have been anyone. It could have been a school girl who saw a mad woman chasing a bus and decided to join in the fun. You're losing it and fast, Dolly. The short woman with puppy eyes, Dolly, only exists in your mind. Start to accept that fact. That fact is as true as your presence right now. The day you will accept that fact, your life would change for the better." He continued blindly cutting my heart into shreds with his words. He has a talent of turning simple words into sharp knives, *ingqamu ezisika nxazonke,* double-edged knife. After another deliberate pause, he asked, "What do you hope to get from the rubbish you pick from the streets?"

That was a very good question. Like a blind man he stumbled into a good question. Should I tell him that once I started picking rubbish from the bins it soon became an obsession? I asked myself. That I got hooked into the habit? I got addicted into it? That I lost the will to stop. It became my only hobby. Getting up early in the morning, leaving him sleeping on the sofa, gave me something to do. It gave structure to my day. Suddenly I had a purpose in life. I enjoyed opening bins, stooping and picking the rubbish - after all dipping into people's bins also served as a useful exercise for my pregnancy, my midwife told me that exercising the stomach and back muscles was important for both the mother and the baby. Instead, I said to him, "To get her address Ice, so that I can visit her and ask her why she is stalking me? I have a thousand and one questions to ask her," I said confidently.

"To find her address? By the way, Dolly, what's her name?"

That was a very bad question to ask me. I had not considered it during my investigations. While picking up the rubbish and shoving it into black bags, that question never crossed my mind. How could you find the address of someone from a document if you didn't know their name? That was a very, very bad question indeed. It dawned on me that I didn't even know her name. In my mind her name was 'short woman with puppy eyes.' I expected to find a receipt with a name 'short woman with puppy eyes.' With one bad question Ice proved beyond all doubt, not only to himself, but to me too, that I was mentally unstable. I didn't have time to think things through before I acted. I dipped my hands into people's bins without thinking straight. I actually dipped into them with my brains, my hands just followed orders. I remained quiet for a long time and then I said;

"I might not know her name Ice, but I'm not mad. I'm not stupid either. All I was looking for in those bins was a document with a Zimbabwean name or surname." Buoyed by this near genius response that came out of my mouth unintentionally, which left Ice agape, I continued, "If that name or surname leads me to the short woman with puppy eyes, it's job done. But if it leads me to a wrong person, still I wouldn't mind, it would have proved that my plan could work at least."

After a very long deliberate pause, Ice finally snapped up, "I have had it. I have had enough of your madness in one day. I might pick up your symptoms if I continue to listen to you. Let's go to the nearest forest for the body ash smearing now. Let's go for your bush treatment right now. You might be getting worse because you haven't had your ash smearing treatment yet. Your condition is getting worse, Dolly. If you're left untreated, soon you will be chasing elephants and giraffes at the Castlepoint shopping centre. Remember that you saw the short woman with puppy eyes wearing a burka in Luton at midnight. I don't want that to happen again." He put some warm water in a plastic container with a lid and put it in the boot of the car, together with another small container for ash mixing. He shoved the witchdoctor's concoction into my hands before he got into the driver's seat in a hump. I picked up the bits and pieces that I would need for the treatment and took the white sheet too. I didn't trust Ice anymore, as he could shove me into the car while naked after the treatment, he would not allow me to dress in any other attire except the one recommended by his witchdoctor. I followed him into the car.

It was one of those June twilights, where it took time to get really dark. The sun was setting as we drove from our house to the Holdenhurst village forest, a mile or so away from our flat. If the bush treatment had to be done, it was certainly the best twilight to do it because it was warm and nice. The ash would certainly dry on my skin quickly enough to allow me to return home early. But because the weather was warm, many dog walkers would be out in full force that would enhance my chances of being found naked in the bush.

We drove quietly without talking to each until he found the space to park his car on the side of the road, at the beginning of the forest. We had already argued enough about the bush treatment that day that we didn't need to revisit it again. It was obvious that Ice had invested a lot into the bush ash smearing treatment to go back on it. He had also done his homework very well about the spot near the road. He parked his old BMW, black man think they are not man enough if they do not drive a BMW once in their life time, got out of the car, took a lidded plastic bucket full of warm water from the boot and led the way into the bush. Reluctantly, I got out of the car too, took my toilet bag and my witchdoctor's concoction and I followed him. One hundred or so metres away from the car he put the plastic bucket on the ground, that would be my treatment spot, my bathroom, my twilight smear-room. Travelling all the way from Zimbabwe to the United Kingdom, paying huge sums of money for air tickets, begging my way through the vigorous immigration system, only to have a bush treatment - no-one would choose a better life than mine.

Once Ice had chosen my bathroom, he went back to the car, but I didn't know how far as I was given instructions by the witchdoctor not to look back from the treatment spot. I had the a car engine start, but it didn't bother me as the witchdoctor had given both of us strict and clear instructions that we should follow without even a minor deviation. He should guard me and I should walk without looking back up to my smearing spot and then walk backwards after smearing, until I got to the car. Once I was on my treatment spot, I mixed the concoction with the water, took off my clothes and started my bush treatment. After I finished bathing, I poured the water left in the bucket into the smaller container that had ash and mixed the two. I then started to smear my whole body with the ash as if I was applying Vaseline or lotion. Fortunately enough, it dried quickly, as I had anticipated due to the warm weather. What I imagined while I was at the witchdoctor's house came to pass. There I was, in the bush, pregnant, naked and as white as snow.

Suddenly a police siren sounded, it became louder and louder and stopped about a hundred metres away, around where Ice had parked his car. I had just finished, I searched for my white sheet in my laundry bag and I couldn't find it. It then dawned on me that I must have left it in his car. I stood in the bush, white and stark naked *njengomthakathi*, like a witch. There was nothing I could do about my situation at that point. I couldn't look back, as the witchdoctor had warned. I waited for Ice to say something, but he said nothing. Instead a female Dorset accented voice said behind me,

"Is everything OK ma'am?" Left exposed, I threw the witchdoctor's instructions in the air and turned. About fifty metres away a white female police officer approached me asking, "Are you OK ma'am? Can I help at all?"

I was stunned and muted.

She hesitated and asked again, "Why are you naked in the bush ma'am?" I remained mute. It was getting really dark.

"What have you covered yourself with ma'am?" I kept quiet. Then, suddenly, *ngafikelwa lidlozi,* my ancestors took over and I ran. I took the police officer by surprise and ran, but that did not dissuade her from pursuing me, "Please stop ma'am. I mean no harm ma'am," she shouted. 'Mean no harm, mean no harm' I thought to myself as I got deeper into the forest. When I looked back I saw that I had opened a distance between us. I was obviously quicker than her. If I wasn't pregnant, I would have easily outpaced her. She ran like a pregnant woman, I ran like a police officer. With my adrenaline literally doing my running, and borrowing some from my baby, I increased the distance between us, I heard a male voice joining in and calling me to stop too. When I glanced back, a male white police officer had joined the chase. But I had actually opened the gap between us, it was getting darker and I started to dream of freedom. Although I was panting and huffing, I kept going. The determination to avoid arrest was overwhelming. I would evade them for now, wait for the nightfall and make my way back home under the cover of the darkness, I thought to myself. I grazed and scratched my naked body against the shrubs and branches of trees as I ran for my freedom. I received bruises all over my body, but I didn't feel any pain. That didn't slow me down either. I kept going. It was either escape or embarrassment. Escape was the only option. The drive I had to evade the police surpassed the determination I had when I first entered the country. I kept running. I told myself that I wasn't going to provide the police with naked evidence in court. I wasn't going to allow them to take my naked pictures.

After a while I slowed down and I was convinced that I had evaded them. I was getting dark, the furthest I could see was about fifteen to twenty metres away. But sooner than later I heard the sound of a helicopter hovering overhead. When I looked up the search light from the helicopter almost blinded me. It dawned on me that the officers had called for rein-forcement. The helicopter fluttered above my head. It was so low that it blew the branches of the vegetation around me. The branches swayed like a drunkard. Despite the deafening noise, a loud speaker pierced through the noise, saying, "Please ma'am give yourself up to the officers, they want to help you. They know where you are. Please give yourself up." I tried to run away from the helicopter's search light, but I couldn't leave it behind. It was like trying to run away from your own shadow. I knew the game of hide and seek was over. With the helicopter floating above my head, it would follow me until the police got the ground support or I dropped dead due to fatigue, which ever was first. The energy was sapped out of my body and my strength deserted me. My brain let me down again, as it ordered the energy and the strength to leave my body. I was transfixed. I just stood there, like a ghost, one hand on my breasts and the other hand on my bulging tummy. Tears flowed from my eyes, down my cheeks, then on the side of my mouth, then onto my chin, then skipped from my chin straight onto my bulging stomach, before they jumped from my stomach to their death on the ground under my feet. My tears marked strip roads over my white ash smeared face and body, like streams running down a mountain. I cried like a baby. Soon the male officer arrived, the female officer was not far behind. There I was, stark naked and as pregnant as a fat man! I must have made a very impressive picture under the helicopter's search light. That was exactly what the lying scandalous witchdoctor ordered. The female officer, still panting, handed me my clothes. I had expected her to handcuff me. I had already outstretched my arms ready to be handcuffed, instead she said,

"Could you please dress up ma'am? Please put your clothes on. Do you understand what I'm saying? Do you speak English?" The officer was killing me with her kindness despite what I had put her through. She had even brought my clothes with her. It then dawned to me why I managed to open the distance between us. She had to pick up my clothes first. I said to her,

"Yes, I can speak English, officer," as I received my maternity dress and my panties and put them on. I had seen these police officers wrestling drunkards to the ground in the streets on Friday nights, when some youths had had one too many. Now that she had caught up with me I had to follow her orders, I did not want any wrestling skirmishes with her. She led the way to the car and the male officer walked very close behind me. I thought that I heard him muttering something like; '*You can take a monkey from the bush but you can't take the bush from the monkey! Immigration helps Britain! Immigration helps Britain my foot,*' under his breath. I stopped short of shouting at him. But who would believe me, after having been chased, pregnant and naked in the bush. If I could see people who were not there, surely I could hear things that were never said, I thought to myself and decided to say nothing.

On our way back to the police car, the female officer said, "You didn't have to run away from me ma'am. Just follow me to my car. I would like to get some information from you." We got to their car quicker than I thought, that explained that I had only run a very short distance indeed, despite the huffing and puffing I went through. The male officer was behind me, ready to pounce if I tried my tricks again. Bournemouth was white, that was in 2009 and there were still no ethnic police officers employed by that police force. Among all the ethnic minorities in the United Kingdom, some of them unemployed, they still couldn't find among them, some with the right qualification to employ as police officers in Bournemouth. When we got to the car, the female officer asked me, "Are you alone ma'am?"

"No." When I looked around I realised that the police car was parked where Ice had parked his car. "My husband brought me here and the witch-doctor told him to guard me until I finished the bush treatment."

"Did you say the witchdoctor told your husband to bring you here?" asked the suddenly excited female officer.

"Yes."

"Where's your husband?" asked the male officer.

"His car was parked here when I had the bush treatment." Whether they believed me or not, was neither here nor there. The helicopter had gone by that time but I didn't think of running away again, it was too dark to try that again. The police politely asked me to get into their car and took me to a Bournemouth police station.

110

Chapter 12

ENGUTSHENI

Sitting at the back of the car I just thought about the direction my life was taking. Running from the police wasn't the right direction, it wouldn't take a genius to figure that out. Thirty-two weeks pregnant and running heptathlon? What kind of woman was I turning into? What was the short woman with puppy eyes turning me into? Jessica Ennis? Was I pregnant of a human being or what? Who knows what happened that night at Limpopo when I was unconscious, that hyena's behind had male genitals written all over its back. It is a known fact that male hyenas also look after their young ones too. Who knows, I could have been impregnated by *impisi*.

The police locked me in a cell before I was seen by a psychiatrist. The psychiatrist saw me in the presence of a social worker and a doctor. I told them the whole truth, nothing but the truth. When the interview finished, I was shocked when they said that they would like me to be admitted to a psychiatric hospital for further assessment. "You have just interviewed me, I don't need further assessment? There's nothing wrong with me," I protested.

"From what you have told us we feel that you need further assessment in hospital. You can get admitted voluntarily or under a Mental Health Act section," the psychiatrist said calmly.

"What is a Mental Health Act section?"

"It's part of the law under the Mental Health Act, that allows us to admit you to hospital against your will."

"Admit me by force?" I asked him, horrified by the suggestion of being detained in Engutsheni.

"Pretty much."

"What if I refuse to go to hospital? Would you ask the police to frog march me into a psychiatric hospital? Would you? You wouldn't do that to a pregnant woman. Would you?" I was getting agitated. He was really pushing the wrong buttons.

"We would ask the police, but we don't want it to get to that. You have a choice to go in voluntarily. Make up your mind. It's your choice."

"You call that a choice? Choice means I choose to go to hospital or not to. Choice is not about choosing between two evils. Choice is about choosing between good and evil."

"Do you want to be admitted voluntarily or under a section?" That was the first time that the psychiatrist interrupted me. Although he remained calm, there was something in his voice that told me he meant business. He was not going to let it go. I had to make a choice between two evils called patients choice. Then I asked him, "How long would I remain in hospital?"

"That would depend on the outcome of the assessment." The response came from the female social worker. She did not say much during the interview, she appeared only interested in taking down personal information about me, about my family and my husband. She took volumes and volumes of information about my family.

"You mean it could be a day or ten years?"

"All I can say at this moment is that it would depend on the outcome of the assessment." It was obvious that they thought I was insane. I, insane? Those people should go to Zimbabwe and see what insanity means. To see insanity walking on its two legs. Where insane people walk the streets naked or half-naked. Where they eat from the bins. Where they are homeless. Where they have no money and no one bothers about them.

It dawned on me that I could argue until the cows come home, but those people were bent on admitting me to a psychiatric hospital, not tomorrow, not next week, but that night. That was one of the reasons that I didn't want to see a psychiatrist in the first place. Now I was going to be admitted to a psychiatric hospital, to Engutsheni, in the United Kingdom. The short woman with puppy eyes had really succeeded in messing my life. I told them that I would rather be admitted to hospital informally.

To my pleasant surprise, I was treated very well in the psychiatric hospital. When I went in I had this idea of toilets without doors, of being chained to my bed, of a nurse going around with a stick, ready to hit those who misbehaved, just as it was in Engutsheni, in Bulawayo. I had feared that I would be racially abused and no one would believe me if I reported it, since I was mentally ill. Nobody would believe a nutter. To my surprise I was treated humanely. Nurses would come and have a chat with me, a genuine chat, where both parties were free to air their views. I was encouraged to say how I really felt about being admitted to hospital. But I deliberately avoided Zimbabwean nurses who worked at that hospital. On the night I was admitted one of them spoke to me in their language, I ignored him. I pretended that I did not understand his language. He had not even asked me which part of Zimbabwe I come from or which Zimbabwean language I spoke, he just assumed that since I was a Zimbabwean I would speak his language. I didn't only distrust Zimbabwean nurses, I didn't trust any of the black nurses in that hospital. I was concerned that they might know someone out there who knew me. Eventually the whole of Bournemouth would know that I had been admitted to Engutsheni hospital.

One of the white female nurses introduced herself as my named-nurse, her name was Nana. She appeared to honestly believe and empathise with my story. She understood that women would do a lot of unthinkable things in an effort to save their marriages. She understood why I made those decisions. She listened to me and on my second day she told me that there would be a multi-disciplinary meeting the following day where I would be given time and space to explain my condition and my situation. Where I would be allowed to express my views about my treatment in hospital.

Mental health professionals have an interesting way of softening a difficult situation, like the police, they killed me with their kindness. They had a way of making me feel that I was part of the system when I wasn't. To feel empowered when I was being disempowered. The last time I was told about choice, it wasn't choice. I believed the meeting was not about my treatment but a tick box exercise, to meet their legislative requirements and policies. Because Nana was nice to me, I agreed with what she said. She also asked me if I wanted someone from my family, a relative or a friend, to attend the meeting. I certainly didn't want Ice to visit me in hospital. He called me once over the telephone the night I was admitted, he didn't say much. He was in a hurry to put the phone down, I couldn't blame him. I felt embarrassed for what I did, running away from the law enforcers! I was happy that he quickly put the phone down, because I didn't have nice things to say to him.

Nana explained to me why I wasn't prescribed any mad people's medication, because, she said, "Most of the psychotropic medication would affect the unborn baby, sometimes resulting in serious deformities including heart defects, missing limbs and stunted growth when the child is born." She went on to advise me to watch a BBC Panorama programme about babies born of mothers who were taking a certain mood stabiliser while they were pregnant. I almost screamed when she told me that information. That was one of the main reasons why I didn't want to see a psychiatrist in the first place - until I saw that witchdoctor who referred me to a psychiatrist via the back door. Thank Heavens, I had not been prescribed or forced to take any medication that far. I didn't want to give birth to a baby with many heads like a snake. A baby with a thousand feet *njengetshongololo*, like a millipede.

I agreed to attend the meeting with my friend Molly, in order to raise my concerns about their baby deforming medication.

The meeting took place in a relatively big room, with nice pictures hanging on the walls. It made me feel like I was at a meeting of equals. It gave me a false sense of security, that was another way of tricking unsuspecting patients, like me, into taking their baby disfiguring medication, I thought.

There were six of us, Molly, Nana, the psychiatrist, the ward manager, the junior doctor and I. We all sat on chairs of the same size and height. We sat in a semi-circle, with no table separating I and the rest, like at the real Engutsheni in Bulawayo. I had thought that the psychiatrist would be sitting on a higher chair to show her power, authority and influence. I was surprised that I sat on the same type of chair with everyone else. Molly and I were offered a cup of tea, just like the rest. Talk about all animals being equal. I was so impressed that I started to revise what I was going to say to them about their foetus mutilating concoctions, before I was even asked to say my piece of mind.

When the meeting started, I was asked to go over what led to my admission to hospital. I narrated the whole story to them, starting from the time I was attacked by the hyena in Uganda up to the ash smearing in the bush in Holdenhurst village.

Eventually, the psychiatrist said, "Well, Dolly, we don't think that you are suffering from a serious mental illness. I sincerely understand why you had what you call bush treatment. But I'm not here to judge people's beliefs, I'm here to help those with serious mental illness. I also believe that you are suffering from Post-Traumatic Stress Disorder, but I don't believe that you need admission to hospital or chemical treatment to deal with the problem. The nightmares you reported are clear symptoms of PTSD. The sightings of a short woman with puppy eyes, as well as the nightmares could be flash backs. I would therefore discharge you back to your GP, with the advice that you engage in a therapy called Cognitive Behaviour Therapy, CBT. I mean talking therapy. I wouldn't recommend any psychotropic medication intervention at this moment due to your pregnancy."

I would have challenged her claim that seeing the short woman with puppy eyes was a flashback, if she had not quickly followed that with the words that she was discharging me from hospital and she wasn't going to prescribe me any medication. But there was no need for that. I had got what I wanted, the discharge from Engutsheni without medication. Why rock the boat, when you don't even know how to swim?

I sighed as we left Engutsheni with Molly. I sat in her car relaxing and wondering where my life would go from there. Would I have to tell people that I had been admitted at Engutsheni? What would I say when people genuinely asked me where I have been in the past two days? Or what would I say when they tell me that they had heard that I had been admitted to a psychiatric hospital? What will I say? *'That's right, I had an achy mind, that lost its way for a bit, but now it's fine? Mad people get well as well you know, just like those with broken limbs, they get admitted to hospital and get discharged when they get better. Although they would still be on crutches or limping, they get discharged. You might still think that I'm limping in my mind, the truth is that I got better and got discharged.'* Would that be enough?

The problem with me though, was that I had not been treated. I just went in and out of hospital as if it was a toilet. Just like someone suffering from early senile symptoms, they would get into a toilet, forget what they had gone in for and walk out without doing any business, only to wet themselves later.

I also wondered where Ice had gone when the police car arrived, during the bush treatment. He was supposed to have been guarding me. Making sure that I was safe. He was supposed to have alerted me that the police were coming. It appeared he had gone by the time they arrived. The police told me that someone called them and told them that a black pregnant woman who appeared disoriented and disinhibited had removed all her clothes in the bush. But did that person see my husband? Did the person see his car? I didn't ask the police those questions as I thought they would further question the state of my mind. I didn't check him during the bath because I followed the witchdoctor's orders and it was getting dark anywhere. Molly couldn't understand why I went along with Ice's and

Beans' crazy suggestion to see a witchdoctor. She said that if anyone should see a witchdoctor, it was either Beans or Ice, not I.

When I got home, I challenged Ice about the events of that day.

"The witchdoctor told me that I should not watch you while undergoing treatment because his concoction would not work. He stressed that watching you while self-treating would certainly cause me bad luck too."

"So since you didn't watch me it worked then? Did it? You have good luck now, ye-e?" I barked at him annoyed by his response, "You're lying Ice. The witchdoctor told you, in my presence that you must guard me. Why are you lying now?"

Looking down he said, "When you left us behind as we were leaving his house he whispered to me, 'Leave her alone in the bush, for the treatment to work. It wouldn't work if a male watches her ash smearing, especially her husband. I have only said that you should guard her, for her peace of mind, since it would be getting darker. Just quietly slip away when she starts undressing. Walk away, if you don't, her bad luck might come to you too,' he warned me."

"How would I have returned home then if you left me in the bush? Ye-e? Did he tell you that I should walk all the way back home, in darkness, covered by a white sheet like a witch, for his juju to work? In order for you to be lucky, did he, ye-e?"

"I was going to come back to pick you when you were done."

"How would you have known that I had finished when you had gone away? How would you know, ye-e? I suppose his juju would have alerted you that I had finished. *Bekuzaluma ezibunu*, your backside was going to be itchy, to alert you of that, ye-e? The police took sometime chasing me about and also noting my story and taking my details down, why didn't you return during that time if you were going to pick me up?"

"I..."

I could not bear to listen to his lousy responses any more, I interrupted him with another question. "Why didn't you visit me in hospital?" I didn't want him to visit me in hospital, but still he should have tried, "Why didn't you visit me?"

"You know after uni I do night shifts, Dolly. We need money for the bills and the baby. I had planned to visit you at the weekend. I didn't know that they would discharge you early."

"So you wanted me to stay in hospital until the weekend?"

"No."

"You don't make sense, Ice. I'm wasting my time talking to you."

"But..." I didn't alow him to finish, I left the room, *ngigonyuluka njengo-mangoye*, retching like a cat due to his lies.

Ice appeared to have all the answers but the better part of my mind, told me that he was lying about the police and about the hospital visits. But why would he lie to me? We were husband and wife, we were not supposed to lie to each other. We both wanted the same things. We both wanted me to get better for our baby's sake. Who called the police? I suspected that he wanted to get me detained in a psychiatric hospital forever. Those were just my suspicions, I didn't have any tangible evidence to support them.

My experience of living with Ice made me think that he had developed cold feet again. When it came to the crunch, he wriggled his way out of situations, leaving me in deep trouble. He developed cold feet during the ash smearing as he did at Heathrow airport five years ago. It was in his blood, it was his personality. Fight or flight, it was always run for him.

I couldn't understand him anymore. He changed his mind about the witchdoctor. One minute he was supporting me, being Mr Nice. The next minute he didn't want to know about my condition, being Mr Nasty. He sometimes joked about what I was going through. He didn't care anymore. There were times when I felt like giving up on our marriage.

Chapter 13

BABY SHOWER

When I fell pregnant Molly offered to hold a baby shower for my baby. I wasn't keen on it at first because of my disturbed mind. I tried to avoid any place where Zimbabweans congregated, except the church. We didn't go to church to judge others, 'Don't judge or you will be judged,' my pastor would warn. He taught us that when Jesus said, 'Cast the first stone if you have never sinned,' none did. *Akusoka lingelasici,* we all have our weaknesses - weak moments as we live our lives. I was always comfortable in church, knowing that whoever was judging me was playing God.

I was therefore concerned that holding a baby shower would take me out of my comfort zone. 'Why give a bunch of Zimbabweans a chance to play psychiatrist with my mind?' I thought every time Molly offered to hold a baby shower for me. Fortunately enough, Ice was also reluctant for me to have a baby shower. He said it would be stressful, despite Molly offering to do all the preparations for me. He argued that there was no reason to put myself under unnecessary stress that could trigger premature birth or even cause still birth, under extreme circumstances.

But when I returned from hospital and Molly made the same offer again, I couldn't turn it down any longer. I assumed that now that I had been to Engutsheni in Bournemouth, every Zimbabwean knew, so there was nothing to hide anymore. Molly started the baby shower preparations as soon as I gave her the go ahead.

I had two reasons when I accepted Molly's offer to host a baby shower. There was a chance of killing two birds with one stone. Firstly, there was an opportunity for those Zimbabweans who had heard about my admission to Engutsheni, to see for themselves how well I was. It would shut up all those who gossiped about my state of mind. Secondly, I hoped that the short woman with puppy eyes would also pitch up. In my language we say *zithiywa ngezikudlayo,* we snare animals by what they eat. To catch a dung beetle, you go to the cattle shelter, you don't go to the supermarket.

But I was also realistic that not all Zimbabwean women who lived in Bournemouth would turn up, so I went off on an advertising spree. I put posters in shops, halls, churches, people's cars, buses and anywhere else they could be seen, advertising my baby shower. I fly posted as if I was campaigning to be the mayoress of Bournemouth.

Ice didn't like the way I was going about advertising my baby shower party. I didn't care what he thought anymore. Since he left me stranded in the bush, naked, white as snow, holding onto his witchdoctor's concoction, then fabricated the reasons why he did it, I didn't trust him anymore, so what he thought didn't matter to me. Our relationship as husband and wife was surely dying a natural death. What was left in our relationship was *udokozana*, a heart murmur. We needed each other to put on a good front in the presence of friends and relatives. To pay our bills. For the sake of our baby, it needed two parents. I didn't want it to be brought up the way I was brought up. When I was growing up my mother was called by all sorts of names, including *umazakhela*, single mother, for raising my brother and I without a father.

I worked reduced hours at the local corner shop, so I wasn't totally dependent on Ice, I could look after myself. Both men and women wear trousers in the United Kingdom because they are equal. Women are not men's doormats, where they can leave their dog poo, knowing that women are fully dependent on them.

When I first came to the United Kingdom, I registered with a teaching agency and I worked as teaching assistant. What a classroom culture shock! As a Zimbabwean teacher, I was used to the fact that the teacher was the mistress of the classroom. I owned the class, if the students misbehaved, I would pull their ears, slap them and even give them a stick on their backside with the full permission of their parents. Not in the United Kingdom. Students were masters and mistresses of the classroom. They did as they pleased, they owned the classroom. There were reversals of roles. I begged them to behave and pay attention until my voice went hoarse. And I had to be careful too, raising my voice could be misconstrued as an act of aggression towards poor students. I could be blacklisted for that. The students were in charge of the classrooms, at least where I was an assistant teacher in North London. The lunatics were in charge of the asylum, as some people would say. That put me off teaching for good and I preferred to stack shelves at a local shop. I was not the only one; I knew a number of former Zimbabwean teachers, who left teaching for good in the United Kingdom and preferred to retrain as nurses or became *omahobho*, security guards. Some became care assistants, my Engutsheni nurse escort called them BMWs. Comrade Moment of Madness referred to Zimbabweans in the diaspora as bum cleaners, irrespective of the jobs they did.

Ice didn't become a teacher for the same reason and began training as a nurse five years ago. If it were not for his poor performance on his nursing course, he could have been a qualified nurse by the time I got pregnant. He blamed it all on the amount of shifts he did, but there was nothing he could show for those shifts. Later he blamed it on my nightmares and visual hallucinations. He blamed everyone and everything for his failures, but not himself.

Ice wasn't the only one who was worried about the way I went about advertising my baby shower, my friend Molly was concerned too. I was open with her, saying that I wanted to take advantage of her generosity to end my hallucinations. I told her that if I managed to find the short woman with puppy eyes, through my baby shower party, my problems would be over.

"But sticking the leaflets with glue on people's cars without the owners' permission might not be lawful, *shamwari*, friend."

"It's not as if glue is not removable, Molly," I said, smiling. "Has anyone complained to you?"

"No, Dolly, bu..."

"Molly, I really appreciate your support and I wouldn't want to offend you. If I've offended you I'm sorry. I hope you won't change your mind about my baby shower."

"No no no Dolly, it's not like that. I don't mean it that way. I am just concerned that plastering people's cars with your posters might land you into trouble."

I listened to her carefully and I thought she was rightly concerned. But the problem was that when I sensed a chance of catching the short woman with puppy eyes, I just went crazy. I lost my mind, like when I started collecting the rubbish from the people's bins, in the hope of getting her details, it soon became my only preoccupation and sooner than I thought our loft was overflowing with rubbish bags. Anything or any thought that could lead to the short woman with puppy eyes became an obsession. I still believed that if I had continued searching the bins, I could have eventually got to her. Molly had come to share ideas about my baby shower, but look who took our time; the short woman with puppy eyes. Somehow she dominated whatever I did. I asked Molly, "How far have you gone with the preparations?"

"Everything is falling into place, but people would like to know the colours you prefer for the baby."

"Since I don't know its sex, unisex colours would do."

"By now the scan can show the sex of the baby, why don't you find out Dolly?"

"To be honest Molly, I'm losing the love of this baby."

"Don't talk like that Dolly, *muromo unoroa*, the bad things you say come to pass."

"It's not easy Molly. I'm trying to be normal in an abnormal situation. My mind is racing, it's full of all the wrong things. No, I'm lying it's not full of wrong things, but it's only full of the short woman with puppy eyes and the nightmares. Sometimes it looks like my mind just walks out on me. Leaving me pleading for it to come back. Begging it to become my friend again. Just imagine. I can't think straight anymore," I said, getting agitated.

As if to distract me, Molly said, "Ok, let's make a date to go to Mothercare to pick the baby clothes you want and put them aside, they allow such a scheme. I will then ask those who want to buy presents to pick from there."

"Good plan."

"Remember its only four weeks to go before your baby's day," she said as she left.

The baby shower party day arrived. Molly's house was full of mostly her relatives and friends. On Ice's side there was only one person, his cousin. On my side there was no one, not that I expected anyone, I didn't have a single relative in the United Kingdom. People were milling around greeting and hugging each other. Some of the relatives present, had never seen each other since they came to the United Kingdom, although they would spend hours on the phone to each other, they did not have time to visit one another, for obvious reasons - shifts. So, my baby's party had made it possible for people to meet their friends and relatives - that was a consolation I had for holding the party. Music was blazing and women were dancing, *skokotshi*, where women's shock absorbers were put through serious gym work. It was the *skokoshi* dance that I loved to see women dancing especially in the absence of their husbands. The hyena and the snake *tsabatsaba* dance was nothing compared to that one. The women were provocative, they really danced the love making game, they twisted, they wriggled, they writhed, as if their waists were made of rubber. Out of nowhere, the short woman with puppy eyes entered the lounge, where most of the women were dancing. I was stunned and for some reason the crowd was stunned too. They all stopped dancing and playing music at the same time. They watched her as she walked to the middle of the dancing floor. She was carrying her present like the rest of the attendees. I gazed at her amazed. The really short woman with puppy eyes graced my party? The Limpopo River goblin. I couldn't believe my eyes, was I dreaming? Excitedly I said to Molly,

"Molly, my fly posting paid off. Look, look, who is here? The short woman with puppy eyes."

The short woman with puppy eyes stood in the middle of the lounge with stern looks. She looked like the goddess of the Limpopo River. She appeared proud to be at my party. She had the pose of being the main invitee without saying a word. She didn't have to say anything to set my mind wild. She owned my mind, it was her toy thing to play with.

"Oh, is she really?" Molly said excitedly too. The short woman with puppy eyes said nothing, she handed a parcel over to Molly. "Oh, she bought you a present too Dolly," but instead of handing the parcel to Molly, she unwrapped the parcel herself, and out came dead baby body parts. Chopped body parts hit the floor. The blood and maggots splattered on the floor too. Shocked Molly instinctively withdrew her hands. She sprang back screaming with terror and she was joined by the rest of the women. I was paralysed with shock. There was pandemonium in the room. Women headed for different doors screaming at the top of their voices, as the baby body parts squirmed on the floor. I pushed Molly's 60-inch 3D television to the floor and it split into many pieces of glass and plastic. I picked up the glass pieces and cut and cut and cut the short woman with puppy eyes. I cut her like a mad woman. Then I woke up, sweating, breathless and screaming. My wardrobe was lying face down. I had also smashed my dressing table. I had cut myself with the glass from the dressing table. My arms, legs, neck and my back were all bleeding. There was blood everywhere.

Ice stood at the door of my bedroom, watching and tears rolled down his cheeks. I felt humiliated and defeated. Those were the tears of triumph not sadness. The tears of the mouse playing with the dead body of a rat. He said,

"Dolly, you're not the woman I married? You have changed. What is your head telling you now? To make a suicide pact with the baby? You're not only a danger to yourself but to our baby too. What's happening to you? Why should I be part of this madhouse? Tell me Dolly, why?"

I had no answer. I was equally lost, yet he expected me to explain my actions while I was asleep. Sleep-walking. Sleep-screaming. Sleep-fighting. He abruptly turned and left the bedroom. He had obviously heard my screams in the middle of the night and came upstairs to check. He obviously heard the sound of the falling wardrobe. He usually ignored my screams at night.

I was shaken. My body was in shreds. The short woman with puppy eyes that night managed to trick me into hurting myself. She came into my bedroom that night and made a joke out of my baby shower. It was the first time that she was involved in my nightmares and she turned them into bloodmares. But Ice was wrong as I was not only dangerous to myself and the baby, but to the property too.

I couldn't go back to sleep after that dream. I didn't want to close my eyes and dream again. I didn't want to shut my eyes again in my lifetime. When I had a shower, I checked myself in the mirror. The blood stains on bed sheets didn't tell a true story because the cuts were superficial. They were self-inflicted but they were not life threatening. But I had to be on the look-out for myself during my sleep. Guard myself against myself, I didn't know how to do it, but it had to be done.

I cleaned my scars, got dressed and went downstairs to the lounge. I found Ice sitting on the sofa not sleeping, his chin resting on both his hands. It was obvious that *wayesidla amathambo engqondo,* he was thinking hard, as my mother would say. I didn't know what he was thinking about. Divorce me? Waste of time. I felt like a divorcee already. Hit me? Never. Not in England. The Queen would fall on top of him like a ton of bricks. Shout at me? Neighbours would report some disturbances next door where a pregnant woman lives and the police would be there in a flash. He could be hit by anti-social behavioural order, ASBO. He wouldn't like that, he still had his pride.

I felt sorry for him that night, despite his hurtful words after the dream. Marriage shouldn't be a battle ground. Instead of hurting each other that night, we should have been sleeping, cuddling and mating as normal couples do. I was convinced that he was regretting the wedding vows he made to a lunatic. He would go to his grave a disappointed man, cursing the day he put his hand around my shoulders as he protected me from the madding crowd, the day we first met. He should have joined the mob and saved himself, like what my ex-boyfriend did. Poor Ice.

"Dolly you should cancel the baby shower," he said softly, "This's exactly why I was against this party, it's stressing you up and you can't handle this kind of stress in your condition. I will ask Molly to cancel it, if you don't want to disappoint her."

"No, Ice, I can't cancel it now. It's tomorrow. People have bought the baby stuff. Some of them are already here, in Bournemouth. I can't disappoint them now. They will think I'm really mad. What kind a woman waits and only cancels the party at the last minute as if she has lost the child? No, I'm sorry Ice, I can't cancel the baby party. It's too late now."

Smiling sarcastically he said, "Dolly, you are mad, just take it from me. I'm your husband, I won't lie to you." With those words, Ice rubbed salt into the fresh wounds, they were painful, cruel and unnecessary. They sliced through my heart like a knife through butter.

"What would you do if I don't cancel it, Icecoldbeer?" That was his full name on his birth certificate.

"I will call for the mental health assessment. I will tell them what you have just done in your nightmares and I'm sure they will not hesitate to section and detain you under the Mental Health Act." He might be a failing student nurse, but he knew the Mental Health Act, he must have researched it thoroughly. I suspected that it was not the first time he had thought of it. He knew that he was my only next of kin and nearest relative, with his consent I would be locked at Engutsheni for life, Nana in Bournemouth Engutsheni hospital explained to me how the system works. Those were not empty threats. If only he knew his general nursing as he did the Mental Health Act, he would have qualified as a nurse years ago.

"Icecoldbeer, if you call them, I will tell them that you did this to me. I will tell them that we had a fight and you cut me like this." He was stunned, but he had left me with no choice. I had to save myself from being detained in a psychiatric hospital. I had to come out with my guns blazing. If he was going to play dirty, *lami ngizamjikijela ngothuvi*, I would throw poo at him too. Fight poo with poo. That was no longer a marriage dispute but a battle ground. Icecoldbeer versus uDolly kaNaKissmore. Bring it on. I didn't want to be sectioned to Engutsheni.

"What?" He thundered.

"You heard me Coldbeer. I can't cancel the party now." I thought, I didn't go through that nightmare for nothing. It might have been warning me of nasty things to come, but it might also bring the short woman with puppy eyes to the party too and that could be the only chance for me to meet her. I was prepared to go to any length to stop him from cancelling my baby's party. I then said to him, "I have let you play with my life for too long, Beer. I agreed to have your caca smearing treatment hoping these nightmares would go. You and your witchdoctor convinced me that after the treatment they would go. Did they go?"

"Don't you try to blackmail me Dolly. I can't believe what you have just said. That you can even think about it. That you could be so evil."

"Just let the party take place tomorrow, Ice and all these threats will come to nothing. Do you think that if I showed the social workers and the police these cuts, which are all over my body and told them that I did them to myself, they would believe me? They would think I'm an abused woman who doesn't want to report her abusive husband. They will think I was in a violent relationship." That left him stunned, looking like someone who has been caught making love to a baboon. "The party is tomorrow Ice, live with it or face the consequences," I said as I went back upstairs.

When the real baby shower party took place it was opposite of the nightmare baby shower. Molly's house had big gardens both at the back and the front. Some women came in and sat in the lounge, some in the kitchen, some stood talking in the front and back gardens and some in their cars parked on the streets, reminding themselves of the good old days. Molly sent word to everyone to come to the lounge and she ordered me to go into her bedroom upstairs.

I was dressed in a maternity dress that covered most of my neck, arms, legs, in short, I made sure that it covered most of my body to hide the scars I inflicted on myself. Once I was upstairs Molly's sister in law from Brighton covered me from head to toe with a see-through white bed sheet and led me downstairs, holding my hand. When we went into the lounge, women ululated and the stereo volume went through the roof.

"Please *madzimai*, women, if you want to see who is under the bed sheet, put money on the wooden plate. She's not for free, she's special," said Molly, although I had been mingling with the women only a few minutes ago, all of a sudden I had acquired exceptional features that required the women to spend their hard earned cash on.

They put some money in the plate and then demanded to see my face. Molly's sister in law from Brighton unveiled my face and the women came face-to-face with the first time mother to be.

Many women came to my baby shower, they gave up their shifts for me, I considered that as an honour. Just like in the nightmare party, most of them were Molly's relatives or friends. But the numbers outstripped those in the nightmare party. Ice's cousin and her friend attended the party too and my church friend was also there. Then Molly's cousin from Leicester said,

"Dolly what is your bedroom name?"

Bedroom name? Ice and I calling each other by bedroom names? We'd been trying for the baby for ten years for God's sake. After ten years of calling each other with bedroom names, with nothing to show for it, we stopped that nonsense. They jinxed me from conceiving a child. Bedroom names after ten years of toiling for nothing? She was having a laugh for sure.

"We want to know your bedroom name Dolly." Most of the women joined the chorus.

"I don't have a bedroom name," I said.

"Punish her," Molly's sister in law from Brighton said, quickly adding "She's too lazy in the bedroom. She must be provocatively active to deserve a bedroom badge. How shall we punish her *madzimai?*"

"Dolly get to the centre of the lounge and show us how you got pregnant after ten barren years of non-performance," Molly's cousin from London said, as I made my way to the centre of the lounge. Ice's cousin from Southend-on-Sea, said,

"I will take the punishment for her," as she made her way to the centre of the lounge. "Money or action?" She asked the women. The crowd shouted in unison,

"Action! Action! Action!"

Then she said, "I want you to play me Devera Ngwena Zhimozhi by Devera Ngwena." In English the song is called Follow the Crocodile by the group called Follow the Crocodile. I didn't know whether it was on purpose or by coincidence that Ice's cousin chose that song. Was she trying to tell me something? Was that the reason she was taking my punishment? Telling me to follow the crocodile? Laughing at my problems? But maybe she didn't mean any harm at all. She then said that she was going to dance a 'bottle dance' invented by a dancer called Bev, affectionately known as Zimbabwe's Biyonce and even made more popular in Zimbabwe's shebeens. She asked for a wine bottle, stood with her legs apart, placed it on the floor between her legs. She was wearing a mini-skirt and she started twisting her hips and bums in a suggestive way in tune with the song. She slowly got down, bit-by-bit, drop-by-drop, twisting, coiling, swirling and belly dancing until her female genitalia came face-to-face with the mouth of the wine bottle and kissed. The bottle got lucky. The crowd went wild. They loved what they saw. I had never seen her dancing like that before. She was really a show woman.

After her dance, Molly's sister in law from Brighton asked everyone around the room to say their bedroom names, surprisingly everyone had a bedroom name, even my church friend had one too. Molly's sister in law from Brighton hers was 'round bums', Ice's cousin from Southend on-sea was '*Mzekezeke*', Molly's cousin from Leicester was '*Zora bata*,' Molly was '*Mafohloza*' Molly's cousin from London was '*D-square*', Dollar's cousin from Luton was '*Bora mughedhi*,' Ice's cousin's friend was '*Small house*', Molly's sister in law from Brighton's friend was '*Green machine*,' Molly's friend from Bradford was '*Bosso*,' Molly's friend from Southampton was '*Juice*,' my friend from church was '*Sodoma neGomora*.' When all the women finished saying their bedroom names, Molly's cousin from Brighton said to me,

"Which love making style did you use most when you got pregnant?" The woman was crazy. Style, what style? She didn't understand my situation, did she? Anything that would make my husband fire a live bullet was allowed, forget about how he fired it or how I was gunned down under.

"We used all sorts of styles," I said.

"Which one did you use most?" She pressed.

"The doggy one," I said and the women shouted,

"Doggy Dolly Go! Doggy Dolly Go! Doggy Dolly Go!" They pointed me to the centre of the lounge again. At that time no one offered to take the punishment for me. I asked the DJ to play me Tina Turner's When The Heartache Is Over. I got to the dance floor already twisting, writhing and side-sliding like the Limpopo snake that thought it could outwit the hyena, at its peril. I then knelt on all fours, and gave it to the man they couldn't see, the man of my imagination. Ice believed that I saw things that other people didn't see, so be it. The women went wild, shouting, "Doggy!

Dolly! Go! Doggy! Dolly! Go! Doggy! Dolly! Go!" in rhythm with my actions and the song too. And I thought, *I'm loving this. I'm loving this. This baby shower should go on forever. It is distracting me from the short woman with puppy eyes.*

"I love that action Dolly," said my friend from church, "Never in a million years, would I imagine that you could be that active, especially with that big belly. If you don't correctly guess the present I bought for you, I will tell the pastor what I saw you doing today." Women laughed as I went back to my seat, breathing heavily as if I was in labour already.

"It's time to guess the presents your friends or friend's friend, or friend's friend's friend bought you," said Molly's sister-in-law from Brighton. "If your guess is correct, you choose the woman to go into the centre and perform. But if your guess is incorrect, the parcel owner will choose who goes to perform. But *vakadzi,* wives, don't ask Dolly to do any more performances, she has done enough for today. We don't want her baby right here and now. I heard that in one baby shower the woman gave birth during the party, so we don't want that to happen here." Many women chuckled. I obviously guessed Molly's present and I asked her sister in law from Brighton to perform in the centre of the lounge so she went to the centre shaking her big bum. I guessed Molly's sister in law from Brighton's present wrong and she asked Molly's cousin from London to perform. This went on until I had a chance to guess, correctly or incorrectly, every parcel that was handed over to me.

Men began to arrive around 6:00pm, which was the time the party was open to everyone. We had started our party four hours before. It was summer time and the sun wasn't going to sleep any time soon.

Ice didn't carry out his threats of using the Mental Health Act against me, he got the message, loud and clear as if I had shouted it from the top of the roof. In my adopted country the police and the law listened to the children first, women second and to men last. It was not his uncle Comrade Moment of Madness' country, where the police and the law listen to men first. If I set the police on him, he could be locked up in a police cell until he gave me a new bedroom name.

Dollar, Molly's husband, requested the DJ to play a song by Oliver Mutikudzi, called *Wasakara,* you are wrinkled. He got to the dance floor, and danced the dance called *zora bata* apply butter. In this dance, with the left arm stretched, like holding a slice of bread, the dancer pretends to apply butter on a slice of bread with the right hand; waist twisting provocatively at the same time. When Dollar got to the dance floor, some men and women joined him, they danced and moved forward in a circle. There were a lot of men by then, Benz and Beans were there, those were the men I knew, but there were a lot of other men I didn't know, I suppose they saw my posters and decided to join the fun. The party came alive for sure. It was no surprise that God created man first, if He had created the woman first, by the time He created man, the woman would have been married to the snake already, because *sithandizinto,* we like stuff.

Benz then asked the DJ to play a song by Lovemore Majaivana, called *Umoya Wami,* my heart, and he started to dance a type of dance called ingquzu. The women circled round him, clapping their hands and ululating and I was glad that my party was going very well. An hour later, Molly stopped the music and said,

"Congratulations to Ice and Dolly, at last, the man has taken a proper aim," Everybody laughed. I sat next to the window, so that I could see all the passers-by, in case the short woman with puppy eyes passed by or paid us a visit. Ice stood near the lounge door that led to the kitchen and the back garden. We both smiled. We were not sitting next to each other, those days were gone, we were miles apart by then.

Then Benz added, "To say that these two have gone through turbulent times would be an understatement of a decade. It has all been Ice's fault, firing blanks." Everybody laughed, including Ice, I just smiled. Then Molly said,

"Thanks very much *bomama, madzimai, women* for your gifts, without you this party would not have been possible. As you can see, men are..."

"Please, Molly, don't forget to thank the British's NHS," said Benz, "Without the NHS's viagra, Ice would have died seedless." Many people laughed again. Benz was certainly playing the clown. I was surprised that Ice laughed too, it was nice to see him laughing at himself, enjoying a joke. He seemed to be enjoying his baby's party which he would have cancelled, had I not stood my ground.

Molly talked over Benz, saying, "You see men are already taking over. I would like to just say enjoy yourselves, *siyabonga, tatenda,* thank you."

As soon as Molly finished Benz went on, "But be careful in whatever you do, the British government doesn't trust us, they think our big bums are sinking their island fast. They're blaming us for the floods. As you know the London vans are telling us to go to hell."

I thought to myself that one day Benz would find himself in hot soup with such kind of careless talk. But the inscriptions on the London vans telling illegal immigrants to go back to wherever they came from were the worst kind of immigration intolerance and hatred in Europe since the fall of Hitler.

From my vantage position I saw a police officer entering Molly's gate. He talked to a few people and one of the men came into the lounge and went over to Dollar. And I thought the police were paid more for strictly policing gatherings by black people. He might have come to tell us that we should be finished by 11pm. Surely we had lived in the country long enough to know that.

Dollar and Molly followed the man out of the house. Dollar talked to the officer and Molly listened. She appeared surprised about what the officer was saying and began talking and pointing towards the house. She hurried back into the lounge and came over to me and said,

"The police officer wants to have a word with you."

"With me? What have I done now?"

"Come and answer for yourself."

I followed her through the front door and to the police officer. The officer said to me,

"We have received a number of complaints about fly posting and in some cases super glue was used on people's cars, advertising the baby shower party today along this road. I would like to talk to the person who fly posted."

"I did it Officer. I was just excited about my party, this is my first baby after trying for ten years, Officer. I'm sorry if I offended anyone."

Ice joined us.

"We would like to ask you a few questions at the police station ma'am. Can you accompany us to the station please."

I was surprised that the Officer wanted me to accompany him to the police station right then, disrupting my party. "With due respect Officer, why can't you ask me those questions here? Or I could come to your station some other day. Is it necessary for me to go to your station now?"

"As you can see Officer, she's pregnant, is it really necessary for her to go to the station now?" Molly pleaded on my behalf.

"Would you drag her to the police station leaving her party behind if she was white?" Asked Dollar and I wasn't sure whether his statement was helpful or not. The officer looked at him and just shook his head. Dollar continued, "I'm serious Officer. This is an unnecessary show of power to drag a black pregnant woman to a police station, for putting a few posters on people's windscreens."

The officer ignored Dollar's statement and said to me, "Due to the number of complaints made, we suspect that a crime might have been committed. There was no house number on the posters, so we waited for the day of the party. We need to question you at the station, ma'am."

"Why can't you ask her those questions here?" Dollar insisted.

"We have got a procedure to follow sir. We would like to interview her at the station."

"Do you mean a procedure designed to deal with the blacks sir, which is institutionally racist? Do you mean that Officer?" Dollar's comments of institutional racism made me think. Stephen Lawrence's inquiry coined the term 'institutional racism.' Was I about to be a victim? I have had a number of stories of black people being unnecessarily detained and some dying in police custody without explanation. Why was the police officer so heavy-handed in dealing with my case? The fact that there were no police officer present from ethnic minority background, made me to further doubt the officer's intentions. Wasn't it mind boggling that United States of America elected a son of an immigrant as president, but Bournemouth police couldn't find a single qualified enough minority police officer to employ in 2009? Would the white only police officers seriously investigate racism levelled against themselves or and white people? I wondered?

The officer ignored Dollar again and said to me, "Please follow me to the car ma'am."

"Officer," persisted Dollar, "What I mean is that the police institution is corrupt and racist. I don't mean that you wake up in the morning, have a wee, a shave, a bath, put on your police uniform, kiss your wife and kids goodbye, look yourself in the mirror, and say to yourself 'I am going to be a racist today.' No. You're too clever for that, as an individual you can hide it very well officer, but collectively as a police force you're damn racists."

"Sir if you want to complain about how I am handling this case I can give you a number to call and make a complaint."

"To make a complaint to another white officer or person sir? What do you take me for officer? Dim-witted? You think my brain is dark like my skin? I've just told you that the whole system is racist and you want me to complain to another white man."

"Sir you can accompany your wife to the station if..."

"There you go again officer. There you go, jumping to conclusions. So typical! Who told you that she's my wife. She's black, I'm black, she's my wife. Stereotyping! Just like you always assume that if a black man is driving a nice car, it's either stolen or he's a drug dealer. I'm not happy with the way you're going with this case, but she's not my wife. For your own benefit officer, she's a friend of my wife. There's absolutely no need to take a pregnant woman to your station for fly posting. You can easily carry out the interview right here."

The officer ignored Dollar and said to me, "Are you coming or not ma'am?" He was determined to take me to the station despite Dollar's tantrums. I remembered Molly's words that plastering people's cars with my posters might land me in trouble. She was right.

"But offi..." Before I could finish my sentence, I saw the short woman with puppy eyes behind a van. I just took off, sprinting in her direction. "It's the short woman with puppy eyes. She's here Molly," I shouted excitedly, running towards the gate. I initially caught the police officer by surprise, but he recovered quickly enough to catch me before I could exit Molly's gate.

He held me by my arm, "You have to go to the station now ma'am." He sounded a bit irritated by my actions. I tried to wriggle out of his grip and a struggle ensued. I tried to pull out of the officer's grip but he wouldn't let go, he held my right arm with both his hands.

"No officer. Please let me catch the short woman with puppy eyes. Please officer I can't go to the station now. Please leave me alone. I want to talk to her right now. You can even arrest her, she's a stalker. Please let me go, officer." I was almost crying. No one came to my rescue, not even Dollar. No one told the officer to let me go. I said to Molly, "Did you see her? Did you?" Molly shook her head. "Did you see her officer?" He ignored me. "Did you see her Dollar? She walked past that red car and went behind that white van," I said, pointing with my left arm. "She's stalking me." No one responded.

She obviously got hold of one of my posters. She didn't come in, but loitered around the house. I knew she was stalking me. Did she tip off the police? She was capable of anything. Ice might have thought that there was no chance that someone would stalk me all the way from Zimbabwe

132

to the United Kingdom, but he was wrong. She deliberately came to the party that day, with full knowledge of my baby shower, but she didn't come in like all the other guests. Her actions were deliberate and amounted to stalking. I knew I had never bumped into her by chance. In Bulawayo, she chose to board the same kombi with me. In Johannesburg she knew where I lived...but how? At Oliver Tambo airport, she knew I had been pulled out by the immigration officer, and she deliberately showed up. In the plane she knew that I was in business class and she showed up in the toilet. At Heathrow airport, she saw me as I was leaving with Ice and showed up. At Castlepoint bus stop, she was loitering around my flat, when she saw me coming out, she quickly boarded a bus. She even showed up in Luton... but...no...forget it...that has madness written all over it.

And that day she knew that I was hosting a party and she pitched up right when I was in the middle of being arrested. She appeared a bit fatter, than she did at the Limpopo River. She was having a good life in the United Kingdom. If that wasn't stalking, then I was mad.

The officer didn't let go and his friend who had been on the phone in the car came out and joined her colleague. The short woman with puppy eyes had escaped again. The fact that the police, Dollar and Molly didn't see her – that nobody saw her except me, made everyone think that I was insane. But she was very good at picking her timings, leaving the stalked one looking mad and vulnerable. She was a perfect stalker.

The police officers dragged and shoved me into the back of their car, as the male officer said, "In addition ma'am, I'm charging you for resisting arrest." First I was arrested for fly posting and next I was charged for trying to flee from a police officer. A pregnant woman charged for attempting to flee from a police officer? I just wanted to catch the short woman with puppy eyes. I wanted to thump her face in for stalking me.

At that point, all my guests had come to the front garden to witness my arrest. That was a drama they didn't expect to witness. I felt so humiliated. Humiliation was now my second name. I was probably the first and the last woman to be arrested at her baby shower party. What does that say about the baby I was carrying? I will name it Humiliation when it is born, as there is a story behind every name.

I couldn't see Ice anymore. He must have left. I didn't see him leave, he just disappeared like the short woman with puppy eyes. I had no doubt that I had humiliated him enough. If I was in his shoes, I thought, I would

133

have done the same. I would have left the sham marriage some months ago. I didn't deserve a husband, I was a nightmare myself. But Molly offered to accompany me to the station and she followed behind us in her car. Very few people have a friend like her, if it hadn't been for her I would have killed myself by then for sure. It never rained, but poured.

I sat at the back of a police car alone as usual - people might have thought that I used police cars for my personal errands. I was never picked up by police cars, in Comrade Moment of Madness' police state. United Kingdom created a monster out of a pussy cat like me. I wasn't a criminal. I was a law-abiding citizen. If I hadn't put up those posters, I wouldn't have been in the police car that day. I would be collecting my presents like all other baby shower mothers. Whatever I did made people think that I was insane. 'She has been arrested on her baby shower,' they told each other at Molly's house when I left in a police car. 'Did you know that she has been admitted at Engutsheni before?' Others inquired. 'Did you see how she danced, you wouldn't believe that she was pregnant.' They poked fun at me. 'Many women who are not even pregnant would not manage her moves,' they laughed. 'You mean those dodgy Dolly moves?' 'Yes, I mean those doggy Dolly disgusting moves.' Laugh out loud girls. 'Why was she admitted to Engutsheni?' As if they didn't know. 'For bush ash smearing.' Laugh girls, laugh out loud. 'Bush ash smearing in Bournemouth? *Usihlekisa ngamakhiwa lo,* she makes whites laugh at us.' 'Why did she ash smear in the bush?' Too nosey. 'She saw a witch doctor in London?' Don't listen to them. 'Why?' Don't tell them. 'Because when she fell pregnant she thought she had been impregnated by a goblin.' Liar, liar, liar. 'Ha-ha-ha,' they laughed.

Once we got to the police station, I was quickly interviewed, given a police caution for fly posting and a slap on my wrist as a first offender, then allowed to return home. I couldn't tell what softened the police's stance at the station, maybe it was Dollar's ranting. The police did warn me though that some of the complainants whose cars may have been damaged by the glue might take further action through the common law route, but they allowed me to return home.

Chapter 14

JOE AND BEN

It was a sunny day, such days are few and far apart in the United Kingdom. Sometimes you could experience four seasons in one day, summer, autumn, winter and spring. When it was sunny like that, Bournemouth residents wasted no time and took to the beach. It wasn't only the local residents who clogged our roads with traffic, people from all over the United Kingdom came there, some from abroad too. People spent their year's savings in order to share a piece of warm weather with us in Bournemouth. It was a nice feeling to know that you lived in a place where others spent money just to be part of it, to be your neighbour, even if it was only for a few hours. The beach's fine sand caressed your feet. Bournemouth beaches were once voted the best not only in the United Kingdom, but in Europe too. I had never been to the beach since I returned from Zimbabwe. I couldn't face the sea, where for some reason, most of my nightmares were centred.

Molly popped in to see me at home. Just like me, she was worried about the appearing and disappearing of the short woman with puppy eyes. She always associated my visual hallucinations with what happened at the Limpopo River. Her concern increased when I told her that while everyone was worried about my injuries on the fateful day, the short woman with puppy eyes was only concerned about missing the kombi at Musina. Molly suspected, just as I did, that maybe she had something to do with the accident, so she began making her own enquiring about what happened. She wondered why I should see only one person from the whole group and that person followed me, not only to the United Kingdom, but to Bournemouth. Why were my visual hallucinations fixed and centred on her only? Why had I not hallucinated about the other people who were present? She honestly believed that I saw a real person despite all my sightings coming to nought. Although she didn't see the short woman with puppy eyes at my baby shower, she still believed that I saw a real person and that I wasn't losing my mind. She was the source of my encouragement. She kept me believing that I was normal and that one day I would come face-to-face with my stalker.

When Molly visited me that day she said, "That's Joe's mobile number," handing me a piece of paper, adding, "Call him," She handed me her mobile phone. "I will foot the bill, just call him."

She set my mind firing in all cylinders. "You managed to get Joe's mobile number. The Limpopo River Joe? And you want me to call him now? Call him and say what?".

"Ask him if he knew the short woman with puppy eyes and whether he was aware that she was on her way to the United Kingdom? Ask him what happened to the rope that day. Ask him anything you want. I have done my own investigations and I have been told that these escorts are thorough in their job. They work in cohort with the soldiers, because serious accidents could cause ripples that touch the soldiers too and go beyond and touch the untouchables of the state. They should have done their own investigations after the accident. You might think that they are criminal gangs, but escorting people across the border puts food on their tables. Accidents like yours Dolly, jeopardised that. I was told that they do their own investigations after such accidents. Of course there have been some bad apples among them, who sometimes rob their clients."

"No Molly, to me Joe is not a criminal, he saved my life," I said as I put Molly's mobile phone on speaker and rang Joe's number in Zimbabwe.

Joe answered the phone with his clear Zimbabwean accent. He boomed from the other side of the world, "Hallo talk to me."

The words stuck in my throat as I thought, '*This was the man who saved my life. Would he think that I was accusing him of attempted murder, by asking questions? Would he think that I was ungrateful for even thinking about it? But he also dumped me for the dead, although I forgive him on that one, because, I suppose, he thought that I was dead. When I was kicking, screaming and asking for help in the Limpopo River, when it mattered most, he came to my assistance.*'

Joe said again, "Hallo? Don't waste my time. Who is this?" he sounded a bit annoyed.

Nervously, I responded, "It's Dolly t..."

"Dolly who?" Getting impatient.

"I'm Dolly the woman you saved from a croco..."

"I've saved many women from crocodiles my sister." He interrupted me.

"I'm the British woman who fell into the Limpopo River, although you saved me from the crocodile you left me for dead lat..." I bleated out my response. I could hear his heart racing on the other side of the phone.

He stammered, "You're...you mean..." He paused for a while before he continued, "I know you. I remember you. But you...you are de...dead I mean...I mean alive?" He said as he tried to gather himself up. The fact that he had recognised me gave me confidence to go on, "Yes I'm alive by God's Grace."

"We left you for dead. I knew you were dead. I swear on my mother's life you were dead. But you were not. You are not. You're alive. How did you live? How did you survive?" There was a drawn out silence before he continued. "I'm sorry, but how did you get my cell number?"

"It doesn't matter or does it?"

"No. No of course, it doesn't. But how did you survive?"

"Thank you for fighting off the crocodile. I survived because of you. You saved my life. However there is something I want to know. How did the rope break?".

"That's still a mystery. But, yeyi...the rope appeared to have been cut by a sharp instrument. I'm sorry I..."

"Appeared to have been cut? Someone cut it? Who cut it?" I interrupted him again. It was my turn to experience a racing heartbeat.

"If the truth has to be told, the rope appeared to have been deliberately cut."

"Who cut it?" I questioned him impatiently. Did someone want me dead? I didn't have enemies. I didn't always agree with everyone but they didn't want me dead? They didn't possess that kind of intense hatred towards me, I believed.

"It doesn't matter who cut the rope, but whoever cut the rope wanted you dead for sure. The Limpopo River is very high at our drop-off point, that is the reason we pay the soldiers for their rope. The soldiers who examined the rope before and after the accident said that it appeared to have been deliberately severed."

"Who cut the rope?" I was now pacing up and down the lounge. Molly was watching and listening. She didn't interfere in my conversation with Joe. I knew none of those who were present that day, so why would they have wished me dead? It wasn't like I was working in the secret service like Molly's brother, Ndodana, where someone would have wanted to silence me.

"There are only three suspects. You, Ben or that short woman."

"Me? I?" I was shocked and surprised that he could even think that I cut the rope myself. How dare? For what benefit?

"You were the only three people left to use the rope," he said calmly.

"Why would I cut it?"

"You tell me." I was stunned. I was biting my lower lip with rage. He went on, "To commit suicide perhaps. Your husband might be seeing a small house, who knows. I also understand that those pastures are not as green as you try to portray them to us you people. You sometimes try too hard to make us believe."

"You're mad. Yes, you are." I couldn't hold back.

"So I rule you out. The next suspect is the short woman. Do you know her?"

"No. Do you know her?" I asked him shaking with expectation.

"No, I don't."

"Did you know if she was on her way to England too?"

"No, I didn't know that. Have you seen her in England?"

"I haven't, bu..."

"I was about to say that - iEngland *isihanjwa langabopopayi kulenzinsuku*, every Jack and Jill goes to England these days." He spoke laughing.

"I haven't seen her here." I didn't want to tell Joe that she had been appearing and disappearing every day since I returned. I only wished that Joe could confirm that she was on her way to England too.

"Then we rule her out too. That leaves Ben, my fellow escort. He was seen splashing some British pounds the following day."

"My money was stolen from my purse that night."

"So we've solved the mystery, my sister. I'm sorry because the safety of those I escort is my primary responsibility. Worse still if they are put in danger by those who are supposed to protect them. By those I trust."

"If you had not risked your life to save mine I would have pointed a finger at you," I said.

"I for one wouldn't blame you British woman. But why would Ben want you dead? If it's not Ben, then yeyi...someone really wants you dead for some reasons. If I were you I would sleep with both my eyes open *njengomvundla,* like a hare. I wouldn't trust anyone, not even my own husband."

"Thanks for your warning," I said, resigned to my fate.

"Be careful British woman. Till we meet again, *ubingelele uLizy,* pass my greetings to the Queen." And he hung up.

He left me with more questions about what happened in the Limpopo River than before. I found myself repeating his last words, *"If it's not Ben, then yeyi…someone really wants you dead. If I were you I would sleep with both my eyes open njengomvundla like a hare. I wouldn't trust anyone, not even my own husband."* My head was spinning, my paranoia hit the roof and I found myself saying out loud, "Did Ice hire Ben to kill me? Do they know each other?"

"That you have to find out, Dolly. But don't rule out anyone yet." Molly paused before she continued, "Joe ruled out the short woman because you don't know her, but she might know you. But at least one thing is clear, your fall wasn't an accident, but an act of pure evil because the rope was deliberately cut. But who did it? We will have to think outside the box to get to the core of this. Don't rule out anyone yet." As she reached for the door she said, "Leave it to me I will work something out. You concentrate on the baby, just let me help you. If you have any suggestions please let me know. I am prepared to go out of my way to help you Dolly, see you later."

One week after my telephone call to Joe, Molly paid me a visit again and she said, "I have tracked Ben down to Tottenham."

"Ben is in London?" I was excited, "He must have used the money he stole from my purse to buy himself a ticket to England."

"Not Ben himself, but his relative."

"Ah…I'm not interested in his relative. I want him to answer for himself." That punctured my excitement. I prepared tea for both of us. Then I asked Molly, "How would his relative in London help me?"

"If he has a relative in London it means that the pounds he was seen spending might have been sent by his relative. So he didn't cut the rope to steal your money."

"He could have cut it to kill me because he was paid by someone," I said.

"Kill you? For what Dolly? You're stretching your imagination here. Personally, I doubt that Ben cut the rope." She shook her head.

"So we rule him out then? Is that what you are saying?" I handed Molly a cup of tea.

"Yes," she said, sipping her tea.

"No, I don't agree with you Molly. Do you have his relative's address in London?"

"Yes, it's in Chandos Road, N18."

"I have an idea that we should pay Ben's relative a visit, to get some information…is his relative a man or a woman?"

"A woman, why?'

139

"I believe that Ben cut the rope. He could have been paid to do so, he couldn't do it for fun would he? People don't kill others for fun, except if they were psychopaths. You see, I think Ben's relative in London could have paid him to cut the rope."

"Why?"

"Who knows, Molly? She might be seeing my husband. There is every reason why Ice's girlfriend would wish me dead."

"Going by what you have said before, you don't think your husband is seeing someone. But, do you suspect that he is seeing someone?"

"No." After a long pause, I said, "I'm confused Molly. But the honest truth is I don't know."

"Maybe you are right, Dolly. It won't hurt to take a trip to the capital. From Tottenham we can pay Finsbury Park market a visit and I might buy one or two things for my brother." When Molly mentioned Finsbury Park market, we both looked at each other, with naughty eyes and smiled. We both knew that was the cheapest place to buy clothes for relatives back in Zim. We agreed to go to London the following day.

Molly picked me up from my flat. She was playing music in her car radio, by Lovemore Majayivana, called *Lelilizwe Alilamali,* this country has no money.

"Lovemore sang this song in the 1980s, when Zimbabwe was the bread basket of Africa, when she could still feed her people and even have surplus for her neighbours." I said to Molly, "Did he see it coming, or is it the power of words? You say something repeatedly, for sure it comes to pass."

"We are careless with our words Dolly. We say many things we don't really mean, especially the bad ones and you know what? They come to happen exactly as we said them. *Vakuru vanoti muromo unoroya,* elders say mouth is a witch," stressed Molly as we went past Ringwood historic market town.

"So as we all sang *'lelilizwe alilamali'* we jinxed and bankrupted Zimbabwe?"

"Partly yes Dolly. But Zimbabwe was mostly bankrupted by Tony Blair and the West?"

"By Tony Blair and the West, Molly?"

"As soon as the Labour Party came to power in 1997 they demanded a land audit. A Zimbabwean land audit. Britain had been paying for the land stolen by the British colonialists, since the Lancaster House agreement in 1979. Out of nowhere, out of the blue, seventeen years later, they demanded a land audit."

"Wouldn't you demand to know how your money is being spent, Molly?"

"It would depend on what I'm paying for," said Molly. "If I was paying for the land I stole I wouldn't turn around and demand an audit? Let's put it this way Dolly, if you stole something from me and the courts rule that you repay me, or you agree to compensate me, you can't then demand to see how I am using that money. Would you? It's my money, you stole it, you are paying it back, you cannot put your nose into how I'm spending it."

"But Mugabe used the British money to buy the land from the whites and gave it to his cronies, not to the black majority. He abused that money, Molly."

"Again that has nothing to do with Britain, Dolly. How Mugabe used that money is a Zim problem. It's a problem made in Zim not in Britain. It's not a British problem."

"And when Britain refused to continue paying for the land without an audit, Mugabe killed white farmers as he forcibly grabbed their land. Surely that was thieving and cold blooded murder."

"If you broke the promise to pay, what would you expect me to do, Dolly? Allow you to get away with it? No. I would forcibly grab what you stole from me. Repossess what is mine."

"But why take from those who had legally bought the land. By 2000 most of the whites had legally bought their land, they had not inherited it. So their land had nothing to do with colonialism?"

"Why did Great Britain offer to pay for land that was legally and fairly acquired? By offering the compensation they admitted guilty, weren't they? What are whites doing occupying more than eighty percent of the land in black Zimbabwe? Occupying tracks and tracks of land." We were travelling past New Forest when Molly said to me, "Look," pointing outside through the window. All that I could see from the car were acres and acres of empty land. She went on, "Imagine if the Germans had originally won the First World War and occupied all this land. But then when the British won the Second World War by defeating Hitler, their land remained in the hands of the few Germans up to this day, would they have allowed it?" I thought that was Dollar speaking through Molly. I suspected that she got those strong pro Comrade Moment of Madness views from her husband. He was a staunch support of the ageing Zimbabwean leader, some people suspected that he was a CIO that claimed asylum and got it. She continued, "As for those whites who managed to buy the land when the black majority could not afford it, tough love, they took advantage of their ancestors' privileged role they occupied during colonisation."

"But how could you support the killing of innocent whites Molly?"

"That's when you see Britain and the West's double standards shining like a beacon, Dolly. Mugabe killed more than twenty thousand of my people in 1980s in Matabeleland, while Great Britain and her friends were knighting him and giving him useless honorary degrees. But when he killed only ten whites, during the land invasion, they demonised and hit him with sanctions and everything they could throw at him. Why? Are the lives of twenty-thousand black people less important than that of ten white people?"

We soon encountered traffic congestion on M27, we therefore slowed down, travelling at just about twenty miles an hour. When we overtook a National Express coach I saw the short woman with puppy eyes sitting in the window.

"Slow down, Molly. Please slow down!" I shouted, "I've seen the short woman with puppy eyes in the National Express coach that we have just overtaken." Molly slowed down, but she couldn't just stop in the middle of the motorway. The traffic in front of us started to move faster. She had to increase her speed to avoid holding back the traffic. "Please Molly go to the slow lane and allow the coach to overtake us." She did as I asked. The coach overtook us on the middle lane, but I couldn't see the woman with puppy eyes because she was sitting on the driver's side. "Try and overtake the coach now and slow down," I said and continued. "She's sitting on the driver's side, slow down as you get in line with the coach." Molly overtook the coach and slowed down once it was in line with us. "There she is," I exclaimed, pointing at her, I couldn't hold back my excitement.

"I can see a black woman," said Molly.

"It's her," I confirmed. The woman with puppy eyes glanced at us and she quickly looked down. "She has seen me Molly." I was excited that Molly also had a good look at her, but she had to increase her speed because we were holding back the traffic behind us. She then slowed down on the slow lane, letting the coach overtake us again, and over-took it and by the time we managed to be in line with the coach again, the woman with puppy eyes was no longer sitting there. "She has disappeared Molly? Can you see her?"

"No I can't see her."

"You see, this is what she does to me all the time, the bi...! Excuse my Xhosa Molly."

"She must have moved to the other side of the bus," said Molly getting sucked in. She overtook the bus without my instructions, then slowed down to allow the bus to overtake us again, "There she is...she's moving to the other side of the bus Dolly. She has gone to the other side. She's gone."

" She is playing with your mind too Molly. She's moved to the other side of the bus. She does this to me all the time. Be careful with her, Molly, if you are not, you might be accused of visually hallucinating. I've been called all sorts of names, for saying that she's stalking me. But today she's stalking you too, Molly." Molly only smiled and said,

"My mind is made up of sterner stuff Dolly," quickly adding, "Not that yours isn't. I sounded worse than I intended," She said smiling again. She continued, "Changing her seat means that she recognises you, Dolly. She doesn't want you to take a good look at her. She's obviously shying away from you."

The coach took the M25 South and we took M25 North and I said to Molly,

"I wanted us to follow the coach indefinitely."

"The next stop for that coach is Gatwick, Dolly. I don't want to get out of our way that far. In any case the coach driver might report me to the highway police for stalking his bus. Even for driving like someone under the influence of something."

"I wanted us to keep the short woman changing her seats like pepper sprinkled knickers. To make her think we're stalking her. To test her own medicine," I said, smiling.

"Forget about her Dolly. Let her continue with her journey, getting hold of her might not solve your problems. She might have nothing to do with your experiences," she said pouring cold water on my case.

"I guess you're right Molly, let's leave her. After all, each time I'm about to get hold of her *ngisala ngibambe insiba*, I'm left clutching feathers. She's slippery like a fish. But I bet, I will get hold of her one day. She will call her mother by her first name, for making people think that my mind was kaput." After a pause I added, "At least you have seen her too. So it's not in my mind, unless you are suffering from some form of visual hallucinations too."

"Dolly, all I saw was a short black woman, not a short black woman with puppy eyes. I didn't see her puppy eyes."

"Because she avoided eye contact?"

"I don't know about that. But one thing is clear to me Dolly, she recognised you and she tried to avoid you."

As we headed towards North London, Molly asked, "What exactly do you want to know from Ben's relative?"

"The truth Molly. Does Ben know Ice? Does she know Ice? Was Ben involved in any way in my accident? Did he cut the rope? Does she have a clue of what happened that night? I just want to piece together something, the missing link that would let me know why someone wanted to kill me."

"What if she doesn't cooperate?"

"If the worse comes to the worst, we could persuade her the Mugabe way. Threatening her with degrees of physical violence might do the trick, Molly. Who knows?" With that thought hanging in the air, we made our way through Edmonton Angel, past White Hart Lane football stadium, onto High Road, took a few back yard roads, then we arrived in Chandos Road.

We rang the doorbell and a black big woman opened the door and Molly asked to speak to Bahle.

"I'm Bahle, just call me Beauty. Please come in." She directed us into her bedsit. She was really masculine, with bulging muscles like a boxer. Pointing us to a worn out, filthy, leather sofa for two, she said, "Do you want some tea or coffee?"

"No thank you," we responded in a chorus.

"The little one might be thirsty, you need to drink something *sis'wami,* my sister," she said, pointing her finger at my bulging tummy.

"I'm ok, thank you anywhere," I said.

"Sure? Not even squash or juice?" We both thanked her and passed on that too. Who would have wanted a drink in that pig sty? The smell coming out of her bedsit could knock a fly unconscious. I couldn't tell where the smell was coming from. Beauty's clothes were all over the floor, she did not even attempt to pick some of them up when we came in. I could see a pile of her knickers and the dumbbell under her bed. Her bed had not been made up and the sheets were dirty and full of stains. Her stove had clearly never been cleaned since it was bought. Unwashed plates and other utensils cluttered the sink area. I could see inside part of her toilet, where toilet paper was thrown all over the floor. The carpet was covered with stains and dried food and seemed as if it had never been hoovered since it was laid down. I just thought to myself, *'she left her country, friends and family behind to live in a dingy bedsit like this. Only Comrade Moment of Madness could force you to live like this.'*

"I'm Molly and my friend is Dolly," Molly introduced us.

"Oh, I spoke to you over the telephone last week? Didn't I? Oh, but was it last week or last month, sometimes my memory lets me down terribly? So how can I help you?" Beauty asked. My eyes had been fixed on a picture on the wall showing Ben and a female. Pointing to the picture I said, "That's Ben, yeh?"

"Oh, so you know *umalume*, my uncle. That's him with my mother. I miss both of them. Bless them. How do you know him?"

"I met him in Beitbri..."

"Oh, my poor uncle, he sometimes escorts border jumpers, to make a living in Beitbridge. He is a heavy drinker, you see. He was a teacher before he left his job to become a border jumper escort. Escorts are paid more than teachers, did you know that? When I send him some money he spends it all on alcohol. A few months ago he told me how he and his colleague, a former teacher too, saved this British woman, without proper papers." Smiling, she continued, "A British border jumper ha ha ha ha! Have you ever heard that?" Her laugh was loud. Her chest expanded as if it will explode. Molly and I exchanged glances. She continued, "I told him not to call her a British woman, but a Zimbabwean asylum seeker. But he then told me that he actually saw her blue passport. I told him that a proper British passport is red. The blue passport is for asylum seekers." She reached for the exercise dumbbells under her bed and she started exercising her arms as she continued to talk to us, "I claimed asylum myself as a lesbian you see, so I know that the blue passport is for asylum seekers. You see most of Zimbabweans have claimed asylum in this country. Did you hear about a Zimbabwean girl who claimed asylum and told the immigration officers that her buttocks were burnt by Mugabe's Green Bombers? Did you? They had not burnt her buttocks, she had lied. When her friend told her that the Home Office would want to see the scars on her bum she

145

panicked and asked her friend *ukuthi am'ayine izibunu*, to iron her bums. She deliberately roasted her own bum. She lay there on her bed, face down, as her friend ironed her bum, she couldn't walk for weeks due to the pain. She went through all that to remain in this country. When the Home Office interviewed her, they didn't check her bums. *Abasakhulumisani lomgane wakhe*, she no longer talks to her friend. The Home Office turned down her asylum claim and deported her back to Zimbabwe with a scarred bum, imagine. She went home with scarred shock absorbers, ha ha ha ha! I feel sorry for the man who will marry her? If she marries one of those docile church boys who only test the pudding after marriage, he would realise very late that he bought a car with broken shock absorbers ha ha ha! He m..."

"Did Ben tell you what happened to the so-called British woman?" Molly asked, trying to bring her back to what was relevant to us.

"Oh, yep. He said after saving her from the crocodile jaws, they dumped her in the bush when she died from the crocodile wounds. He said that she had lost too much blood, that's why she died. He also said that they tried to resuscitate her. They frantically tried to revive her but she was gone. Gone to her ancestors. Uncle Ben also told me that, Joe, his boss, cried when they couldn't revive the British Zimbabwean asylum seeker." I was crying too at that point. "Oh, you have a feminine soft heart too *nkazana*, girl, do you know her? Or is it the little one that makes you a pussy cat?" She asked as she handed me some tissues to wipe off my tears. I shook my head and she continued, "Ben told me that he had never seen Joe so emotional. He had always believed that Joe's nerves were made of steel, of iron, but that night he cried. He cried like a baby, ha ha ha. But then Ben also cried over the phone as he told me the story!" Beauty broke off as if she had heard something that distracted her before she continued, as if she had not stopped talking at all, "How could two men cry over a dead British Zimbabwean asylum seeker? How many Zimbabwean border jumpers have been eaten by crocodiles while attempting to cross Limpopo River? How many *bomaGe*, mates? Maybe they really believed that she was British, ha ha ha."

"Ben cried too?" That was my life she was narrating, I could not help but get interested. Was he remorseful? Why would he cry?

"Oh, Ben usually cries when he has had one or two glasses of spirits. He becomes a little girl you see. He blows all his money on spirits. So I was not surprised when he cried. He cries as if crying is his hobby or best friend. But that day he told me that he cried because he felt guilty because of what he did that night." She began pacing up and down in the room, still exercising her arms.

'So he cut the rope. The devil cut the rope, but why?' I thought to myself,

"Why did he feel guilty?" Molly asked.

'He said that when they dumped the body, he remained behind, searched the poor asylum seeker, took her British pounds and he almost took her passport too, but he didn't."

"Why didn't he take her passport?" Molly asked again.

"He is also human you see. Of course he stole her money, which was not right, but he didn't still her identity. He told me that it would have been difficult to identify the body if it was found, if he had taken the passport too. And he didn't need the passport anyway. But I told him that in London, Nigerians sell other people's passports like vegetables."

At that point I was crying aloud. Molly put her arm around me, consoling me. Beauty gave me more tissues, as if they would stop my tears. That was a part of my life story that I didn't know. That was part of my life that was lost to me. I never thought that I would ever know what had happened to me before they dumped my body. It was bizarre how my heart connected to my horrible past and it bled as if it has been sliced into two halves. Evil Ben had a heart too, I really appreciated the fact that he left me in possession of my passport.

"Did he tell you why the rope broke?" Molly wanted to know more.

"What rope?"

"Didn't he tell you what had happened before the British woman was attacked by the crocodile?"

"What do you know about the rope? I haven't mentioned the rope." Oh oh. She stopped exercising and stared at us and I was concerned that if that mountain of a woman sensed that something was wrong, we would be in big trouble. 'If she found that we were playing detective, we would be in hot soup.' I thought to myself.

"You mentioned the rope earlier," Molly said, trying to wriggle out of trouble. Her detective inquisitive skills had let her down.

"Oh, did I?" She looked confused.

"Yes you did." I joined in to help out, Molly. "Yes you did." I took advantage of her hesitance.

147

"Oh, yes they do use ropes, but he didn't mention the rope to me. Oh - I have remembered something! They also considered burying the Zimbabwean British asylum seeker in a shallow grave, but the only woman in the group kept telling them that they did not have time to bury her. Ben told me that this woman kept on saying they should go, otherwise they would miss their kombi. He said the woman annoyed Joe a lot and at some point he told her to find her own way to Musina if she could not just wait to see if the dead woman was dead, ha ha ha. Just to pay some respect to the dead. He said she was heartless." She stopped exercising put the dumbbells back under the bed.

"Did they find out why the woman was in such a rush?" asked Molly.

"She was on her way to her wedding in Johannesburg, which was so important to her that she would not be patient with a dying woman, ha ha ha." She went into those distracted moments again before she said, "Ok girls, you have been listening to me, now, how can I help you? You didn't come all the way from Bournemouth to listen to my rambling. Did you? I talk too much I know."

We had nothing more to talk to the mountain woman about, she had told us all what we wanted to know. But there she was, asking how she could help us. We had to find out a way to get out of that sticky situation quickly. And the help came at that very moment. There was a knock at the door and she looked at her watch and said, "Oh, it could be my nurse, I'm due my depot injection today, around this time." We seized that opportunity to tell her that we would visit her again in a few weeks' time. As she let her nurse in, she shunted us out. Her nurse was not wearing a uniform as I had expected and was carrying a small black bag. That could have been a nurse or a drug dealer, I thought to myself. I couldn't help wondering what could be in that bag - injections or *mbanje,* cannabis? Beauty was certainly on something.

As we walked to Molly's car I asked, "Was that a nurse?"

"Without a uniform it could be anyone, Dolly." Concurring with my thoughts, she continued, "But you wouldn't believe that she is unwell. Would you?" Molly said.

"Molly, she talked rapidly and volunteered too much information without prompting. Did you notice that she laughed incongruently throughout her rambling. She laughed when she talked about Joe crying over my dead body? And she appeared distracted sometimes, stopping in the middle of a sentence as if listening to something. Some patients behaved like that during my admission to Engutsheni in Bournemouth."

"Oh, so you're an expert now." We laughed as we got into her car and set off towards Finsbury Park market. We were quiet for a while. I will never know what was in Molly's mind, but I sat in her car stewing on what Beauty had told us. There was nothing I could do or talk about without that short woman with puppy eyes popping up. She was like a spam. She appeared everywhere in my life. Finally, I said to Molly, "Isn't it ironical that the short woman with puppy eyes unintentionally saved my life in her hurry to get to her wedding in Johannesburg?"

"I thought about that too, Dolly. Your life and hers appear to be intertwined. Wherever you are, she is lurking around the corner, literally. If she is not stalking you she's saving your life, it's an unbelievably interesting story. If you told someone about your life journey with the short woman with puppy eyes they would think you were making it up."

"I must write a book called 'I and the Short Woman with Puppy Eyes.'" We both laughed, before I said, "Isn't it a bit curious that Ben chose to mention that he rescued me from the crocodile and stole my money, but didn't tell Beauty what had happened earlier. He chose not to say anything about the rope. Why didn't he say something about it? Maybe he did, but Beauty's brains got muddled and confused under the influence of something."

"I believe that Ben left out the rope because it was either insignificant, or too risky to mention it to her," said Molly as we arrived at Finsbury Park market.

Chapter 15

CASTLEPOINT SHOPPING CENTRE

Beauty told me the story of my life that was lost to me. The part of my life I wouldn't have known, when I was deemed dead. I wondered if I should also thank the short woman with puppy eyes for unintentionally saving my life. But something at the back of my mind told me that if she knew that by stopping the group from burying me she was saving my life, she would have forgotten about missing her wedding and made sure that I was buried more than twenty feet under. I hated her even more for the fact that her selfish deeds were intertwined with my survival. She was a selfish stalker, everything had to revolve around her. Even when I was being resuscitated, they had to stop, so that she would get to her wedding in time. The fact that she selfishly saved my life made me angrier. She was playing God to me. The rage that I carried against her was a danger to her as well as to me. It was like I was holding a burning log, at some point I would have to throw it away or it will set one of us, if not both, alight.

I was still wrapped in my angry thoughts when Ice burst into the flat and announced, "If you want me to help you with the shopping, let's go now because I have got my own plans later."

I picked up my purse and followed him as we headed towards Castlepoint Shopping Centre. I was lucky to have him offering to help out with the shopping those days. He was too busy with his assignments and friends most of the times. When he offered his services like that, I had to grab them with both hands and thank God for giving me such a caring husband. He had never said a word about the police baby shower incident. He never asked me how it was resolved. In his mind it was as if it never happened. I suspected he had some bottled anger too. I prayed that when it came out I would be a million miles away. I was convinced that it was going to be messy when it exploded.

I didn't tell him about our London journey. I didn't see the point. He believed I suffered from visual hallucinations and that the short woman with puppy eyes only existed in my mind. Telling him that I had gone to London trying to solve the mystery of my hallucinations was tantamount to telling him that she existed. I wasn't sure how far I could push his frustration. I didn't want him to call for the Mental Health Assessment, and have me locked in a psychiatric hospital. Having gone there once, I didn't want to tempt the devil. I was playing my cards close to my chest at that time, at least I had a witness that the woman existed - Molly. Even though she didn't see her puppy eyes she saw a short woman who avoided me. That was all that mattered to me. What Ice thought, he could as well shove it in a hyena's behind, I wouldn't care a hoot.

Castlepoint Shopping Centre was a short walk from our two floored flat. We crossed Castle Lane West at Woodbury Roundabout traffic lights, briefly followed Woodbury road before we turned left into the Castlepoint Shopping Centre. Walking side-by-side, we passed some shops on our right before we took the escalator and as we reached the top, I saw the short woman with puppy eyes leaving a supermarket pushing a shopping trolley. I had no doubt that it was her. That was an appearance that she didn't plan very well. *Indwangu yakhutha ugatsha,* even the baboon misses the branch sometimes. She badly planned that journey that day, because it backfired spectacularly, right on her face. If she thought because I was pregnant, I wouldn't chase her, she blundered horribly.

The sight of her sent me loopy, I even forgot that I was pregnant. The rage I retained inside me took over. I once chased her in a bus and came out with an egg on my face. That day I made sure that it wouldn't happen. It was payback time. The memory of being chased by the police and the helicopter hit me like an avalanche. I told myself that the cat and mouse games she played with my mind were over. I felt anger and humiliation mixed together and how do you describe that? I made sure that she wouldn't escape that day. I wouldn't allow that to happen. I was in control. I was prepared to chase her until I laid my bear hands on her. I was ready to do anything to get hold of her, if it meant losing the baby; so be it. My eyes welled up, my heart rate increased and my hands started to itch - symptoms that meant I had finally found the woman with puppy eyes who stalked and haunted me from Zimbabwe to the United Kingdom. That was my lucky day and her worst day. I knew that that day would come, every dog has its day. The fact that Ice was with me was an icing on the cake. He would see for himself the face of the woman he had accused me of hallucinating about. He would see for himself that I've been stalked and abused. That confrontation could not have been better timed, in an open car park at the Castlepoint Shopping Centre. If I couldn't catch her, I was convinced that Ice would. She couldn't evade both of us. It was time to work as a team. He wanted to meet the woman with puppy eyes more than I did. I was sure that he wanted to mete out his own justice too, for ruining our marriage to that extent.

I ran towards her shouting, "Short woman stop! Short black woman, stop there! Witch, stop right there!" The short woman turned, saw me rushing towards her and she dumped her trolley and ran away. I chased after her, shouting, "You stop there, witch!" The words, which Ice once said when we were having a heated debate about that short woman, came rushing back to me, 'Next time you see her confront her, challenge her, talk to her, because I don't believe that she exists at all.' I wasn't going to let her get away that day. I wanted to convince him that she existed so much.

I ran after her as fast as I could with Ice hard on my heels, saying, "Be careful Dolly, you don't lose our baby."

I ignored him and I appealed to the public, "Please help me to catch that short witch running away from a pregnant woman! Help me catch that stalker! Please help me." The people around me didn't join in and I was bitterly disappointed. If it was in Zimbabwe, someone would have tripped her without any hesitation. People look after each other in third world countries. In Zimbabwe they would have fallen over each other trying to catch her for me, especially since I was calling her a witch and I was pregnant. Not in Bournemouth, they didn't lynch. Only a few of the shoppers stopped to watch as the drama unfolded, the rest went about their business as if nothing was happening. That was more than a drama to me. What happened there would be used as evidence to show that I was either sane or insane. I had to prove to Ice just how sane I was, once and for all.

I didn't only run on my adrenaline, but that of my unborn baby too. Each time the short woman with puppy eyes appeared and disappeared, she left my baby at risk of being still born. She couldn't get away from the three of us that day, with its father behind us like a dog's tail, she had no chance. Finally, I caught up with her as she stopped and tried to get into her car. She was a poor runner, to be caught by a pregnant woman. Or did she have a lung or heart condition? She was only good at appearings and disappearings. She was good for nothing.

I was panting, crazy and frenzied when I caught up with her. I grabbed her by her sleeve and she was as frightened as a goblin found by its owner making love to his wife. I smashed her eyes with the back of my right hand.

That was exactly what I had been praying for for some time, to smash her face in and God had answered my prayers. Her car keys flew out of her hand. She staggered and fell face down onto the bonnet of her car. I pulled her up by the collar of her blouse and my right fist caught her jaw. Ice tried to pull me off, but I pushed him away as my left fist landed on her ribs and she fell to the ground.

She bled from her mouth. I had done some really damage to her, but she deserved it. At that point Ice literally lifted me off the ground to stop me doing her further damage. Gesturing at the back of the bus, hiding and seeking at my baby shower and on a National Express coach and playing goblin games in the aeroplane, had to come to an end. I had been humiliated enough. I was foaming at the mouth like a dog with rabies. I was crazy. That was the part of me that I had never known that I possessed. I was punching and swearing like a possessed woman, throwing punches like Mike Tyson and dancing like Mohammed Ali.

When the short woman lifted her head, bleeding from her nose and mouth, to my utter shock, she was not the real short woman with puppy eyes. That was a stranger. She was as scared as a hare caught in the headlights at night in the middle of the road. I turned to Ice and said, "It's not the short woman with puppy eyes." I shook my head and screamed, "It's not her. Oh God what have I done?"

"You mean you have assaulted an innocent woman? You have assaulted a complete stranger!" He went bonkers, crazier than I. "I knew all along that there was no short woman with puppy eyes. I knew it! I knew it! The short woman only exists in your diseased head Dolly! You are going to prison now and you deserve it! No one should attack strangers and get away with it! I will personally make sure that you go to prison. I promise you."

A crowd began to gather around us. The police and the ambulance arrived, obviously some people who ate and breathed other people's affairs had called them. The paramedics attended to her and the police handcuffed me and politely asked me to get into their car. I made a spectacular picture. I was in a state, my hair was all over my face. I was frothing from the mouth like a sick dog. Eight months pregnant, handcuffed and getting into a police car, crying rivers of tears. It was like when I was attacked by the crocodile, my eyes sucked all the Limpopo River water and I just let it out to flood Castlepoint Shopping Centre car park.

Ice refused to get into the police car with me. I had embarrassed him enough. I didn't blame him. My moment of truth had changed to a nightmare as usual. I had proved to him how insane I was. He went over to talk to the poor woman, although she was shocked, she was not crying like me. She could have been too shocked to cry. People don't cry when they die, the shock of death dries their tears and blocks their airways. The police car drove off with me.

I sat at the back of a police car again. It was like wherever I was, a police car was lurking. I sighed, dropped my shoulders and closed my eyes. I was beginning to frighten even myself, let alone those around me. If I couldn't control myself who could? If my mind went off track that far, who would believe me? I was never violent, where was it coming from? It was a question of horrible mistaken identity. I didn't need to hit her. Catching up with her and showing her to Ice would have been enough. But in my mind that would not have been justice done. I had turned to a person I didn't know and I certainly didn't like. As I chased her I thought I was about to throw away the burning log I was holding, but I was still holding onto it and to make matters worse, it had started to burn my hand. I had to let it go before it was too late. The problem was I didn't know how.

At Bournemouth police station two female police officers led me into an underground cell. They took away my shoes, my watch, my earrings - everything that I could use to harm myself. It was a dingy place, the kind of place you should read about, not find yourself in. Certainly not a place for a pregnant woman. That was my third visit and I believed it was for good. My husband wouldn't shed a tear for me, he had already said it. The first time I was here I was admitted into a psychiatric hospital. The second time I was given a police caution for fly posting, but the third time meant the last time, as I would never be set free again. I had been violent and attacked a complete stranger, as Ice would say, as if there was such a thing like a half-stranger, or semi-stranger. The third time I believed that they would put me in an asylum for life. I could only imagine the headlines in the Bournemouth Echo, *'A Pregnant Black Woman Goes Crazy' 'Innocent Shopper Attacked By Lunatic At Castlepoint Shopping Centre' 'Are We Safe From These People?' 'Bush Ash Smearing Woman Now Targets Fellow Immigrants'.* I also imagined my picture on the front page of the newspaper, dishevelled as a witch, with my hair covering my face. I would certainly make headlines for all the wrong reasons.

From the streets and at the reception, the police station almost looked like a trendy place. Down in the cells it felt as if it was haunted. From outside it was like any place in the first world. In the cells it was worse than a place in the third world. The two faces of Britain, of the West. The walls were dirty, the floors were filthy with what appeared to be human waste and the whole place was stinking of all kinds of human fluids. Perhaps it was kept in that state deliberately, as a way of punishing suspected or real criminals. Real criminals like me.

I started to question my personality. I wondered if I had travelled too far to remember who I was. Had I allowed the imagined or the real appearances of the short woman with puppy eyes to take me too far? Had her appearances and disappearances changed the person I was? For the first time I seriously started to question the existence of the short woman with puppy eyes. Was that how people start to lose their minds? Was it the onset of insanity? Did I see things or people who didn't exist but believed that they existed? Was mind out of order? Was that what is called madness? Did the short woman with puppy eyes really exist? Did I really see her on the motorway in the National Express coach? Did Molly go along with my madness because she didn't want to disappoint me? Was she so concerned about the fragile state of my mind that she didn't want to weaken it further by challenging it? Did she really believe that I wasn't mad but she had no guts to tell me? She couldn't put her hand on her heart and say that it was the short woman with puppy eyes, but she agreed that a short black woman moved seats to avoid us. Was I seeing the real short woman with puppy eyes who was at the Limpopo River, or someone similar? I had just attacked a stranger. Was I seeing one woman or many similar women?

My fixation with the short woman with puppy eyes was not only destroying my marriage, but my life too. The nightmares had been chipping away at whatever was left of my marriage, too. A few nights ago, when I experienced the nightmare where I was swallowed by a fish, I screamed and went to hide in the wardrobe and Ice had to come upstairs to pull me out. The nightmares were vivid, relentless and real. They changed the way I thought and behaved. The combination of the short woman with puppy eyes and the nightmares had stripped me of my dignity and humanity. They had reduced me to a raving mad cow. I cried again at the police station. I felt sick and sat in a foetus position at the corner of my cell and cried floods of tears again. The tears kept coming

155

like Victoria Falls waterfall. If they didn't stop soon, I thought to myself, I would run the risk of getting dehydrated, putting the poor thing I was carrying into further danger. I just wanted to be put out of my misery. Let the psychiatrist assess and send me to an asylum and throw away the keys. I was certainly not fit to be a mother. I didn't deserve to be anyone's wife. I was not fit for anything. I was a violent woman and a danger to society. I should be locked away. I cried a good cry. Reality had finally sunk in. It had hit me in the face. I was a low life who deserved nothing. My tears kept flowing as if my brain was melting into liquid. It was as if my heart was pumping out water through my eyes. The police kept on checking me. It dawned to me why people kill themselves in police cells. You were not only stripped of what you are wearing, but you were also stripped of who you are; stripped of life itself.

Finally the two female officers opened my cell and led me into a private room. They told me that I would be assessed by a psychiatrist first and the police interview would follow, depending on the outcome of the psychiatrist's assessment. My interview with the psychiatrist was also attended by a social worker as usual, but this time my own GP was part of the assessment team, so I felt that those professionals were trying to understand rather than persecute me. My GP was smiling and reassuring. I was asked many questions, such as *has anyone ever committed suicide in your family*. I wondered what that had to do with my offence. My maternal grandmother committed suicide when she was fed up with my grandfather's continual marrying of new wives, some as young as her own daughters. I didn't tell them about it, because it was none of their business. The last psychiatric assessment taught me a few things: lie, lie and lie, they are not mind readers. Psychiatrists are nosey but they are not mental telepathist. They will never know what you don't tell them. One thing that I did very well though was remorsefulness. I didn't pretend on that one. I was really disgusted with myself on what I had done to an innocent woman. I would not like it if it was done to me, my relative or friend. I was therefore genuinely contrite.

After the assessment they all agreed that I did not need to be detained under the Mental Health Act, as my mind was sound and intact and I was insightful and remorseful to what I had done. They agreed with me that the incident was a question of mistaken identity and said it was up to the police to charge me for public disorder and for the woman to press charges against me if she wanted to. The psychiatrist felt that I might need some medication for my anxiety but advised my GP to prescribe it for me only after the birth of my baby, which was a few weeks away.

The police interview followed immediately after the psychiatrist's assessment. Before the police interview started, a woman introduced herself and said that she was required by law to sit in on such an interview because I was a 'vulnerable adult.' She told me that she would want to make sure that the interview conducted by the police was done orderly and fairly. If it wasn't for the gravity of the charges I was facing, I would have laughed when she introduced herself. I, a 'vulnerable adult'? The poor short woman I attacked at Castlepoint was a real 'vulnerable adult,' not I. I was a pregnant monster. A danger even to myself. I didn't even trust myself that I wouldn't repeat what I had done in the future. How could I trust myself, when my mind was by then my number one enemy? I was careful not to mention that to my assessors and the police.

After the interview, the police charged me with assault and public disorder and let me return to my flat on bail. However, they warned me that the woman I attacked might press some charges against me.

Molly picked me up from the police station and drove me home. When I got home Ice went crackers again, "You are mad," he said, almost poking my face with his finger. He was pacing up and down the lounge. "Why did they let you out?" He held his head in his hands. "How could they let a mad woman out? They don't know what they are doing. Are they setting you up to fail? You are dangerous! You are dangerous, Dolly!" He pointed a finger at me threateningly, "How could you embarrass me like that? How could you? How could you attack a complete stranger?"

"You told me before that I should challenge her..." I said, trying to defend my actions.

"I meant the real woman with puppy eyes. Not every short, black woman with puppy eyes on the streets," he shouted at me. "You have changed Dolly. You are not the woman I married. You are like a total stranger now. I know it's not the baby, but I don't know what it is. I don't know what happened to you in Zimbabwe, I really don't know." As he sat down, he said slowly, "I think you will have to move out."

The man was mad. I, move out? He must be thinking that Great Britain was ruled by a Queen by accident, did he? That was not Zimbabwe, where men return women to their families when they fall out of love with them or they have served their useful purpose. Sometimes he appeared to use *amaphambili akhe*, his testicles to think, I thought to myself.

"I'm not moving out Ice," I said to him, adding emphatically, "This's England. You will move out if you so wish, not me. It's your choice."

"So you are deliberately destroying our marriage so that I move out. Is that what you call England? If England means broken marriages, you can keep it. If England means you disrespect your husband, you can keep it. If England means you attack strangers and go scot free, you can keep it. I don't need it. I still need my dignity, affection and respect, if your England doesn't have those, you can keep it."

It was as if he had stolen my words. I was the one who had been stripped of dignity, affection and respect and he thought it was him. Selfish man. Why did I marry him in the first place? *Ngangingenwe yini,* what had entered my head? Slowly I asked him, "What about the baby?"

Both of us went quiet for a while, before he finally said, "You can keep it too if your England wants it. The baby mustn't be the reason I should be denied a normal life, which every human being aspires for." After he said those words I left the lounge and went upstairs to my bedroom to cry myself to sleep.

Chapter 16

NO BODY TO CRY FOR

Exactly two weeks after the shopping centre incident, I received a telephone call from my uncle in Zimbabwe saying that my mother had passed away peacefully in hospital. The truth was I had been secretly waiting for that telephone call since I left Zimbabwe about eight months ago. I also thought the Castlepoint Shopping Centre incident, *yayingihlolela*, pre-empted my mother's death. I had already said my goodbyes to her. She had finally left this hopeless world. I didn't cry. I didn't have the tears anymore to shed. My situation since I left Zimbabwe, had drained all the tears and I was empty, there was nothing left to show grief for my mother. When my brother did not return from the liberation war, I didn't cry. There was no body to cry for. History repeated itself that day: my mother had passed on but again I did not have the body to cry for. That was the story of my life. With Ice turning his back on me, I was left on my own. 'When does life become useless? Lose meaning and relevance! Does one has to live a painful and useless life for the sake of living? To keep within the norms of the society.' I wondered.

I sent some money to my uncle in Zimbabwe for her funeral and asked him to buy my mother a white casket and make sure everyone was properly fed on the day of the funeral. I wanted people to remember the kind and generous woman that she was, not the body they would have just viewed. There was nothing she had left behind for the relatives to fight for. I had promised her a house with a swimming pool, high walls and electric fence in low density areas, when I first headed to the diaspora. That promise died with her. *Yayisizilalele intomb'enhle*, the beautiful lady was asleep. I remembered that I asked my mother to move on only when she knew where she was going, and to keep a place for me. I trusted that she would reserve a place for me. With the way things were going in my life, it wouldn't be too long before I took my reserved place next to her, I thought.

Everything was going downhill in my life. Ice and I were hardly speaking to each other by that time. I never thought that I could be so lonely in a marriage. The fact that I was now signed-off on maternity leave meant that I didn't have to spend time with work colleagues who knew absolutely nothing about what I was going through. Fortunately all those Bournemouth Echo headlines I had imagined, remained exactly that, imagination. My imagination appeared to be pregnant too. Even though I attacked the wrong woman, I still believed that the short woman with puppy eyes existed. Now that Ice and I hardly talked, I didn't have to be explaining or justifying things to him anymore. The other good thing was that my childhood friend Molly completely believed me and she always reassured me. She was by that time actively helping me hunt down the short woman with puppy eyes. She completely believed in my cause. But I was still recovering from the Castlepoint incident.

My friend from church spoke to our pastor after she saw me being arrested at my baby shower. She convinced the pastor that Satan had taken over my life and that I needed God's intervention and the pastor arranged a special service for me. She was really angry with Ice and Beans when I confessed to her that I had seen a witchdoctor. She couldn't believe that I could betray Jesus that way. She asked me why I didn't seek her help when they were leading me astray. I told her that in my situation of trying to please everybody and save everything, time to pose and reflect was like luxury. The more I realised that I was no longer in a position to please everybody or save anything, the more I tried. The result was that I failed in everything.

My special prayer service eventually came. Our congregation rented a space in another church. Their service was in the morning and ours was in the afternoon. That church's bishop was a Zimbabwean, that made it easy for my pastor to negotiate the deal. The morning service was always half-empty, as it was meant for the indigenous. They had lost God and they had even stopped seeking after Him. When the immigrants came in, in the afternoon, the house of God was packed, welcoming everyone legal or illegal. There were no illegal immigrants in the house of God. There was singing, dancing, preaching and fun. My church provided the twenty-first century type of worshiping, *uNkulunkulu ngenkani,* God by force.

What is happening in the United Kingdom is that they are importing priests from Africa and all over the world, enticing them with work visas, as if they needed enticing at all, to come and preach in the land that has lost faith in everything. This gracious land has lost God, lost Jesus and if it's not careful, very soon it will be persecuting Christians. This is a country whose constitution is based on Christian values. Basic human survival, conscience, hope, empathy, fairness and forgiveness are the cornerstones of the Christian faith. Without these, humans are as good as other animals. Greed takes over and Satan triumphs.

Those who live their lives by the word of Faith are in a win-win situation. My mother used to say to me, "Dolly, let's say that I discovered that there is no Heaven in the end, what would I lose if I had lived my life by the Christian faith - nothing. But if there was Heaven what would I lose - everything." She used to tell me that a faithless society was a dangerous one, because it had no boundaries about what they can and can't do. Faith provides boundaries. A faithless society expects to solve all its social, spiritual, mental and physical health through the overuse of medication and a bit of psychology, because it doesn't know the power of prayer. Yet what psychology or talking therapies offer, is exactly what the prayer offers - exploration and addressing of human ills through their belief systems. Therefore, I decided against spending my money on psychology or therapies, which do not come cheap by the way, and sought free healing from the church. NHS psychology waiting list was as long as my arm, taking months, sometimes years to get treated. Yet prayers were free every Sunday, sometimes during the week too. I didn't think that the United Kingdom government would dish out its sort-after visas to priests, for a laugh.

On my Big Sunday, the pastor announced that the songs that would be sung, the dance that would be danced, the prayers that would be prayed and the preaching that would be preached, would all be mine. I really felt special that day. All eyes were on me. I was the centre of attraction, for good reasons for a change. The church went wild when they sang;

Ndamhanyamhanya, kwese kwese I ran around, everywhere
Ndatswagatswaga, kwese kwese, I looked around, everywhere
Ndatenderera, kwese kwese, I circled, everywhere
Hakuna hakuna wo, there's no one.

The song just nailed my encounters with the short woman with puppy eyes. I ran, looked and circled to no avail. As we sang the song we ran, looked and circled around. It felt unbelievable. Yes, I did enjoy myself at the baby shower, but in the church, *ngadakwa yibunandi,* I got drunk with sweetness. I left behind my earthly body, riddled with visual hallucinations and nightmares and soared like an eagle in a body that had never sinned. I felt free from police arrests and detentions. I was in God's tender hands. God was there with me, with us.

161

The pastor then asked me to come forward, so that he could lay his holly hands over my head and bless me. Set me free from the devil that was playing games with my mind and cast the demons away, as my church friend would say. She was present too, but I didn't know how much she told the pastor. Did she tell him that I was barking mad for him to arrange a Big Sunday? Did she tell him that I needed help with prayers and quick? But what I knew was that after the service my life would go back to normal. Whether that included Ice coming back I didn't know and I didn't care anymore. I majestically walked to the front of the church and stood in front of the pastor. I opened up my arms like Jesus on the cross as the pastor put his holly hands over my head. Two of his male deacons came forward and they too placed their hands over my head. I felt very safe, honoured, protected and assured to be among God's faithful disciples. They prayed for me, beginning in low voices and increasing the volume as each demon was cast out. The pastor also prayed in tongues and I felt saved. I was praying too.

In our church you choose whether to close or open your eyes during prayer. That made me feel safe because I remember very well when I was growing up that my cousins, when the food was put in front of us and my mother made us close our eyes and pray, they took that opportunity to pick the big pieces of meat and eat them during prayer. That taught me to pray with one eye open. So when the pastor said that there was no fast rule on whether one closes or opens their eyes, I really felt assured. Experience had taught me that many unthinkable things happened when eyes were closed.

Right in the middle of my special prayer, a short woman with puppy eyes walked past the church window. She walked to the window, paused as she looked in before she calmly strode on. She certainly gorged me in front of God. In the presence of my pastor and fellow worshippers. She was brave bordering on stupidity. She wanted a response and she got it immediately. I did what I always did when I saw her. I immediately went after her.

I shouted at the top of my voice, trying to drown the pastor and his two deacons' voices. "The short woman with puppy eyes is here! She's outside! She's going past the window!" I screamed before I took off, catching the pastor and his deacons by surprise, but at an arm's length, one of the deacons got hold of my maternity top, the force causing my dress to tear under the armpit right down the rest of my body, leaving part of my body partially exposed as I hit the ground. "Please let me go! Please let me catch the short woman with puppy eyes. Let me free! She is here!" I shouted, screamed, yelled, shrilled, and howled to no avail. The three priests held me down, praying and shouting even louder. Drowning my voice out. I was no match to three bellowing men. I struggled, kicked and fought to get out of their grip, but they held me down like metal vices.

The pastor's wife came forward in an attempt to cover my partially naked body. I was struggling and hitting out with my fists and kicking with my legs like a donkey. One of my fists accidentally caught the priest's wife on her eye and she screamed as she fell backwards. It was pandemonium. Hell broke loose. It was dog eat dog. My church friend joined in the position of the pastor's wife. She was big, *elamandla endlovu,* with elephant strength. She held both of my hands down with one hand and used the other to cover me up. Job done. Her bedroom name was not Sodom and Gomorra for nothing. She then said to the pastor, "The short woman with puppy eyes is the devil." I struggled and shouted at her saying that I had actually seen the real short woman with puppy eyes. The prayers got louder, as I tried to tell them that I really saw the short woman with puppy eyes passing by the church window. I tried to bite my church friend, who shouted, "This is your end Satan! *Phuma Sathani,* get out Satan! You have come to your end today. Leave my friend alone, devil. You hear me? Leave her. Leave her now!" She shouted at the top of her voice too. It sounded like a shouting competition between the pastor, his deacons, my church friend and I.

When I realised that by then the short woman with puppy eyes had escaped, ironically with the full blessings of my church; I stopped struggling. The grips on my body loosened and I was allowed to sit on the floor without anyone holding me down. It was at this point that I realised that the male church guitarist and drummer had joined the struggle to hold me down and they had stopped me from catching the short woman with puppy eyes. It took five men and two women to hold me down. That was the power that came with the appearances and disappearances of a short woman with puppy eyes.

Eventually, the volume of the prayers came down; and sounded like whispers. Then the pastor said, "Amen." His tie was on the floor. I remember at one point trying to choke him with it, hoping that his assistants would then concentrate on saving him, and let me off to run after the short one. That tactic didn't work because his tie was similar to those worn by prison guards, male psychiatric nurses and doctors -if you pull them they come away. His jacket was a bit creased, a sure sign that the demons of the short woman with puppy eyes gave a good fight.

The timing of the short woman with puppy eyes was too good to be true, especially her last two appearances and disappearances. During the baby shower she appeared when I was under arrest and at the church she appeared while I was in prayer. The fact that no one saw her, left me having to face awkward questions. I accepted that I was possessed by the demons to save myself from explanations. Otherwise how could I have explained the pastor's wife's black eye. I played it safe. After prayer sessions, when the demons had been cast out, you're not expected to explain what you went through.

I was a bit concerned about the pastor's wife. Her eye kept ballooning, but she kept singing with the rest of the church as if nothing happened to her. Maybe that's why she was a pastor's wife, she was patient, forgiving and always exuding confidence.

I wouldn't have thought in a million years that my special service, dedicated only to me, would have ended that way. I had just punched an innocent woman, a few weeks ago I attacked a total stranger, what next? If I wasn't careful, I might end up killing someone or maiming them for life. Whenever the short woman with puppy eyes appeared, I became a danger to people around me.

Privately I was really becoming more concerned about the state of my mind. What if I was not seeing a real person? What if? What if? Because I didn't like that thought, I would quickly banish it from my mind. To get through what I was going through, I had to repeatedly reassure myself that there was nothing wrong with my mind, despite what everyone was saying. They were all wrong, I was the only one right. Anything else, I would be admitting madness.

Had God forsaken me? But my friend from church would console me by saying, *minduro yake inonoka,* His response is slow to come. I was beginning to accept the inevitable. I was mad, I knew it, the church knew it, Ice knew it, the whole of Bournemouth knew it too, especially the black community. They were ululating over my condition. The women were waiting to snatch my husband away from me. I wasn't taking psychiatric medication not because I was well, different psychiatrists had told me that if I were not pregnant they would have prescribed some psychotropics for my condition. I was a nutter for real.

The poor woman I attacked had not pressed the charges against me yet, but I was sure she was taking advice about it, unless she was an illegal immigrant. The people who were affected by my fly posting had not pressed charges either. I was in limbo, my world was collapsing around me and very fast. Those were the times when I started asking myself, about the whole purpose of my life. Was it worth living? Who should make that final decision?

One week after my church service Molly came to visit me; she had been visiting me frequently since I lost my mother and the church fiasco. For some reason, despite all the misfortunes that surrounded the appearances and the disappearances of a short woman with puppy eyes, Molly still believed that I saw a real person.

That day she brought a spying device we secretly put on Beans's flat some months ago. I had almost forgotten about it? We bugged Beans' flat when I heard that Beans was living with a short woman, Molly reluctantly bought into the idea. Any mention of a black short woman excited my imagination. But if the business of bugging Beans' flat was that slow, we might as well kiss goodbye to trapping her.

We had agreed to engage in some unorthodox means, with the help of Molly's husband, to get to the bottom of my crocodile accident and the whole stalking situation. We both wanted the truth about what happened at the Limpopo River and the short woman with puppy eyes to be exposed. We both believed that if the truth came out my nightmares and my over arousal would stop. It would untangle my mind and make me a better person. That day she played the device on my radio. "Just listen to this," she said to me,

"*You look stunning tonight,*"

That was a male voice that I recognised straight away, "Its Beans," I said to Molly,

"I know, just listen."

A female voice I didn't recognize said "*I dressed nicely for the man and again he let me down, he didn't come.*"

Beans went on, "*I don't blame the man for cheating on his wife. Girls like you can make a priest commit adultery. It was just lucky that you were not Eve.*

165

The snake might have swathed you and refused to let go. Adam would have lost a would-be wife. Who knows, we might have been preaching a different gospel today. You represent the perfection of Eve in every sense, I don't blame Adam for eating the forbidden fruit."

"Forbidden fruit?"

"Every bit of your flesh is at the right place and in the right proportions. And right now you are a forbidden fruit to me. You're untouchable," said Beans.

"Why?" asked the female voice, giggling.

"He wants you for himself alone, doesn't he? He can't share you, can he?"

"So you want this forbidden fruit too? You want this too, do you?"

"Why not?" asked Beans *"Give me one reason why I shouldn't."*

"You are lying." She giggled again. *"You are a good liar too. You lied under oath in court when you married me. Didn't you? Liar, liar liar."*

"He made me lie. There are good lies and bad lies, that one was a good lie. We all lie to protect those we love don't we?"

"I will never forget what he did for me. His idea of you marrying me was a master stroke. A game changer. It really changed my life forever. Tomorrow I am starting a new job. If it wasn't for him, I would be hopelessly jobless in Zimbabwe today. He's a life changer and giver. I will never forget him for that."

"Ndingafe nenyota makumbo arimvura sei? How could I die of thirst while my feet are in the water," Beans' last words come straight from a song by the late Zimbabwean musician, Paul Matavire.

"Are you thirsty? Why didn't you say so when you came in? Tea or coffee, black or white?"

"No amount of coffee or tea, black or white could quench my thirst."

After a pause the female voice asked, *"Juice then, orange or apple?"*

Beans, *"Only you can quench my thirst, only you."*

"Ah....Ah Oh...Oh..." I heard smooching sounds in the background and some groans, as the tape ended.

"Is that all?" I asked. "It was ages ago since we bugged Beans, and this's all what we get?"

Molly appeared disappointed, "I thought the female voice would jog something in your memory"

"Like what Molly?"

"The woman's voice did not sound familiar to you then?"

"No, it didn't. Should I know everyone who Beans smooches, Molly?"

"How about 'the man'?"

"What man?"

"Come on Dolly, the man being referred to in the tape"

"You mean it could be..." I paused, giggled a little and continued, "No, it can't be your husband Molly."

Molly looked up and rolled her eyes, "No Dolly, I mean your husband."

"You think Beans could be bonking Ice's mistress Molly?" I paused, "You think Ice has a mistress and that's the reason he wants me to move out?" I had never openly told Molly that Ice might have a mistress. My choice of words might have appeared to suggest that sometimes, but I have never intentionally told her that. Maybe my body language spoke louder than words. That's the problem with the body language, it says everything that you don't say verbally. It betrays your inner thoughts. I continued, "No Molly, Ice is cold because he can't handle my situation. I'm the one driving him away. Do you think he has a mistress?"

"No Dolly. I don't know," said Molly shaking her head, "maybe I'm just trying too hard to find fault with him because of the way he is treating you."

"Be honest with yourself Molly. You don't have to be diplomatic about it, I've lost my mind. Who would like to live with me? I'm the problem. I..."

"Stop it Dolly. You didn't invite your problems."

"Maybe I did Molly. Maybe I did. I don't trust my mind anymore, Molly. My mind has its own mind now. The dialogue in the device should have stimulated something in me. But there is nothing to stimulate Molly. This body and its mind divorced the day I was attacked by the crocodile. My forehead is written 'out of order' as the Engutsheni nurse would have said."

"How about 'the man' asking Beans to marry the woman on his behalf in the tape? What do you think? What do you make of that?"

"Beans and Ice are soul mates Molly, they can't bonk each other's mistresses behind each other's backs."

"Ok Dolly." You could hear the disappointment in her voice as she prepared to leave.

"At least the dialogue confirms that Beans lives with a woman."

"Be strong for your unborn bab..."

"Wait Molly, wait," I said with excitement, after something crossed my mind, "Do you remember that Beauty in Tottenham told us that the short woman with puppy eyes was on her way to a wedding in Johannesburg? Do you remember?" Suddenly my heart beat increased. There could be a breakthrough after all.

"Yes, I remember Dolly."

"The woman on the tape had a sham wedding," I said.

"She didn't say in Johannesburg, Dolly." Dampening my excitement.

"But she comes from Zimbabwe and she had a wedding."

"On the other hand, what's Beans doing in sham marriages. Maybe we should aggressively bug his flat," she said as we parted.

Chapter 17

STALKER

My baby was due anytime, my doctor had told me. When we were trying for a baby for those ten long years, I thought it would mean the world to me, to us, but if anything, it was a rope forcibly tying us together. If it were not for the baby we would have gone our separate ways long ago. I didn't think that I needed it anymore and Ice didn't care about it either. It didn't feel like a baby anymore. It felt like a lump. It was sitting there, bulging my stomach, hurting me and making me ugly. When it kicked in my tummy it further distanced its father and I.

The baby was conceived just before I went to Zimbabwe. I suffered from some form of sickness while in Zimbabwe and I put it down to out of date foodstuff. I also remember not feeling great while I was there and I assumed that it was due to my emotions regarding my sick mother. My husband had just returned from his own trip to Zimbabwe, and making love was like eating chocolate, we could go on and on and never have enough of it. It was like taking benzodiazepines the more you took them the more you wanted more. Unlike benzodiazepine, instead of being addicted to love making, the nightmares and the short woman with puppy eyes took over our lives. I had missed him and he said he missed me too while he was away. We made love anytime and anywhere in the flat like we have never done before. Like we were newly married. Like we never knew that both of us were so good at the game of love-making. They say that distance makes the heart fonder. For us the distance made our baby. And for the first time in his life Ice took a proper aim like a man. But a few weeks after his return, my mother got ill and I had to go and see her. The baby had already been planted. The baby that we had been trying and praying for, for ten years, was growing in me. It helped me fight the crocodile. It defended me against the hyena. It survived the animals' attacks. It was a survivor. I hoped it would survive and heal the strain between its father and I.

Molly and I had been to Beans' house twice since we wanted to know more about the woman on the tape. On the first day we rang the doorbell and no one answered. We thought that we heard some footsteps inside, but nobody came to the door. On the second day Beans opened the door and he was alone. We looked for clues that he lived with someone, but there were none. He seemed a bit distracted though and he tried to be excessively friendly. We could not put our fingers on anything tangible. We couldn't tell if he was actually living with someone or not. We didn't want to ask him because we didn't want to raise the alarm in case it sent our target underground, we also didn't want to be openly too intrusive in whatever we said or did in his presence. At one point I had a sixth sense, which urged me to open one of his bedroom doors and check, but I thought against it because if I had opened it and there was no one, I would have blown our plan open and Beans would have been in a position to hide her, move her to a safe house. I didn't want to do that, so I ignored my sixth sense. Again we left empty handed.

When we returned for the third time, we had a more sophisticated device to bug Beans' clothing than the first one. We decided to place two devices on his jackets to enable them to record whether he was in or out.

On that visit, I kept Beans busy with a small talk, "You look well, Beans, *amakhiwa akuphethe kahle, yi*, the whites are treating you well, right?"

"*Kambe ngidlani ebabayo, dadewethu, ngaphandle kwengizifakele khona,* I choose the type of food and spices I eat, I'm sitting pretty." He smiled revealing his missing front tooth. Because his tooth had been missing since he was born, the lone front tooth became greedy and grew more than normal, covering most of the other missing tooth's space. His front tooth looked like that of *indlegu*, squirrel's two front teeth formed into one.

Molly asked to use the toilet and Beans directed her, it was along the hallway. He appeared interested in me more than Molly and I took advantage to keep him distracted as I said to him,

"*Kanti ungaphi umalukazana,* when are you going to get married?" At the corner of my eye I could see Molly looking at some jackets that were hung opposite the toilet door on the hallway.

"I have no time to look for one, Dolly, I am married to shifts, they are a jealous lot," he replied, smiling, showing his massive loner. Molly pointed at the jackets. I got the message and distracted Beans even further. I walked towards a picture on the wall and said while pointing at it, "Is this your mother?" He followed me, giving his back to Molly, who took two jackets into the toilet with her.

"*Yebo*, yes, it's my late mother, Dolly. By the way you never met her."

170

The picture reminded me of my own late mother too, bless her, I thought. I then said to him,

"No, I didn't. She's tall like you."

"If you think she was tall, you should have seen my father before he passed away." Molly quietly and slightly opened the toilet door and quietly closed it again. I got the message, she wanted to come out with the jackets hopefully having successfully planted the device. I had to attract all of Beans' attention at that moment. I said to him,

"As you are aware, I lost my own mother recently," I said as I covered my eyes with both hands. He moved closer to me, put his hand around my shoulders and said,

"*Siyabe sesifikile isikhathi dadewethu,* time will have arrived my sister." He consoled me as he helped me to sit on one of his sofas and continued, "Our turn will come too." Molly came out of the toilet and quickly hung back the two jackets. I thought to myself, *mission accomplished* and I sighed and said to him,

"We will all go one day when our mission has been accomplished here on earth." Agreeing with him. Molly came back to the lounge and said,

"I don't know what's wrong with me these days, I'm peeing buckets like a pregnant woman," we all laughed. Beans offered us some tea, we kindly turned it down and Molly pretended to be in a hurry to go home and we bid him goodbye and left his flat.

Once we got into Molly's car, she said, "Those devices fitted his jackets' buttons as if they were real buttons. *Ungadlali ngamakhiwa,* don't play with the whites, it could be one of the devices they created while they were hunting down Bin Laden. The batteries of those devices can record for more than a month before they run out."

"So we have a full month to fish Beans' goblin out," I said.

"Not only that, whatever is recorded will be transmitted to this receiver," showing me a device that looked like a recording stick, "wirelessly but we will have to be between twenty and fifty metres away to record or hear directly from the device in the flat. But if we manage to be fifteen or less metres away, we could get clear pictures too. As you saw, I planted two devices on two jackets, which had similar buttons. The jacket that he leaves behind will take care of the goblin."

"But, how would we manage to get that close, Molly, fifteen metres?"

"Dollar is trying to work out how we could get close without being seen.

He told me that he was going to talk to the private detective he borrowed the devices from, on how to get closer," she said still excited.

"Wow," I said and continued, "Who needs Wikileaks?" We laughed as we had a hi five and Molly said, "My husband always says when you discover the hole where the rats hide, you decide on two things. If you want to catch them alive, you pour cold water into the hole. If you want to kill them you pour in boiling water."

"So we are pouring cold water, because we want to catch the rat alive so that it answers a few questions."

"Exactly," concurred Molly.

"But what would happen if Beans discovered the devices before we got the information we wanted?" I wondered aloud.

"*Apoka, kuchapindira midzimu*, in that case, the ancestors will have to intervene, Dolly," she quickly added, "We will cross the bridge when we get there."

"That would give Ice all the ammunition he needs to divorce me through the meerkats court. Meerkat Beans would sign the divorce papers and Meerkat Benz will hand me the divorce certificate," mimicking meerkats accent on adverts, I said, "'*uxolo nkosazana, umtshado wakho wephukile lamhlanje*, sorry madam, your marriage has been broken today,' and that would be the end of my ten year marriage. Just like that. Gone. Kaput!" I said jokingly. As far as I was concerned my marriage broke a few months ago. At that moment it was just limping on like an old wounded donkey. But nobody appeared interested in putting it off because its meat is considered inedible.

"Is using electronic surveillance legal or illegal?" Molly Inquired. I had not thought about that. If it was illegal, the police wouldn't give me another bail again, they would lock me up for life. I wouldn't allow myself to be locked up by the police again. I would rather die than be locked up again. That couldn't be the right way to lead a life. I responded, "I don't know." We were both quiet for a while before Molly said, "Well, we will cross the bridge when we get there."

Those were desperate times that needed desperate measures. If stalking a stalker was illegal, so be it, I reassured myself.

Beans and Ice had been friends for as long as I cared to remember. Molly's suggestion that Beans might have been smooching Ice's mistress on the tape was ridiculous to say the least. The guys respected each other.

I shared the same bedroom with Beans in Johannesburg and nothing happened between us. Ice knew it and he trusted him. I'm sure he would do the same with Ice's mistress. Molly was wrong, the man referred to in the tape couldn't be Ice, it could be anyone. But something was not quite right whatever way you looked at it. If you put it upside down it appeared upside up, if you put it upside up, it appeared upside down. Something was crooked, but I couldn't put my finger on it. Beans was asked to marry a girl by a married man. Who was that married man called 'the man' in the tape? Why were they not calling him by his name? It could have been Benz. Beans and Benz were like meerkats. They were both tall, dark and bald headed. Benz could be 'the man' referred to on the tape, and maybe that's why the poor woman had her knickers twisted, because she couldn't differentiate between the two of them.

A few days after bugging Beans' flat, there was a loud knock at my door. When I opened it Molly rushed in looking excited to the point of being delirious.

"I saw the woman on the tape - she is very short. She just went in while I and Dollar were watching Beans' flat. Hurry! We need to get there before she leaves. She has the keys to the flat too. So she must live there. It must be her. My husband borrowed a people's carrier with dark tinted windows, and we parked it less than fifteen metres from Beans' flat. Once we saw the short woman going in I left to pick you up. Hurry up – let's go." She stood at the doorway, with the door wide open. She left me with no choice but to follow her orders. I was so grateful for her support, despite everyone else doubting my mind, she stood by my side. We might even have broken the law together in bugging Beans' flat. That was a matter to look after itself, to be dealt with some other day.

I just thought, would we find her, or that was another wild goose chase? I was used to them by then. Our hopes had been raised before, only to come down crashing like a tonne of bricks. But she was more excited than I have ever seen her before that day. I locked the door behind me and followed her to her car. She continued to say,

"Before she went in we had this recorded conversation between Beans and Benz on this memory stick, just listen. I'm sorry this will shock you, but after all you have gone through I'm sure nothing shocks you anymore. You are better off knowing the truth. I hope you are prepared to learn the truth, Dolly. Unfortunately there are no pain relief tablets for bad news. If there were, I would give them to you before you heard this," she said as she inserted the recorded stick into her car radio and pressed play.

We heard Beans' voice first. *"Eh, Benz, come in. Thanks for coming. I've had this thing for too long now. You know what? I've a confession to make man. I can't keep it a secret anymore, I have to come out.*

"You have to come out?," Benz asked him. *"Are you gay?"*

They both laughed.

"Come'n Benz, I'm serious."

Benz replied, *"You really have a confession to make to me? I'm now father Matibili..."*

Beans broke in, *"I have fallen in love with Dots. We're madly in love."*

"Seriously? You and Dots? Ice's lunch box?" Benz asked.

"We are planning to get married soon."

Benz digested the information *"You and Dots are an item? First it was Ice's plan that you marry Dots in South Africa in order to bring her into this country. You sham married her in Johannesburg and now you want to double sham her. You have tasted the blood you now want the flesh, I can't believe you two?*

"We have fallen in love big time man."

We could hear Benz giggling *"You're fleecing Ice's lunch box Beans.*

"She's no longer Ice's girlfriend. She's my wife to be."

"Boy oh boy, so you have proposed! You're brave Beans, yes you are. You're bending Ice's woman and now you want to marry her."

"Please show her some respect, she will be my wife soon," said Beans.

Benz continued, *"Somehow I had this niggling feeling about your arranged sham marriage in Johannesburg. I had a feeling that it would end in tears. Talk of keeping a cat and a mouse in the same cage. Women break friendships Beans. The first woman broke the long standing trust and friendship between Adam and God. Be careful for what you wish for."*

Beans protested, *"Falling in love is not a sin Benz. I'm neither the first nor the last man to fall in love with a friend's girlfriend."*

"You know it's taboo in our culture to marry a friend's small house. It's seen as self-hatred. It's viewed as self-disrespect, and you know it."

Beans took a deep breath, *"She's pregnant with my child."*

"Pregnant? Dots is pregnant? This is worse than what I thought!"

"That's the end of the recording," said Molly.

I kept telling myself that that was one of those nightmares. I would wake up as I always did in my worst nightmares. I would wake up and only realise that I have strangled myself to death. I prayed to God to turn that situation into a real nightmare. I begged for a nightmare. I didn't want to wake up. Molly was right, there were no pain killers for bad news, or I would have overdosed that day.

We didn't talk to each other until we arrived at Beans' flat. We parked close to Dollar's hired car and got out of Molly's car and got into his car and found him recording and listening to the device and there were pictures too on his hand held small screen. He told us that Ice has just gone into the flat. Dollar and Molly sat in the front, I sat alone in the back, it was as if they didn't want to see my face, to see a twenty something old heart breaking into shreds like a teenager's heart. We could all hear and see inside Beans' flat, the picture was crystal clear.

"Eh MaGents" (Slang for 'hi gentlemen') said Ice. Ice and Benz shook hands, standing in the middle of the lounge. Beans walked across the lounge and stood by the window, cutting a figure of a sulking teenager. Benz said, *"Ice, Beans has news for you,"* Looking in Beans' direction, Ice said,

"You have news for me, Beans?" Beans didn't respond. Benz, looked down, smiled and said, *"Yes, Beans spill the beans, sorry for the pun,"* and giggled.

After a short silence, Beans said," *Dots is pregnant!"*

Ice looked Beans straight in the eye and he looked puzzled too and said, *"What? No, she isn't pregnant. I would have known it first."* Benz looked at Ice a bit surprised and said,

"This means you haven't been around then Ice?" And he continued, *"You really put Beans in a very difficult situation, Ice. You put your friend in a very tempting situation?"* He paused before he said, *"I see. You haven't been around, Ice, have you?"*

"What has her pregnancy got to do with you two anyway?" said Ice.

Beans walked from the window and came closer to the two and said, *"He thinks he can sleep with every woman. He walks with his zip open. His hands have been in every woman's bum."* Ice looked at Beans, shook his head and said,

"What's wrong with you Beans today?" He grumbled. *"Why are you on my case like this?"*

"While you have been away, Beans has been keeping the fires burning!" said Benz and laughed.

175

"What do you mean, Benz?" Benz looked at Beans and said,

"Go on Beans tell him,"

"Tell me what? What is going on here? I've just come to see Dots and you start speaking in tongues. What's wrong with you two?" Ice was becoming impatient. Benz looked at Ice and said,

"Beans is sleeping with Dots."

"Beans is having sex with my girlfriend?"

When Ice confirmed that he had a girlfriend, I found myself saying, "No. Not again! We can't travel that journey again," I covered my face with both my hands in shame mixed with rage. Dollar paused the recording. Why? Out of the respect of my feelings? To show that he wasn't recording it to humiliate me? I had looked for answers all along, but what answers? The recording was certainly giving me the wrong answer. Did I take the eye off the ball when I chased the short woman with puppy eyes? Was she a dummy, a non-event? Was she the one who was said to be pregnant? An avalanche of questions went unanswered by my feeble mind. A sell-out mind. There was dead silence in the car.

That wasn't what I expected from my husband. He did that once and I had forgiven him and he had done exactly the same thing again. He never took his wedding vows seriously. He took them like *amadlwane,* child's play. Could I honestly say that I didn't see it coming? I had not been hit by a stray bullet there. I had seen the bullet coming and hoped that it would miss me. Ice's behaviour had been indicative of what hit me that day. He had been sleeping in the lounge for months. Why was I surprised to hear that he had a girlfriend? According to Beans, he had many of them too. He denied me my conjugal rights giving my nightmares as an excuse. I felt humiliated and embarrassed. My eyes welled up and I felt like screaming as loud as my vocals cords would allow, but a lump filled up my throat, making me mute. It's as if the short woman with puppy eyes had just grabbed my throat like a vice, like the crocodile did to my leg. It was as if Ice was helping her to suffocate me. I wouldn't be suffocated. I refused to be suffocated. I said to Dollar, "Continue with the recording. Surely what's left can't be worse than what I have already heard. It can't kill me because I feel dead already."

Dollar apologised for the recording those contents but he resumed playing it back, he had not stopped the recording.

"She complained that you didn't make time for her," said Beans. *"You were too busy with your neurotic wife and the chain of other women."*

"What?" asked Ice as he paced up and down the lounge, between Beans and Benz.

"Tell him everything Beans," Benz urged.

"She's now pregnant," said Beans.

"You've just told me that. Unless you have impregnated her? Have you impregnated her?" Ice thundered, quickening his pacing up and down the lounge, *"Have you? Where is the bitch? Dots is my b...tch Beans! You're sleeping with my b...tch?*

"You know what Beans, in rural areas where people use the bush as toilets, sometimes the dogs follow them and feed on their stools! Sometimes the dog actually brings the ca-ca home. Then the dog eats it in front of everyone. It's disgusting to see your own ca-ca Beans. It smells horrible. You chase the dog away. Why Beans? Why do you chase the dog away? Because you don't want your family to know that you're capable of passing such stinking ca-ca! That you are a stinker! That you can be so reckless with your marriage! That you can commit marital suicide! Beans you are not different from that dog that eats my ca-ca. Beans you are that dog that eats my ca-ca. My ca-ca was supposed to stay in the bush, Beans. Why did you bring it home?"

"You are insulting me Ice. You can't come into my flat to insult me! Get out!" Beans shouted. Ice moved threateningly towards Beans and said, *"Or what? You want to punch me? Punch me."* Benz got between them and said,

"Guys, guys you can't fight over a woman. Not only a woman but a small house. Not in this day and age guys."

Ice said threateningly, *"Be careful Beans. Be very careful indeed. Do you remember your false asylum claim! I can get you deported from this country!"*

Beans came straight back, *"Come'n, Ice. Don't try to black mail me! Your wife needs you more now that she's gone cuckoo. You're responsible for her loss of mind! Leave Dots alone."*

Once again I found myself saying, "Stop it Dollar. Stop it! If you hear something breaking inside me, now, today or tomorrow, it would be my heart! I can't stand this humiliation any longer." I heard of a woman who cut her husband's penis, fried it and ate it and thought what could have possessed her. She wasn't possessed! She had been changed into a new creature. Changed from human to inhuman by her husband cheating on her. Every human being has a capacity to take humiliation and abuse. When they can't take it anymore, they lose it. And I felt I had lost my head big time right then. It felt like my head has been chewed into mincemeat, exactly what the hyena did to the Limpopo snake. I was in the snake's shoes.

I got out of the car and went straight into the flat without knocking. I had rocked the boat until it capsized, it was time to swim or sink. I was sweating and my heart was racing like it did in my nightmares. Molly and her husband followed me into the flat. The three of them were standing in the lounge, with Benz in between Ice and Beans, keeping them apart. He kept them apart from thumping each other just because of a woman. They were startled. They kept quiet. I stood in the middle of the lounge gazing into Ice's eyes. He blinked and avoided any further eye contact.

"Why didn't you divorce me rather than humiliate me like this, Ice? Why Ice? You thought if you did I would be hurt. I might have been, but not this way. Divorce would have left me with some dignity, not like this!" Turning to Beans I said, "Thank you for joy sticking Ice's woman. And a big thank you for joy sticking me too in Johannesburg!"

Both Beans and Ice were stunned, they stared at each other with evil eyes. But they didn't attempt to thump each other over me. I continued looking Beans in the eye, "You have managed a first Beans, for joying sticking both the Mrs and the mistress. You're a best friend indeed. I honestly wish all men with mistresses had best friends like you! You..."

The bedroom door opened and out came the short woman with puppy eyes. She was real. I was almost happy to see her. If Ice had to cheat me, I didn't want him to have cheated on me with any other woman, as that would have left me still chasing the short woman with puppy eyes. I said to Molly,

"This's the short woman with puppy eyes for real, Molly. Thank you for believing me. Thank you for putting up with my non-existent visual hallucinations." Molly stood there stunned. She was speechless, that was what the short woman with puppy eyes did to people. She left them doubting their minds. The stalker with puppy eyes had a way of making people feel vulnerable and frightened.

That day she didn't have puppy eyes, she had devil's eyes. Eyes of deceit. Eyes that took my husband's attention and stopped him loving me. Eyes that led me to bush ash smearing. Eyes that destroyed my dreams. Eyes that led me to attack an innocent stranger. Oh, no, she was pregnant too. The man who fired blanks for so long had suddenly acquired new shooting skills. Hitting two birds with one bullet. Double congratulations Ice, I thought to myself.

"Why are you stalking me? Did you cut the rope?" I asked her. She went quiet. She was not scared. She walked towards me, looking me right in the eye, not blinking like Ice. She was made of sterner stuff than him. She kept coming towards me, till she was right under my nose. I came face-to-face with my tormentor of the past eight months and she had the guts to stand toe-to-toe with me. Face-to-face with the stalked. She didn't understand what she put me through. She had no idea. She thought that was child's play, *bantwana bantwana wozani ekhaya*, children, children come home. Well, it wasn't! That was my life being torn into shreds! When she was close enough, my right fist thundered into her devious, left puppy eye. She fell backwards landing on the sofa. No one moved or said a word in the lounge.

"Did you cut the rope?" I asked her again, she lay there on the sofa, looking straight into my eyes again, stubborn female dog. She was defiant, it was as if she was saying *'You are falling right into my trap. Come'n hit me again. Hit me again. I know everything about you.'* Her eyes were still fixed at me, the left one as red as the setting sun. As she got up I tried to punch her again but my fist was held back by Benz, saying,

"Please Dolly, this woman is pregnant too." Turning to Dots, he said, "Please Dots, answer her."

Dots slowly got to her feet, wiping tears from her left eye with the back of her hand. But this time she was careful, she didn't come too close to me. She got the message. That's what I expected, my personal space was to be respected. I was the wife, after all. Arms akimbo she said,

"Yes, I did."

"Why?"

"Ask your husband." She still oozed with that *'I don't care attitude,'* she had already forgotten that I had just thumped her. Either she was brave or mad. I looked at Ice and he shook his head,

"I don't know what she is talking abou..." She didn't allow him to finish as she said,

"He told me that *uyinyumba*, you are barren." Putting emphasis on the word 'uyinyumba" and continued, "That you were 'inhospitable to his little delicacies' in his own words. Simply put, your ova were hostile to his sperms. You were empty, sterile and unproductive. Because you couldn't conceive, he begged me to have his child. I cut the rope to take you out of the picture. Out of your misery. He told me that he was going to divorce you anyway. So I thought I was doing you a favour. I didn't only cut the rope, I also tipped the immigration officer at Johannesburg airport that you were attacked by the crocodile because I didn't want you to come back to England and interfere with our lives - like you are doing right now."

I turned to Ice, "You see I am not mad. I wasn't hallucinating after all. This is the woman who has been appearing and disappearing. She's a stalker. You pretended that I was mental, yet all along you were sleeping with her. Sleeping with the woman who was causing me nightmares, responsible for the crocodile attack. Sleeping with my stalker. You wanted me to be committed to hospital so that you could have her."

"No, no Dolly I..."

Dots interrupted him again, "Not only that, he also told me that he deliberately left you at Heathrow airport, switched off his mobile so that you would get deported. He didn't want you in England either..."

"No, Dolly I didn't know that the short woman with puppy eyes you kept seeing was Dots." Ice protested his innocence.

"Oh please Ice, don't call me 'short' and 'puppy eyes' in front of your wife. Are you trying to save your dead marriage? You see Ice, I'm pregnant with your child too...."

"No, Dots, no," Beans interrupted her, "You're carrying my child."

Swaggering towards Beans, she said, "You see Beans, your problem is that you are Ice's lap dog. When he says jump, you say 'how high sir?'" She spoke with authority, she was ruling the roost, there was no doubt about that. Two stupid men were fighting over her child. Most men run away from such responsibilities, but not those two. She continued, "You lick his back side. You see I was already pregnant when I started sleeping with you. Ice visited Zimbabwe, just before I came to the United Kingdom. We had a good time, as you can see," Pointing to her stomach. "Married men have experience Beans, something that you are short of. This is Ice's child, not yours. Ice might be horrible to his wife but he has been special to m..."

I couldn't stop myself any longer. I had been humiliated and insulted enough. I ploughed my full fist into her bulging stomach. I could feel the punch breaking the soft bones of the little devil inside her womb. She screamed and staggered backwards, this time she was not so lucky, she missed the sofa and hit the floor with her head and I could see her eyes turning inside out. I didn't care. As soon as she hit the deck, there was a big kick inside my rib cage and I passed out.

Chapter 18

WAGES OF SIN

I woke up in a maternity ward in a Bournemouth hospital, early in the morning. The nurse told me that I was unconscious when they admitted me to hospital and I had an induced labour. He congratulated me and showed me a healthy baby boy, but I didn't feel like hugging it. He realised my lack of interest in the baby and he put it back in its cot. She checked my blood pressure and temperature and said that I was fine. She left my cubicle after showing me the button to press should I need some help.

My head was still spinning from what happened yesterday. Too much happened at once leaving me dazed. I was still fuming from what Ice and that short woman with evil eyes had put me through. They made me to chase shadows when they were nestling and laughing behind my back. To say I was angry is a lie, I was ready to kill someone. I felt some hatred I have never felt in my entire life. I wanted to put them through what they had put me through, but I didn't know how. I wanted to revenge, but I didn't know how to go about it. How could I make them pay for what they put me through. My revenge would never be enough to what I had gone through. Humiliation is worse than physical abuse. How could I revenge humiliation? It has no shape, no form, no depth or extent. It's not measurable. Only the sufferer experiences it. Physical revenge is easy, eye for an eye, job done. I couldn't fathom on how to revenge my humiliation. I thought of using physical violence to revenge my mortification. But I wasn't sure on how to carry it out. Should I get a gun and start by shooting their toes, then legs, then trunk and finally their heads, making sure that they were dead. But would that equal the torture I experienced? Or should I boil oil and pour it over Ice, while he was asleep and disfigure him for life. But would that be enough revenge? Or should I poison their food with *isibindi sengwenya,* crocodile liver? Maybe I could get it from Ice's witchdoctor in Luton. It was the failure to figure out how to revenge and whether it would be enough that fuelled my anger.

When I got up from my bed to visit the toilet and my body felt very light. Ice's cyst had left it. I didn't feel any after birth pains, they were overcome by my rage. On the corridor as I made my way to the toilet, I saw Dots, sleeping in her cubicle. My heart sucked all the blood from my brain and deposited it into my body. I felt light headed and got into a stupor. She looked innocent, her baby was sleeping in its cot next to her, it looked innocent too. I felt intense hatred in that state of stupor. For a minute I detached from myself from Dolly and I became an observer. I read Dolly's thoughts as they urged her 'revenge, revenge, revenge.' They flashed 'it's payback time for all the appearances and disappearances she had put you through. She must answer for each of them.' As weird as it might sound I attached myself to Dolly again. I felt what she felt, we became one again. I liked what she wanted - revenge.

I didn't even make my way to the toilet. I had to deal with Dots and Ice and show them what they had put me through in the past nine months. I returned to my cubicle and grabbed my baby by its legs. It didn't remind me of innocence, it reminded me of cheating and broken vows. I entered Dots' cubicle, grabbed her baby, or should I say Ice's baby, by its feet too. It reminded me of dishonesty and sin. At the end of the building I could see stairs that served as a fire escape route. Dangling the two babies on each of my arm like dead chickens, I climbed up the stairs that led to the flat roof of the building. It was quite early in the morning, most of the mothers were still asleep, so nobody saw me as I made my way up the roof. The two babies were fully clothed, for some reason they were not crying. I suppose they were shell shocked to cry. They were born at the wrong time to the wrong parents. No baby in its right frame of mind would have chosen me as its mother. The poor baby boy on my right hand made a huge mistake by choosing me as its mother. It was fatal attraction. I suppose many babies gave me a pass, delaying my pregnancy, but the baby on my right hand took a chance with me.

I couldn't control my mind anymore, revenge was all I wanted. Revenge drove me crazy. My only focus was that someone had to suffer like I did. Once I reached the flat roof of the building, I shouted at the top of my voice, "These are the wages of sin." Dangling the babies upside down with both of my hands, holding them by their ankles, I continued, "Here are two baby boys, born on the same day by the same man but by two different women. One of the mothers is a stalker, the other is plain stupid. Their father thinks that he is the only man in town. He thinks that everything revolves around him. He is a selfish and heartless man. Born the same day they will die the same day, today and now."

A white male nurse came to the roof via the fire escape stairs, and I shouted at him, "Get back or else I throw down these babies right now!" "Please Mrs Sibanda, just give me the babies."

"Don't call me Mrs Sibanda, my name is Dolly. Give Mr Sibanda his name back! I don't want it anymore!"

"Please Dolly, don't hurt the children. They don't deserve that kind of treatment!" He was standing six metres away. He took one step forward and I shouted at him, "Stay away from me or these babies die!"

The nurse retreated down the stairs. A number of nurses gathered at the top of the fire escape. They kept popping up their heads like meerkats. I heard one of them saying to her colleagues, "I recognise her. It's the bush woman. I saw her at Bournemouth psychiatric hospital a few months ago on my placement. She was found by the police in the bush, body ash smearing and they brought her to hospital." It appeared one of the nurses knew me and I decided to have a conversation with her.

"The nurse who said that she recognises me must come forward," I shouted. No one showed up, I shouted again, "I will drop the babies now if she doesn't come forward now." A timid white young female nurse climbed up to the roof. She had turned white like a sheet, her blood had deserted her skin. "Do you remember what the psychiatrist said I suffered from?"

She went quiet, shaking like a leaf, before she responded, "No, I don't." She shook her head. "And you call yourself a nurse?"

"No I'm not. I'm a student nurse."

"OK, let me tell you what the psychiatrist said. She said that the sightings of a short woman with puppy eyes were flash backs. She blamed my mind for it. She said I was mad as she believed that she could read my mind. She couldn't! Psychiatrists pretend to be mind readers, they are not. To be a good nurse, learn to listen carefully to your patients. You see this baby," I showed her the baby on my left arm, "It's the baby of the short woman with puppy eyes. She does exist. She is in the building below us right now, sleeping. When you see the psychiatrist again, tell her for me that she's no mind reader. I had a bush ash smearing treatment, yes I did. I didn't believe that it would help me in any shape or form, right from the start. But I did it for my husband, to save my marriage. But looking at how it's all ending today, I shouldn't have tried at all. Go and tell Dots, the short woman with puppy eyes, that I have her baby on the roof and she should come and save it."

As soon as she went down the stairs a white male police officer showed up. I could see the police cars and ambulances at the bottom of the building. The officer introduced himself, "Ma'am I'm Sergeant Drinkwater. I've come to help yo..."

"You can't help me sergeant Drinkpoison! I'm beyond help! I'm not going to listen to your usual crap," I screamed at him. He was the same police officer who I thought mumbled a racist statement under his breath when he caught me naked and ash smearing in the bush.

"I can help you. Yes I can. Just give me the babies, ma'am, I'll help you."

"You had the chance to help me during the bush smearing and what did you do? Instead you locked me in your cells and urged a psychiatrist to detain me in hospital."

"Just give me the babies ma'am, I'll help you."

"These are my children, they're both my husband's babies. This one," I showed him the baby on my right hand, my baby, "was given to him by God. And this one," I showed him the baby on my left hand, Dots' baby, "Was given to him by Satan." The officer took one step forward, and I screamed at him, "Don't play games with me officer. Shoot me if you can, move back." He stepped back, I was really living my nightmares and a master of them too.

"When I was crying for help nobody listened, including you officer. Instead, you chased me with a helicopter like a criminal. Everybody told me that I was losing my mind, and at some point I started to believe them." After a pause I said, "But since I was abused and humiliated by their father, I should have the right to end their lives." I felt that the burning log that I had been carrying, while chasing Dots' shadows and pleading to everyone to listen to me, was now burning my hand. It was time to throw it away or my hand would be burnt beyond recognition. I had a chance to do something about it that day. Dots wanted to kill me for love and that day I wanted to kill her baby and mine out of love too. The police officer went down the stairs and quickly returned with Molly. I had never seen Molly in that state. She looked shell shocked. Clutching her chest she pleaded with me,

"Please Dolly don't do it. Please don't." She broke down crying. She kept coming forward, pleading with me. "Please don't. There is a way out of this, Dolly. I understand what you are going through. I've been with you all the way. Haven't I? Don't kill the babies please." She was almost two metres away, when I realised that she could have been coached by the police on how to catch me by surprise. "Stop it Molly! Stop! You take another step forward and I will drop them!" I screamed at her. She took another step forward, I moved to the edge of the roof and dangled the babies threateningly, saying, "If you make one more step forward Molly, *ngifunga ngomama ongasekho,* I swear on my late mother, I will kill them! You will live with your conscience!" She stopped. "Go back to the officer!" She hesitated. "Please go back Molly! This is not between me and you, it's between Ice, Dots and I! Please don't get involved!" I begged her and she moved back to the officer.

"Killing those babies will not solve anything Dolly, instead it will put you into deeper trouble," she said in a trembling voice. "I don't want to live after this nightmare Molly. What would I live for? Life has to have a purpose. To me, Molly, it doesn't have a purpose anymore. My mother is already gone to prepare my place." Molly, choked on her tears and she cried out loud.

"Please sergeant, don't use my only friend this way!" I shouted at Sergeant Drinkwater. "Take her downstairs officer!" Molly went downstairs. Both the babies suddenly wailed as if they knew that they had lost their last chance to survive. My arms were aching too from dangling them, therefore, I rested both of them on my chest, and they both suddenly stopped screaming. They hugged my chest with their little arms and that fuelled my anger.

"You have brought the wrong person officer!" I shouted at him. "Bring Dots upstairs! Bring the female dog on heat! Bring the short woman with devil's eyes!" Each time I shouted instruction at the white officer, he went red, but he followed my orders. He brought Dots up. She came onto the roof trembling as if she was freezing. I ordered her to come forward until she was two metres away. She wasn't swaggering anymore. She was no longer full of crap she had at Beans' flat yesterday. I said to her, "Tell everyone why you wanted to kill me. Why you stalked me." Tears rolled down her cheeks. "Tell everyone why you wanted me dead! Come on, tell them. Your tears are coming twenty four hours late." Showing her both babies, I asked her, "Which one is yours? If you guess correctly, I will hand him back to you." She pointed to my left hand, which was correct, and I said to her, "He has Ice's looks wickedly blended with yours hasn't he?"

You have picked the right baby but I won't keep my promise, just as Ice broke his to me." Beckoning her I said, "Come and get closer to the edge of the roof. Come and take a look. Look." She hesitantly looks down and quickly moves back. Either she was afraid of heights or she thought that I would push her and that idea did cross my mind at that time. Coward. I asked her, "Why shouldn't I throw your baby from the top of this building? Give me just one reason, why I shouldn't."

After a pause, she said, "I didn't cut the rope and..." "Stop lying *mahotsha*, (lady of the night). Try saying something else, liar!" "And I didn't call the police when you were bush ash smearing, your husband did," she sobbed.

"Oh, so that is supposed to make me feel better, does it? That can't save your baby." Then I said to the officer, "Leave this waste of space where she is," Pointing at Dots, with her baby, "and bring Ice to the roof." The officer went red and then following my instructions, he went down the stairs. A thought came to my mind that I could be on television too. Nothing would have embarrassed Ice more than that. The officer returned with Ice. He was there too, he had come to see his twins and say hi to his wife and mistress, what a lucky man. He was living a lie. When he came onto the flat roof, I ordered him to stand five metres away from me. I didn't want him to develop any silly ideas. He looked as if he had lost weight already! Coward. I asked him, "Do you remember our wedding vows?" He remained quiet. "Do you?" He just nodded his head. "I remember them too. They meant nothing to you, they meant the world to me. I kept them till this day. Forget about what I said yesterday, that I slept with Beans, I didn't. I said it because I wanted to see whether you would bash each other over me, as you wanted to for this b...tch. But you didn't. I wasn't worth it. At twenty-nine I'm past the sell-by-date, haven't I? But you were more than prepared to lose a few teeth over Dots. I don't know what I saw in you. It was the biggest mistake of my life. I didn't know that meeting you was equivalent to meeting death. How could I? I thought I'd met a husband, but I had met death walking on two feet. I had met Satan who appeared like God. How absurd! The vows you made on our wedding day were promises of death. But you know what, sometimes I don't blame you, I blame my choice. The choice I made was as good as suicide. I don't want to live and make another suicide choice in this life again. There were a number of decent, intelligent and kinder men, but I chose you. A man who fired more blanks than all the World War 2 shots put together and made up for it by having a mistress. You're obviously insecure. You're a coward too. You were not man enough to divorce me. You even called the police behind my naked back while I was having the bush treatment. What else did you do behind my back Ice?

If you tell me the truth I might save your poor things!"

He remained quiet for a while before he said, "I know I have to come clean Dolly, for tomorrow's sake. I..."

"There's no tomorrow for me Ice. Just tell me the truth for the sake of your tomorrow."

"I'm sorry Dolly, I have a one week old baby with another woman." At that point I ordered him to step back to the officer. I held both babies in my left hand, took Dots by surprise, grabbed her with my right hand and we all jumped from the top of the building to our death.

Chapter 19

MY END, END

So you now know why I'm in a secure psychiatric hospital. I have lost love for life. The nurses here tell me that the babies and Dots' survived the jump too. I thought I was the only one who fell on a pile of mattresses and nets placed on the ground by the police, but it appears that everyone survived as a result. I'm gutted. I don't need this life anymore. I hate it with a passion.

My friend Molly is paying me a visit today. She is the only one who visits me. It's tough when you get ill as an immigrant, especially if you try to kill your family and others. Who wants to be in the company of a "nutter". People from all walks of life regardless of their social background, race, class or tribe are cruel when they give names to people with mental health problems. They pick the worst sounding words, "nutter", "wacko", "geek", "psycho", "cuckoo", "crackpot", "oddball". But my friend Molly sees beyond an illness. Beyond a label. But am I mentally ill? No, I'm not. The psychiatrist thinks that I suffer from PTSD and PPD. The Meerkat Court agreed with him. But I'm not mentally ill.

What's abnormal by wanting to take your own life? What's abnormal about taking revenge? For trying to revenge and to take my own life, the nurses here have told me that I'm likely to spend the rest of my life in a secure hospital. The system, with the help of the Meerkat Court, sentences people who want to take their own lives to life hospitalisation. It's not different to life imprisonment, my liberty is gone forever that is why I still want to die.

Today Molly arrives smart and smiling as always. She hands me some fruit and sits down. I really look forward to her visits. She makes me relax. She makes me feel human again. But when I look around there are not so many visitors. There are some who have not received a visitor since I have been here. I thought it was only the black Zimbabweans in Engutsheni in Bulawayo, that didn't visit their relatives in a psychiatric hospital, they don't visit them in England too. What is it with this illness?

I'm saying for the last time that I'm not mentally ill. But I would like to live in another world not this one. It's my choice to die in this world and live in another one. I've already confessed about what I'm about to do, my sins, to my God. I've made this decision independent of my mental state. I'm aware that I've come to this decision using the supposedly diseased organ. But being admitted to a mental institution has been a blessing in disguise. Some patients have told me how to go quietly, not as noisily as my first suicide attempt. They have also told me about the most effective tablets to overdose on. I have stashed them. I am saying my last goodbyes to Molly today, just as I did to my mother, nine months ago. I believe I am lucky, how many people are able to say goodbye to their families and friends before they die? I'm one of the few.

I hug Molly for a long time. "Please look after my son. I am not worthy to be his mother."

"Please Dolly don't say that. I hope they will allow me to adopt him." I have told the social services that I want Molly to adopt my son. I say to Molly,

"The past nine months of my life are like human creation, from conception to birth and then finally, death. My last nine months started with crazy love making with Ice, just as what happens before most women get pregnant. Some hard labour is put into those home factories called bedrooms. Rotas have to be timed to perfection for successful results.

"The crocodile and hyena attacks as well as carjack are the dreaded pregnancy sicknesses, which, unfortunately, most pregnant women have to endure. The morning sicknesses that leave you regretting the hard labour you put in that home factory.

"The nightmares, appearing and disappearing of the short woman with puppy eyes, are the cyst, you tell your doctor that you are pregnant and she tells you that her ultrasounds tell her that it's a fibroid not a baby. As the visual hallucinations increase in intensity, so is the growth of the baby, or cyst. As the baby or cyst continues to grow, the doctor tells you that since you are almost thirty years old, she will have to remove your uterus, otherwise these cancerous cells might spread to some parts of your body. You strongly disagree with your doctor and refuse to contemplate the removal of your uterus because you still harbour some slight hope that you might fall pregnant one day. You also secretly hope that you are really pregnant and the doctor is wrong. At the same time you are caught in a dilemma, to remove the cyst or risk the spread of the cancer.

"One day you feel like pooing and you go to the toilet, and guess what comes out instead of poo, a baby. You are rightly angry with your doctor for not believing you all along. You are angry with your husband for not believing you too. You're angry with the whole world for conniving against you. But, it's too late. You are now a mother. Although this is something you have been trying and wishing for, for many years, you are not ready to be a mother. To put it bluntly, you are an unfit mother.

"In anger and rage you attempt to flash the baby down the drains, your friend suddenly shows up and tells you to stop it. You then shove your cyst, sorry, baby, in her hands and order her to look after it. The doctor is no longer there to say sorry. You are left on your own to dry *njengomhwabha,* like biltong. To deal with the consequences. After all you are not the first one to suffer like that, you're just a number." Molly shakes her head and I can see her eyes welling up and she says, as we part,

"Your analogue couldn't have summarised the last nine months any better, Dolly. At least the nightmare is over."

I watch her through the hospital window, as she gets into her car and drives off. I take my stashed tablets from inside my mattress and swallow them all at once with a glass of water. I put the last full stop on my suicide note, which I have been writing while I have been in hospital and put it under my pillow and lie quietly on my bed. I close my eyes and murmur, "Please mama forgive me for being so ungrateful, for putting my own life into my own hands. For taking away the life you gave me without charge. The past nine months have been a living hell for me mama. Satan took over my life and turned it into hell on earth. There are things that I will never know about my life, but those I know only serve to complicate it further. I'm so embarrassed for living this life, it's not worth it. Life must have a purpose. The moment it fails to have a purpose, it must be allowed to self-cannibalise. Suicide must be the solution. No one has the right to... to...sto...stop...m..."

When I open my eyes again, Molly, is sitting next to my bed. "Where am I?" I ask her. I'm a bit numb, confused and dazed.

"You are in a Bournemouth hospital," Molly responds.

"Again? What happened?"

"You don't remember?" She asks me.

"So, I have failed in my bid to die again?"

"I'm so happy that you have woken up Dolly. You have been in a coma for three months since you took an overdose. You were found by the nurses lying and puking on the floor and they rushed you to hospital. For the last three months the church and the pastor have been praying at your bedside. Some form of all day and all-night vigil."

My friend from Church was right, *mhinduro yake inononoka,* His response is slow. She reaches for her hand bag and hands me a book. The author and the title of the book are written in bold letters on the front cover of the book. The front cover picture is of a woman ash smearing in the bush, I know who she is. The title of the book is "My Suicide Note" the author is yours truly, Dolly Sibanda. I say to Molly, "What's all this about Molly?"

"I took your suicide note to the publishers, they fought to lay their hands on it. This is the final rough draft. Congratulations, you are about to be a published author."

"I give up on death, Molly. God kept me alive for a reason. It might be a baby not a cyst, after all." I ask for a pen from Molly, I cancel the title of the book and scribble instead, "Why Rock the Boat When You Don't Know How to Swim." Molly smiles and says, "It's actually a better title, I will inform the publisher about the change you have just suggested." I also cancel 'Sibanda' in front of my name and write Nare instead. She only smiles.

END

Acknowledgements

A special thank you to my family, relatives and friends, God bless you all.

A huge thank you to the following online news media; Nehanda Radio, New Zimbabwe, Bulawayo 24, Harare 24, Africa NewsDesk and Africa NewsHub.

Last but not least, thank you to The Writing.co.uk Team, HardRock Media UK and my publishing partner, Paragon Publishing, Rothersthorpe, for their support.

About the author

Daniel Sebata was born in Gwanda, Zimbabwe and after training as a secondary school teacher at Gweru Teachers' College he taught for almost ten years at Lobengula Secondary School in Bulawayo, before moving to the United Kingdom in 1998. He graduated with a Diploma of Higher Education in Mental Health Nursing from Middlesex University, London, in 2002 and with a BSc (Hons) in Bournemouth University, in 2005. He lives in Bournemouth with his family.

Lightning Source UK Ltd.
Milton Keynes UK
UKOW04f1332050914

238095UK00002B/25/P